HALLOWED GROUND

Recent Titles by Margaret James from Severn House

THE ASH TREE
A GREEN BAY TREE
THE FINAL RECKONING
THE SNAKE STONE
A SPECIAL INHERITANCE

HALLOWED GROUND

Margaret James

This first world edition published in Great Britain 1998 by
SEVERN HOUSE PUBLISHERS LTD of
9–15 High Street, Sutton, Surrey SM1 1DF.
This first world edition published in the U.S.A. 1998 by
SEVERN HOUSE PUBLISHERS INC of
595 Madison Avenue, New York, N.Y. 10022.

British Library Cataloguing in Publication Data

James, Margaret, 1949-
Hallowed ground
1. Title
823.9'14 [F]

ISBN 0-7278-5259-0

Typeset by Hewer Text Ltd,
Edinburgh, Scotland.
Printed and bound in Great Britain by
MPG Books Ltd, Bodmin, Cornwall.

Prologue

I had finished drinking my morning coffee, and this was just as well because otherwise there would have been scalding liquid as well as broken china spread all over my desk.

"Alex?" Disturbed by this unexpected smashing of crockery, my secretary looked up. She frowned at me in concern. "Alex, what's the matter?"

"Nothing." Hastily scooping up the remains of the mug which, in falling, had hit my ashtray and taken a jagged chip out of its side, I managed to force a smile. "Just a spot of Monday morning clumsiness, that's all. It's a good job the mug was empty."

"Yes." Gina eyed me narrowly. "But do you feel all right? You're looking very pale. I'm sure you shouldn't be back at work just yet. I mean, that bloke *did* give you a very nasty one—"

"I'm fine," I said, through gritted teeth. I thought, please God, don't let her notice the tremor in my hands, don't let her say anything more.

My prayer was answered. After staring hard at me for a few seconds more, she turned back to her keyboard, went on with her work, and left me to get on with mine.

I really don't know how I managed to turn that page of the *Daily Telegraph*, to leave the exclusive story which some stringer had presumably picked up, and then faxed to the news desk. But, I told myself, it wasn't particularly worrying. Or not yet, anyway.

Somehow, I managed to do some work that morning. At one o'clock, I went out for a walk. Sitting down on a convenient park bench, I took out the *Telegraph* again, and read the story through a second time.

Now, I became more anxious, for the full impact of what I'd read had hit me. They'd be looking, of course they would. So how long might it take them to find *me*?

I stared across the park, towards the children on the swings and slides and roundabouts. But all the time my inward eye was staring at something else.

For I had buried the body they'd discovered – and now the past was going to catch up with me.

Chapter One

"It's strange you should ring, because I actually heard this morning," said Helen Tremain, and Alex Colborn could imagine her opening the letter, which she was probably re-reading at that very moment. "Well, Alex? What about you?"

"My landlord said he'd send my letters on, so I presume my offer must be in the post. I hope so, anyway. I'd better give them a ring then, I suppose."

"I'll get off the line, and let you make the call."

"Right." For a moment, Alex Colborn hesitated. "Ah – Helen?" he began.

"Yes?" said Helen.

"If we *do* get posted to the same department, I was wondering – what I mean is, would you like to share a flat? Or a house, or something? I—"

"That might be quite a good idea," said Helen. She sounded both amused and a little flattered, Alex decided. But before he could turn this to his advantage, Helen spoke again. "So you make that phone call," she continued. "Then let me know how you got on, okay?"

It was after lunch by the time Alex phoned again, to tell Helen that he'd been successful too. He was also posted to the DHSS, so it looked as if he and Helen would end up in the same provincial office, in the ancient Hampshire city of Westingford.

* * *

"I was afraid it would be Westingford," said Helen, when she and Alex met for coffee at the University of London Students' Union.

"Why afraid?" asked Alex.

"You've obviously never been there." Helen licked the foam from her plastic teaspoon, then replaced it in the china saucer. "The place is an absolute dump. It might have been quite picturesque, back in the distant past – but it was flattened during the war, and they rebuilt it in the Marxist-Leninist style, in concrete, chrome and steel. Of course, the concrete's stained and crumbling now. The ring road is a nightmare, the pedestrian underpasses are disgusting, and there's dog mess everywhere."

"But it's in a really beautiful part of England, and I've heard there are very attractive towns and villages nearby." Alex, Helen noticed, was for some reason doing his level best to sell her this lousy package of boring job, dreadful pay and terrible location. "We could check some of them out, if you like," he told her. "If you're not busy this weekend, we might go and look around."

"Yeah, I suppose we might." Helen stirred her coffee, round and round and round. Poor Alex, she thought, he's been trying to get his leg over for ages. Almost from day one of Freshers' Week. Almost for a whole three years, in fact.

Helen could not think why. It wasn't as if she were God's gift to men – and Alex himself was certainly no desperate, rancid loser. In fact, he was quite tasty, if you liked that sort of thing. She supposed it must be the fact that she herself was living with someone else which turned some people on. "I've got Tom Stenton's Metro at the moment," she informed him.

"Excellent." Alex grinned. "Okay, then – Saturday it is. I'll come round to your place."

"All right. But don't be there all bright and bushy-tailed, at the crack of dawn." Extravagantly, Helen yawned. "I've days and weeks of sleep to catch up on now. Finals really stressed me out, you see."

It wasn't only Finals which had taken their toll on Helen's health and temper. Tom Stenton had a case to answer, too. But no, she wouldn't think about Tom Stenton, that was too much like hard work. Talking of work, it had come as quite a blow, this sudden realisation that the rest of her life began here. That unless she could arrange to have an income from some other source – such as begging, borrowing or inheriting, by marrying money or by stealing it – she would now have to flog her guts out in return for her daily bread.

She wondered now if Alex felt it, too. If he knew that the day the pair of them walked into the Westingford office of the Department of Health and Social Security, it would be as if a great portcullis had come clanking down behind them. As if a blind rolled down, for all eternity.

She supposed she should be grateful that she was on the fast track, to guaranteed promotion. If she was a good, obedient trainee, in five years' time she'd find herself in Whitehall, helping government ministers make policy decisions. As opposed to arguing with belligerent claimants, and toiling at the National Insurance coalface every day.

"You're late," she said, when she finally answered the door that Saturday morning.

"You told me not to come early." Alex looked aggrieved. But then he saw that Helen was smiling at him, and he grinned back at her. "Ready for the off?" he asked.

"Just let me find the keys." Helen located these on the windowsill. "Come on, then. Let's get going," she said, walking out of the front door.

Obediently, Alex followed her, closing the door behind

him. They got into Tom Stenton's little car, then Helen drove away.

Although the city fathers of Westingford had done their level best to wreck the place, although they had torn out its mediaeval heart and built wind tunnels of shopping arcades where there'd once existed the most charming higgledy-piggle of lanes in all of south-east England, they had left the Victorian suburbs almost intact. So the area around the red brick university, and the rural districts round about the city, seemed safe in a time-warp of at least fifty years ago.

But property to let proved to be both scarce and surprisingly expensive, so Helen and Alex decided they'd need to broaden their horizons. Alex opened the road atlas at random, then let his fingers walk across the page.

"Let's go and look at Eversleigh and Rettingham," he suggested. So Helen drove Thomas Stenton's brand new Metro out of the windy city and into the open countryside, arriving in the little market town of Rettingham in time for the pubs to be opening, and for the townspeople to be taking their lunch breaks in the August sunshine.

They parked the car, then went to look for somewhere cheap to eat. "What about the Saracen's Head?" said Alex. "They do bar snacks and sandwiches."

"I fancy the Black Swan," said Helen, looking across the street. "It says it's got a garden. We could have our lunch amidst the pansies and sweet peas."

"Yeah, that's fine by me." Alex had seen the sign announcing that the Black Swan sold real ales.

It was in the dark saloon bar of the Swan that they first got talking to the genial landlord. "Not local, are you?" he began, drawing Alex a pint of Old Peculiar, then adding that the young lady here was sure to like it, too.

"No, we've come from London." Alex handed over a green pound note. "But we're moving into the area very shortly."

"Actually," said Helen, giving the man her brightest, most charming smile, "we're looking for somewhere to live."

"To buy or rent, would that be?"

"Oh – to rent, I think." Helen knew she was having the desired effect, so she now stepped up the wattage. "Do you know anywhere? The cheaper the better, of course."

"You need to talk to Jack." The landlord called to a man who was sitting quietly in a gloomy corner. He told them that if they were looking for a place to rent, if they wanted something cheap and convenient, a good mate of his had this house in Sydenham Street.

In that summer of 1984, the Merchant's House was going to rack and ruin. It *was* a ruin, to all intents and purposes, and most probably it ought to have been condemned.

When Helen first saw it, she was quite appalled. As a student, she had lived in plenty of ramshackle and even dangerously decrepit places, and she thought she'd seen it all. But the Merchant's House was something else again. It brought a whole new dimension of meaning to the simple expression 'tip'.

Standing all by itself in huge, untended grounds, set well back from the street and hemmed in by a motley collection of outhouses, sheds and stables, it looked exactly like the prototype for the haunted house of a thousand children's comics, or for the *Scooby Doo* cartoons.

"I'm waiting for the property boom to peak," explained Mr Jarvis, as he unlocked the heavily studded front door, then put his shoulder to the splintering wood and finally forced it open. "I reckon the site alone's worth close to three hundred grand – but it's going to fetch a cool half million quid in six or seven months' time. I'll make a killing, then! Well, I suppose this is the lounge."

"How nice," said Helen. Oh my God, she thought, I'm sure that was a rat.

"The kitchen's through the hallway. There's gas piped from the mains. Or at least, there ought to be."

Alex stared all around, looking for sockets and switches. "But there isn't any electricity?"

"No." Mr Jarvis shrugged. "You want to see the bedrooms?"

"Yes, okay."

"Be careful on the stairs. A few of the boards are a little bit rotten, see."

"Well, at least he's an honest bastard," muttered Alex, as he and Helen followed their prospective landlord up the spectacularly rickety staircase. "Yeah, he seems a candid sort of git—"

"Shut up," hissed Helen, trying not to giggle. She walked across the landing. "It's quite a pretty house," she observed, and Alex found himself agreeing there. He gazed up at what was a beautiful but dilapidated Jacobean ceiling, in urgent need of expert restoration. If he'd had the money—

"Stay here until you find somewhere permanent, eh?" Mr Jarvis grinned encouragingly. "I know it's damp, but open a couple of windows, and it'll soon dry out. I'll be honest with you, okay? You'll be doing me a sort of favour, see."

"A favour?" echoed Alex.

"Yeah." Mr Jarvis sighed. "Last winter, we had dossers, tramps, the lot. They did no end of damage. So if you'll take the place, I'll let you have it cheap."

"How cheap?" asked Alex. For cheap in London meant eighty quid a month, for a squalid basement bedsit. All bills exclusive, and extra for a phone.

"A tenner each a week," said Mr Jarvis.

"A fiver," suggested Alex, trying it on.

"What? Well, all right. If you pay the gas yourselves." Mr Jarvis leered at Helen's legs. "You'll never find anything else as cheap as that."

"I'm sure you're right." Alex met the landlord's subtle gaze. "Okay, then – do you have a contract with you?"

"Oh, don't you worry your heads about none of that." Mr Jarvis grinned again. "Just give me twenty down, and then I'll trust you. I'm always passing, so I can call in."

"I'll give you a cheque, and I'll want a full receipt."

"No problem." Mr Jarvis winked at Helen. "He's very careful, this young man of yours. You hang on to him – he'll see you right."

"He didn't want tenants with any legal rights," said Alex, scowling. He and Helen walked back down the street to where they'd parked the car. "He needs somebody to keep an eye on things. But he's far too mean to pay Securicor, or someone from Group 4."

"So instead, we're paying *him*." Helen shook her head. "That man will go far."

"But it *is* extremely cheap," said Alex, wondering how the hell they were going to light, dry out and heat the wretched place.

"It's very convenient, too. Five minutes from the station. Plenty of pubs and shops just down the road—"

"Exactly." Alex had noticed all the pubs, and had been very much encouraged. "We could ask Paul Graham and Julia Newman if they'd like to join us. The rent would be just peanuts, if we split it four ways."

"Paul has got that job in Fareham, then?"

"Yes, and Julia's doing a load of freelance stuff at present, so it doesn't really matter where she lives."

"So what about it?" Helen had parted with her own ten

quid, but if Alex wasn't planning to stay very long, she didn't fancy living at the Merchant's House alone. "What do you really think? Look, we could get a cat, to deal with the rats and mice. There aren't any other houses within earshot, so we could make a racket and nobody's going to complain about the noise. We could have some *wild* parties!"

"We could indeed," said Alex, and Helen could almost see the next idea forming in his mind.

Well, she decided, that might not be a bad thing, after all. Tom Stenton was becoming too possessive. No, *ob*sessive – that was the actual word. So although she had briefly toyed with the idea of staying in London, and commuting to Westingford, she now made up her mind. "Come on Alex," she whispered, huskily. "Let's do it, yeah?"

"Let's take the Merchant's House, you mean?" he countered.

"Well, that's one idea." Eyeing Alex narrowly, with a green-eyed, feline stare, Helen licked her lips. Lazily, she yawned. "Tom's gone to spend a few days with his ghastly parents," she continued. "He went up to Edinburgh by sleeper, late on Wednesday night."

"So that's why you've got his car." Understanding, Alex grinned. "Actually, I thought it was a bit uncharacteristic, letting you out on a sunny Saturday, to go on a jaunt with me."

"He's getting quite ridiculous these days." Helen scowled now. "He thinks I'm working in the Union bar all this weekend. If he knew I was gadding around the countryside, with another man, it would really blow his mind."

"He always was a nutter." Alex took Helen's hand. "We could go back to my place," he suggested.

"Or to mine." Helen gave Alex's fingers some answering pressure. "By the way, I like to be on top," she said.

Chapter Two

The move to Rettingham went surprisingly smoothly, considering how much stuff there was to shift. It was a help that Alex's best friend, Paul Graham, owned a Ford Transit van into which he, Alex and Helen managed to cram almost all of their various belongings.

Helen said she'd go by train, but then decided she wouldn't mind lying on the pile of duvets, sleeping bags and a dozen assorted cushions after all. So that fine Tuesday morning in September they creaked and rattled over to Rettingham.

"God, what a dump," said Paul, as he surveyed the Merchant's House.

"I told you it was basic," said Alex, mildly. "So did Helen. You were too drunk to notice."

"But there's basic and there's squalid," muttered Paul. "This place is a bloody ruin!"

"It's a Grade One listed ruin." Alex dragged a box of saucepans out of the back of the van. "Stop moaning, and remember what you were paying for that rat hole in Blackheath."

"At least my rat hole had mains drainage, and electric light."

"But candles and lanterns are just *so* romantic." Helen smiled up at Alex. "I think this place is absolutely lovely."

"Yeah, well. As you say, it's very cheap." At the thought of saving so much money, which he could then spend on football, fags and beer, Paul grinned, too. "But Julie's going to have a purple fit, when she realises there's no bathroom."

"She'll get used to it," said Helen, confidently. "If she's that particular, she can always take the hip bath from the scullery up to her own room. But I shall wash myself at the kitchen sink."

"How very *Sons and Lovers*," observed Paul.

"Well, *you* don't wash at all," said Alex, "so you won't have a problem." Drawing Helen close to him, he hugged her, then he kissed her on the nose.

"Don't mind me," said Paul.

"Okay," said Helen, kissing Alex on the mouth.

Paul lit a cigarette. "But doesn't that other bloke of yours object to the fact that you've started carrying on with Colborn here?" he muttered.

"It's actually none of your business, but as of last Friday, Thomas Stenton's ancient history." Helen stopped canoodling with Alex, and regarded Paul severely. "When I told him Alex and I had been down to Rettingham in his precious Metro, he really lost his temper. He called me all the names under the sun. We had a flaming row, and he told me that if he never saw me again, it would be far too soon. So I told *him* he could go and fuck himself, because he certainly wasn't screwing me any more."

"Dear Helen," said Paul, "you were always a perfect lady. But how did you get away from the evil bastard? How—"

"As Helen says," interrupted Alex tersely, "it's absolutely no concern of yours. So why don't you—"

"Okay, you guys," interrupted Paul, "we'd better get on with it." He grabbed a sleeping bag, and a couple of lumpy pillows. "Well, then? Do I get a guided tour of Castle Dread? Or do I have to find my own way round the place?"

* * *

"It won't be too bad at all, once we get everything cleaned up," said Paul, as they ate a Chinese takeaway by the light of a flickering candle. He opened another carton, and dug around inside. "God, what's this stringy mess? It looks like prunes in vomit."

"It's supposed to be shredded duck, with plum and orange sauce." Alex reached across, and forked up a generous mouthful. "It's okay," he said. "But I reckon this particular duck had long, black fur and whiskers."

"Alex!" exclaimed Helen.

"Only joking, sweetheart." Alex poured her another glass of lager. "This is the life," he said.

"Yeah, it's all right." Paul gazed round the kitchen. "Like I say, it's not as bad as it might be, I suppose. If we slap a bit of paint on all the walls—"

"A sort of apricot in here, I think." Helen tapped the bulging wall behind her. "It would only need a couple of coats of emulsion. The plaster seems fairly sound."

"You could rag roll it, perhaps. Or try a bit of dragging, or maybe stippling."

"Yes!" Helen realised Paul was teasing her, but she didn't really mind. For the house was lovely, and the kitchen looked particularly romantic, in the gentle glow of candlelight, with the setting sun bathing the plastered walls in a soft, warm phosphorescence. The scents from the overgrown garden wafted in through the open window, and the shadows obscured the cracks and holes and general dilapidation.

"We'll have to get some firewood in for winter," said Alex, opening another bottle. "But the garden's full of trees, so that's no problem. If we can use that fireplace in the lobby—"

"We could send young Helen scrambling up the chimney. She could sweep it clean—"

"Then we could have log fires—"

"Mulled ale—"

"Or cinnamon toast, and crumpets—"

"We could even roast a pig, on an iron spit." Paul grinned ghoulishly at Helen. "Why don't we get a pig? We could fatten it on kitchen scraps and stuff. Then, at Christmas, one of you guys could go out there, with your little hatchet—"

"Why one of us?" asked Helen.

"Well, *I* couldn't do it. I'm not a country boy. But Alex here—"

"No chance," said Alex. "I couldn't kill anything."

"This place just needs some TLC, that's all," said Helen, bringing them back to reality. "We'll go and buy some paint and stuff tomorrow. But now, I'm ready for bed."

"Yeah, so am I," said Alex.

"I'll wash up." Paul exhaled a cloud of beer fumes, then staggered to his feet. "At least there's running water. When I first saw this dump, I was afraid we'd have to dig ourselves a well."

He ran some water into the huge, stone sink. "By the way, when do you two guys start work?"

"Next Monday." Helen pulled a face. "Oh, God. The very thought—"

"You should have married Stenton, then. *He*'s absolutely loaded. You could have been a Lady Who Lunched, if you'd married old Tom Stenton. Or at any rate, you wouldn't have had to get a boring job."

"Does Thomas have a job yet?" enquired Alex.

"I don't think so." Helen shrugged. "But as our knowledgeable friend here has observed, he's not short of money. His father's some big shot in the Tartan Triangle, you see."

"The what?" grinned Paul, dunking their greasy plates in ice-cold water.

"Old man Stenton's coining it, running a haulage franchise. His lorries and ferries operate between the highlands and the islands, from Inverness to Glasgow, and all points in between. So if Thomas doesn't manage to get himself a proper job I suppose he'll find some sinecure in the family firm. Alex, those boxes can wait until morning, can't they?"

"Yes, of course. Right then, I'm coming to bed." Alex grinned at Paul. "Look here, my man," he said, "you've been on the go all day. Why don't you take the rest of the evening off?"

"Bog off, Colborn." Paul Graham snatched up his faded denim jacket. "I'm going to find a call box and ring Julie, tell her I'm coming back to the Smoke tonight. But I'll be here first thing tomorrow morning. Any chance of getting a phone put in, do you reckon?"

"I'll find out." Helen was half way up the stairs by now. "Goodnight then, Paul."

"Sleep tight." Paul winked at her lasciviously, then opened the front door. They heard his van drive off into the night.

"I wish Paul wouldn't wink at me like that," said Helen, as she and Alex lay in each other's arms, in a tangle of sheets and blankets. "He must think I'm a slut."

"Of course he doesn't." Alex kissed her naked shoulder. "He's just jealous."

"But why should he be jealous? Julia's a very attractive girl."

"Yes, she's very sweet. But she's nowhere near as beautiful as you."

"She'll hate it here. She'll grumble about the lack of facilities, and she'll be terrified of all the spiders. She'll want to have the whole place fumigated, I expect."

"Then it'll be up to her to sort it out." Alex hauled Helen back on top of him. "Oh, God," he cried, "I've waited so long for you! I thought you'd never tell bloody Thomas Stenton to bugger off! I—"

"I'd been trying to dump him for months and months and months. For almost a year, in fact. The trouble is, he's not an easy person to escape from, do you see?"

"Do you reckon he still loves *you*, then?"

"Maybe. Well – I don't think he actually loves me." Helen shrugged. "But honestly, he's a world class obsessive. When I was with him I really couldn't call my soul my own. He always wanted to know where I was going, whom I'd be with, what time I'd be getting home. He once said – and this was after we'd just made love, can you believe it – that if I ever left him, he would kill himself. But before that, he'd kill me."

"Well, people often say things they don't mean."

"But I think he meant that."

"No. The fact is, he was trying to be hard. I mean, if you're a little bloke like Stenton, you have to pretend you're hard. Look at Napoleon. He was a little guy, too."

"Napoleon *was* hard!"

"But Stenton bloody isn't."

"You're sure of that?"

"I'm absolutely certain."

"I hope you're right." Helen still looked troubled. "But I'm very glad you're so much bigger than he is."

"Yeah, he'd have to bite my ankles. Or at best go for my knees." Alex looked into Helen's emerald eyes. She saw his own were huge. They didn't talk again.

They were sleeping the sleep of the totally exhausted when the smoke began to drift up the rotten staircase, and billow across the landing towards their room.

Chapter Three

Alex woke up first. The smoke was drifting across the bedroom now, and there was a sound like the creaking of timber, like a ship in a storm, although there was little wind. The sound of ghostly footsteps echoed on the stairs.

Still not properly awake, for some reason he didn't panic. Getting out of bed, he groped his way on to the pitch black landing, making a mental note that he must buy a torch – no, a couple of torches – first thing tomorrow morning.

There didn't seem to be a blaze, or at least he couldn't hear or feel or see one. Perhaps somebody along the road was having a midnight bonfire? All the same, he went back to the bedroom, and woke Helen. "Get up," he whispered – he didn't quite know why he was whispering. "Helen? Helen!"

"Alex?" Helen opened her eyes, and blinked in the sullen gloom. Then, she smelled the smoke. "Oh, God!" she cried, "there must be a fire—"

"Come on, now." Alex took her hand. Still he felt unreasonably calm, as if he had been tripping. "Perhaps it's that bugger Graham trying to scare us."

They were almost at the bottom of the rather rickety staircase when they saw the flash of light, and smelled the acrid tang of burning sulphur.

"What the hell?" Stumbling against the heaps of books and clothes and cooking pots still cluttering up the narrow entrance hall, Alex ran into the kitchen in time to see the pile of polystyrene cartons, greasy paper bags and disposable plastic dishes, which had contained their Chinese feast, go up in flames.

He grabbed his new cord jacket from the back of a dining chair, and threw it over the blaze. Then, he shunted the whole lot into the sink, and turned the icy water on full blast. The hiss and crackle of fire gave way to a sullen fizzing. The kitchen was filled with thick, black, pungent smoke.

"Alex!" Terrified, Helen grabbed him by the arm and held on tightly. "Alex, what happened, what—"

"It's all right, sweetheart." Alex had recovered a little from his own shock and terror, and now he even managed to find and light a piece of candle. "It's okay, don't worry. Paul must have left a match on a greasy lid, and somehow it ignited."

"What?" Helen rubbed her eyes and stared at him. "Don't be ridiculous!"

"Well, polystyrene's very inflammable. I remember seeing Graham chucking his matches into the heap, and I almost said—"

"But why should a used match suddenly re-ignite, at four o'clock in the morning?"

"I don't know!" Alex stared straight back at her, afraid to consider any other explanation. "How do you explain it?"

"Oh, I suppose I don't." Helen picked her way across to the great stone sink. "That was your new jacket," she observed.

"Well, I didn't have time to make the perfect choice of emergency fire blanket."

"No, of course." Helen laid her head on Alex's shoulder. "Perhaps it was a cigarette end," she suggested. "They can smoulder away for ages and ages."

"That's true," Alex said.

"Maybe we should ask Paul not to smoke when he's in the house. All this wood and plaster – it would go up like a torch, once a fire got a proper hold."

"I'll speak to him about it. Julia doesn't like him smoking, so she'll be on our side." Alex stroked Helen's hair. "You okay?"

"Yes, fine." Helen hugged him round the waist. "My hero," she murmured, giggling.

"Come on, then." Alex edged towards the doorway. "Let's get a bit of shut-eye. We can easily clear this mess up in the morning."

When Alex and Helen finally got up and went down to the kitchen later that same morning, they discovered it was worse than they'd supposed. In addition to the debris from the fire, they found packets of biscuits, bags of sugar and boxes of cereals upended and their contents spilled all over the walk-in larder.

"My God," cried Helen, appalled. "So that's why this wretched place has been left empty for the past however many years!"

"You mean you think we've got a poltergeist?" Alex surveyed the shambles. Then, gingerly, he tapped one of the shelves. "This house is timber-framed, okay?" he said. "Also, it's falling apart. So it rocks in even the slightest little wind. These shelves are rotten. They wobble if I touch them. So, when I came charging in here last night I set up vibrations which sent all this lot tumbling."

"You reckon?" Helen picked up a box of cornflakes. "This inside packet looks as if it's been cut with scissors."

"Oh, but that thin plastic easily tears."

"Yes, I suppose that's true." Helen looked up at him. "So you don't buy the ghostly joker theory?"

"Not at all."

"Perhaps someone broke in?"

"No, I checked," said Alex, and he shrugged. "The doors were locked, the windows were all closed. There's no sign whatsoever of forced entry."

"Good." Helen managed a smile. "I'm glad you're here."

"So am I," said Alex, hugging her. "I'll look after you," he promised.

"You'll be my very own personal ghostbuster?"

"You got it." Alex grinned. "Let's have breakfast, shall we? Then, we'll go out somewhere. Do something really wild."

"But Paul said he'd be over—"

"Bugger Paul." Alex pulled a face. "Remember, the rest of our lives begin on Monday. Our last few hours of freedom are ticking inexorably away."

As he had half expected, Alex really hated his new job. But Helen didn't mind it quite as much as she had feared. Although even she was irritated and almost overwhelmed by the amount of finicking detail, by the sheer volume of material she was expected to absorb.

Great, thick, dark green binders of procedural instructions landed on her desk at least three times a day, and she was told she would be tested at the end of every month. If she passed these little local tests, she'd be going on various courses, in Blackpool, Basingstoke and Birmingham, in order to refine her expertise.

"What I can't stand is all the argument and pointless messing about, just to work out who qualifies for this and who isn't getting that," she complained to Alex, as she pored over the volume calling itself *Discretionary Payments 1982*. "If a single mother's cooker has blown up, and she reckons she needs a new one, the bloody state should give her one. Why should she have to grovel to the likes of you and me?"

"There needs to be a system. Or she'll think, this is all right, and demand a television set next week." Alex had spent the past ten days accompanying a Visiting Officer, round one of Westingford's most deprived estates. He'd been disgusted by the attitude of some of the younger claimants, who seemed to think they had only to ask, for the government to provide.

"The department doesn't buy televisions for claimants. It never has done, either." Helen closed the Code. "Alex, it's lunchtime – are you coming down the pub?"

After Alex, Helen and Julia had given him the third degree, Paul Graham promised he'd try to give up smoking, at least in the Merchant's House. But he vehemently denied leaving any smouldering matches or glowing cigarette ends on the heap of rubbish which had subsequently caught fire.

"I think we'll have to get some proper locks put on the doors," said Julia, who to everyone's surprise had proved astonishingly adaptable, and who seemed to enjoy living in the Merchant's House. "Otherwise, we might start getting people breaking in."

"Right, I'll see about it this weekend." Paul turned to see who had come into the kitchen. "Hello, Helen," he said. "You're late tonight."

"Yes, I know. I had to see the manager, at the office."

"On the carpet, were you?"

"No, he said I was doing fine. He just asked me where I thought I'd like to go, when I apply for posting." Helen dumped her bag on the kitchen table. "Paul, where's Alex?"

"He was in here earlier, but he went down to the off-licence about five minutes ago. I'm surprised you didn't pass him. Helen, are you all right?"

"I think so. Why?"

"You're very pale."

"Yes, you are." Julia poured Helen a cup of tea. "But you've had a long day at the office."

"Yes, I suppose I have."

It wasn't until Alex and Helen were in bed together that same evening that Helen finally told him what had happened. "I'd been doing some easy interviews on my own, right?" she began. "So I went into one of the cubicles after lunch, expecting to see this man about his industrial injury – and there he was!"

"There who was?" asked Alex.

"Tom, of course!"

"Tom Stenton, do you mean?"

"Yes!" cried Helen.

"So what did he want?"

"Alex, he was horrible!" Helen began to cry. "He said – he said I was nothing but a whore. He said that if he thought I was going to dump him and live happily ever after with that arsehole Colborn – sorry, Alex – I could just think again. Because wherever I went, whatever I did, he'd always be watching me. He'd always be there, waiting. He had no intention of being made a fool of by you or me, and if I didn't leave you before the end of this week, I could start counting out my days on the fingers of one hand. Because that's about as many as I'd have left."

"Stupid bastard." Alex glared into the darkness. "He's only trying it on," he muttered. "How did he know where to find you, anyway?"

"Oh, that was simple. He rang my mother and asked for my new address."

"So she just *gave* it to him?"

"Yes, of course." Miserably, Helen sniffed. "She doesn't know what he's like. He's always been perfectly charming towards her. She was saying only last week it was such a pity we'd split up."

"Helen, how long has he been skulking around the place?"

"About a week or two."

"What?" Alex was aghast. "Why didn't you tell me?"

"I didn't want to bother you." Helen started to cry again. "He's t-trying to drive me round the bend, I think. He hangs around the office, he follows me when I go into town, then trails me back here."

"God! Why on earth didn't you say?" Alex made up his mind. "Right, from now on, I'll come with you everywhere. Bugger flexible working hours, and covering shifts – we'll go to work at the same time, and we'll come home together. We'll take the same breaks for lunch. If Stenton comes within six feet of you, I'll knock him into the middle of next week."

"I was wondering if I should go to the police?"

"Why the police?"

"Well, perhaps they could tell him to stop annoying me."

"I don't think there's any need to involve the police." Alex took Helen in his arms, and held her. "I'll make sure he doesn't bother you."

But, as Helen and Alex would discover, it wasn't quite that simple. Thomas Stenton appeared to have nothing to do, and he certainly had no shame about the way he was behaving. As Alex and Helen left for Rettingham station at eight fifteen each morning, they would be trailed by a dark blue Metro. As they walked home at half past six each evening, the Metro would crawl slowly after them, until they reached the house.

But Alex was not particularly concerned. He was almost sure Thomas wouldn't dare to pester Helen, not if he were with her. He took Julia and Paul into his confidence, and between them they mounted what was effectively a twenty-four hour guard on Thomas Stenton's quarry.

"He's bound to get fed up and bugger off," said Paul, as the four of them sat at the kitchen table one cold autumn evening, eating their supper by golden candlelight. "I'm sure that with the winter coming, he'll get sick of hanging around outside, freezing his bollocks off."

"I just hope you're right." Julia shook her head. "All this cloak and dagger stuff is giving me the creeps." She turned to Helen now. "There's a good film on at Studio One this week," she told her, brightly. "Why don't we all go and see it?"

"If you mean the one with Harrison Ford, I've already seen it, when it was on at Leicester Square." Alex collected up the dirty dishes. "But I don't mind if you lot want to go."

"Helen?" Paul looked up at her, and grinned encouragingly. "Come with me and Julie? You can sit between us, if you want to feel extra safe."

"Alex?" began Helen, doubtfully.

"Yes, why don't you go?" Alex yawned, then rubbed his tired eyes. "I've got another test coming up on Friday. So I suppose I ought to spend a bit of time mugging up the stuff in all those blasted Codes."

"You're still living life in the fast lane, eh?" grinned Paul.

"Shut it, Graham," said Alex.

"So the rest of us'll be off, then?" prompted Julia.

"Okay." Bravely, Helen forced a smile.

"That's the ticket, sunshine." Paul gave her a hug. "Don't worry, we'll look after you – won't we, Julie? If we have any bother from the Phantom of the Opera, we'll march him down to the nearest nick, okay?"

"I'm hoping it won't come to that," said Helen.

"Well," said Paul, "that's entirely up to him. But if he wants to be a pest, I'm quite happy to thump him."

So Helen, Paul and Julia went to the cinema, leaving Alex at home to study for his test. Cracking open a can of lager, he sat down at the kitchen table and opened all his books, determined this would be the evening that he'd finally get to grips with *Retirement Pensions – Provisions, Claims and Law*. He was yawning over this when someone hammered heavily on the door of the Merchant's House.

"Stupid bastards," muttered Alex, thinking that at least one of his fellow residents could have remembered to take a key. "Coming," he called, and stumped along the passage.

He opened the front door to find a small, slim, fair-haired man standing waiting on the step. "Good evening," said Thomas Stenton.

"You what?" Alex glared at him. "You've got a nerve!"

"May I come in?" asked Thomas.

"Why?" growled Alex.

"I'd like to talk to you."

"She isn't here, you know." Alex was torn between thumping the little sod, and slamming the door in his pretty choirboy's face. "She's gone out, with friends."

"I know." Thomas Stenton smiled seraphically. "I saw them all go into Studio One."

"You mean, you trailed them to the cinema, sat behind them all through the evening, and generally made a nuisance of yourself." Alex glared. "I have nothing to say to you."

"Please, can't we talk about this?" Again, Thomas Stenton smiled. He actually had a rather charming smile, thought Alex, sourly. It was no wonder Helen's mother had been smitten.

"Oh, all right. Come in." Alex stood back, to let him walk inside.

The kitchen looked warm and welcoming. Despairing of ever getting good enough light from candle power alone, Paul and Alex had gone out and bought some oil lamps, which cast a mellow, golden glow on the ancient beams and roughly-plastered walls. They'd painted the plaster a soft apricot and even managed to sweep the kitchen chimney. Then they'd arranged for the delivery of half a ton of logs, some of which now burned in the open fireplace.

"This is nice," said Thomas. "It's really rather cosy. You've done a good job here."

"You think so?" Alex glared. "But of course. I was forgetting. You've been round here before."

"I'm sorry?"

"You visited us when we first moved in. I didn't tell Helen, but I reckon you got in through the scullery window. You lit a little fire."

"I've no idea what you're talking about." Thomas Stenton shrugged. "I was only saying—"

"What do you want?" interrupted Alex, curtly.

"I suppose I must want Helen, basically." Thomas shrugged again. "It's been a couple of months now, hasn't it? I'm sure she's quite enjoyed her little adventure. But the thing is, I've had enough of being without her. After all – she does belong to me."

"I can't believe I'm hearing this." Alex didn't know what to do. Thomas Stenton was far and away too small to hit. So, Alex supposed, a summary eviction would be the obvious thing. "I think you ought to leave now," he began.

"I'd like to wait for Helen, actually."

"She doesn't wish to see you."

"That's not for you to say."

"I'll give you ten seconds to leave of your own accord. If you haven't gone by then, I'll throw you out." Alex turned away. "Okay, I'm counting—"

He didn't see the kitchen knife until it was just inches from his throat. Until his arm was twisted behind his back, and Thomas Stenton's breath was hissing in his ear.

"You thought you could get away with it," he muttered. "But you were wrong, because I'm going to kill you. I—"

But Thomas Stenton didn't finish his diatribe, because Alex silenced him. Anger had made Thomas brave, but Alex was much stronger. Freeing his arm, he rounded on Thomas, snatched the knife from his hand.

Alex was never sure what happened next. When the brief, undignified scuffle was over, however, Thomas was lying on the cold, tiled floor, gasping like a dying fish.

As Alex stared aghast, he heard the key turn in the lock. As he watched the trickle of blood become a stream, as Thomas Stenton's shoulder became a horrible crimson sponge, as his blue eyes slowly closed, Helen walked into the room.

She didn't waste any time on screams of horror, or on any exclamations of disgust. Instead, she went up to Alex and took his hand, as if feeling for a pulse. "Did he hurt *you*?" she whispered.

"N-no, he didn't." Alex was in shock. "Helen, I—"

"Alex, we must get rid of him, before the others come."

"W-where are they now?" asked Alex.

"Paul fancied a drink, so they walked me to the door, saw me come in, then went on to the Swan. But I thought that was his car down by the shops, so I was afraid he might be here." Helen knelt down beside Thomas Stenton's body. Gingerly, she touched his wrist. "He isn't dead," she murmured.

"Thank God for that." Alex looked ready to faint away himself.

"But he does have a weak heart, so we can't take any chances." Helen got to her feet. "Will you help me take him to his car?"

"What?" Alex stared. "But we can't take him to Casualty!

They'll want to know what happened! How he was hurt – and then I'll be arrested!"

"I'm sure he must have provoked you."

"Too damned right he did!" Alex looked as if he might start to cry. "He grabbed the knife and held it to my neck. If I hadn't managed to fight him off, he'd have cut my throat, I'm sure of it."

"Then you acted in self-defence. There's nothing wrong with that."

"Helen, it's not that simple. It never is, and—"

"He needs medical attention." Helen took off her coat. "I don't want any blood on it," she explained. "Okay then, help me lift him."

"But—"

"We'll take him to Palmer Crescent Surgery." Helen began to pull the now semi-conscious Thomas into a sitting position, preparatory to dragging him to his feet. "If we leave him in the lobby, we can ring the bell, then scarper. Evening surgery will be over, but I'm sure that place has a locum on permanent call, twenty-four hours a day."

"Helen, this is insane. We can't just go and dump him like a parcel—"

"The alternative is taking him to Westingford A and E. Or letting him bleed to death on our kitchen floor." Helen met Alex's gaze. "Come *on*!" she whispered urgently, "I'll drive."

So, they manoeuvred Thomas to his feet. They covered his shoulder with one of Alex's jumpers and tied the sleeves around his neck. He was so small and light that it was relatively easy to half march, half carry him to his waiting car, and for some providential reason, they didn't meet a single passer-by.

Alex was about to start going through the pockets of his

blood-stained denim jacket when Helen noticed Thomas had left the keys in the ignition.

Alex sat with Thomas, in the back. Helen drove very carefully, breathing hard. When they reached the surgery, they did as Helen had suggested, ringing the bell marked Emergency for several desperate seconds, before legging it down the road.

"They'll find our prints all over the wretched car," cried Alex, as they ran.

"Only if they look for them," gasped Helen, in reply.

"We should have taken him to hospital. He might stay slumped there in that porch all night."

Helen stopped running. "Do you want to go back for him?" she demanded, sharply.

"No, not at all." Alex clenched his fists. "I want – I want—"

"You want him dead, and so do I." Helen began to walk very briskly now, in the general direction of the Merchant's House. "We mustn't hang about," she said. "There's bound to be some blood on the kitchen floor. We have to clean it up before Paul and Julia get back from the pub."

They strode along in silence after that.

"Helen," began Alex, as they walked into the house, "is it true what you said about Stenton?"

"What do you mean?" asked Helen.

"You said he has a heart condition – is that right?"

Helen shrugged. "It's what he always told me," she replied, going into the kitchen. She shuddered, then she fainted, falling to the floor.

Chapter Four

"It looks as if Creeping Jesus finally got the message," observed Paul Graham, a week after Helen and Alex had left Thomas Stenton lying on the surgery steps.

"About time, too," said Julia. "Don't you reckon, Helen?"

"What? Oh – yes." Absently, Helen stirred her vegetable soup, made by Julia on the ancient black-leaded range, and served with fresh bread baked in the genuine antique bread oven at the Merchant's House. "This is nice," she said, manfully swallowing a mouthful and trying to be normal, to act quite naturally.

"Anything in the local rag tonight?" Alex was also making rather heavy weather of eating his supper, but he hoped only Helen could see he was forcing it down. "Anything of interest, I mean?"

"What did you have in mind?" Paul was studying the classifieds in the motoring section of the *Rettingham Echo*, but as Julia placed his bowl of soup before him, he put it to one side. He tore off a piece of loaf, and chewed it vigorously. "This bread is ace," he said.

So Alex picked up the paper and looked through it himself. Meeting Helen's gaze, he shook his head. "It looks like we'll have to make our own fun this weekend," he told her, almost visibly relieved.

"Oh – I see." Helen dipped a piece of bread in her rapidly cooling soup. "Well, nothing ever happens in Rettingham."

"Anybody fancy a jar or two later on?" enquired Paul. "Alex, do you want to come down the Swan?"

"Not tonight, mate." Alex feigned a yawn. "I'm a bit tired, and—"

"Yeah, I bet." Grinning, Paul punched his shoulder. "You're like a pair of ferrets in a sack, the two of you. All night, every night – I dunno where you get the energy."

"Don't be such a yob, my love," said Julia, patiently. "More soup, anyone?"

"Not for Casanova here," said Paul. "He wants to go to bed."

Paul's comment had hit home, and Helen was embarrassed. But she could hardly explain, could hardly take him to one side and tell him, that this was the only way they could get to sleep. That they had to be so tired, so absolutely exhausted mentally, physically and emotionally, that shagging each other senseless – as Paul would no doubt have put it – was the only way they could manage to get some rest.

They went over it and over it, then over it and over it again. Helen in particular seemed to need to pick at the scab of memory, refusing to let it heal.

"I *didn't* stab him," said Alex, as he lay on his back in the darkness, worn out by an uneasy combination of too much sex and constant anxiety. But this evening, like all the others since it had happened, he was too wound up to rest. "He pulled the knife on *me*, for heaven's sake!"

"Yes, so you said."

"What's that supposed to mean?"

"Well, it wasn't *his* knife."

"He took it from the kitchen drawer, okay?"

"Okay." Helen rolled away from him. "The thing is, Alex, I never thought that *you* were a violent man."

"I'm not bloody violent!"

"You most certainly are. In fact, you were really hurting me just now."

"Why, what did I do?"

"You bit me, hard. You scratched my arm – look here. You know I don't like you going at it like a battering ram. But tonight, you forced your way inside without a thought for me."

"Darling, I'm sorry." Alex looked genuinely contrite. "I never meant to hurt you, honestly! I–I'm letting it get to me, I suppose."

"Well, I wish you wouldn't."

"I think we should go away, for a long weekend." Alex folded his arms behind his head. "We could go somewhere we've never been before. A pub in the Cotswolds, or the Chilterns – what do you think of that?"

"Yes, we could go to the Cotswolds, if you like." Indifferently, Helen shrugged. "It can't do any harm, I don't suppose."

"It would be a break," said Alex. "Helen?"

"What?"

"I love you," Alex told her.

"Do you?"

"Yes!" Alex touched her hand. "Do you still love me?"

"Yes, I imagine so." Helen got out of bed. "I need a drink of water," she muttered. "Okay if I take the lamp?"

"Of course. But Helen—"

"Go to sleep now, Alex." Helen put on her nightdress. "Try not to worry. We just need a little time."

The weekend in the Cotswolds was not a great success. They'd meant to go for some lengthy country walks, to blow all the cobwebs of guilt and recrimination right away. But instead, they spent two days more or less holed up in bleak little country pubs, watching rain slide down the windows, and trying to be polite to one another.

They arrived back at the Merchant's House tired, irritable and very ill at ease, to be greeted by Paul Graham who grinned and said he didn't know how Colborn stood the pace. "You want a cup of tea?" he enquired, as he watched them hang up their sopping coats, for they'd left their hired car in Westingford and walked up from the station. "The bromide's optional in Colborn's case."

Alex couldn't find the energy to tell him to bugger off.

"Young Julia's gone and got herself a flat," continued Paul, spooning sugar into his mug of builder's brew.

"Well, I can't say I blame her." He was warmed and somewhat revived by the caffeine hit, and now Alex grinned. "So she finally got sick of you?"

"No, mate. Not at all." Paul Graham cracked his knuckles. "Some maiden aunt of hers did the decent thing last month. She left Julie a couple of grand, so she's spent the dosh on a flat in Westingford. Well – the deposit, anyway. We're moving Monday week."

"We?" said Alex.

"Me and Jules, old mucker." Paul scratched his head. "I'll be sorry to leave you two guys stuck in this rat hole. But there's only the one bedroom, and—"

"That's okay." Helen forced a smile. "We like it here. Honestly, we do."

"It takes all sorts," said Paul. "You can come over and visit, of course you can. In fact, we'll be having a party on Saturday. You two could stay the night."

"That would be lovely." Helen smiled at him. "Do you need any help with moving?"

"No, that's no problem. I haven't got much stuff, so I'll just shove it all in the van." Paul shook his head at them. "Why don't you two look for something else? You could afford a place between you, I'd have thought? I dunno – I don't believe in ghosts, or elves or witches. But this old ruin – it gives me the creeps."

"As Helen says, we like it." Alex poured himself more lukewarm tea. "We'll stay here for the present, anyway. We'll both be posted in less than six months' time, so it probably won't be worth finding somewhere else."

"Yeah, I suppose you're right." Paul stood up. "Well, like I said, you're welcome to call round Julie's any time. Whenever Castle Dread starts to get you down."

But Alex and Helen had to work so very hard, and were sent on so many courses, that they never had time to wonder if the old house got them down.

In due course, Helen forgot the horrid details. Although she longed to know if Thomas Stenton had been found and if his injuries had been properly treated, she did not dare make any sort of enquiry. Instead, she assured herself that if a man had been discovered lying on a doctor's steps, dead or dying of stab wounds to the chest, the story would have made the local press.

"Of course it would," said Alex. "Look, stop worrying. Somebody came downstairs, and took him in. They sewed him up, then sent him on his way."

"How would he have explained his injuries?"

"I expect he spun them some convincing yarn. Then later, when he thought about what had happened, he realised he'd overplayed his hand. He decided he'd better leave us both alone."

"I suppose you're right." Helen rubbed her eyes. "They told me today that they're probably going to post me up to Newcastle in March."

"In one of those big, brown envelopes?" Alex grinned. "I'm down for the Audit Office, in sunny Basingstoke."

"That's definite, is it?"

"Well, it's looking likely."

"So it'll soon be goodbye, Rettingham."

"So long, Merchant's House." Alex covered Helen's hand with his. "I'll come up and see you."

"I'll come and see *you*."

"Good." But then, Alex frowned at her. "It *is* all right now, isn't it?" he demanded.

"What do you mean?"

"You know."

"Yes, Alex." Helen kissed him. "It's all right."

"You don't still think I'm a violent maniac?"

"Alex! I never thought anything of the kind!"

"But you said—"

"I remember what I said. But I was upset that night. I didn't mean it."

"I'll be glad to get away from here," said Alex.

"Yes? I've grown to like the Merchant's House, hovel though it is. If I had the money—"

"I think it's beyond repair."

"No, it just needs a little loving care." Helen looked up at him. "There's water coming through the larder roof," she said. "I was thinking yesterday, we ought to tell the landlord. He could send someone round."

"He won't do that," said Alex. "He actually wants the place to fall apart. The quicker the better, as far as he's concerned."

"But our food is getting damp. I opened a bag of flour this evening, and it was green with mould."

"We could easily get up on to the roof ourselves," Alex assured her. "There are ladders in the stables, and some bits and pieces of wood, to make repairs. If we were to climb up on to the kitchen roof, we could easily find the holes. We could patch them up with bitumen, I expect."

"So where does one get bitumen?"

"One buys it from a builder's yard, I think," said Alex. "But before we go to any expense like that, we'll have a rummage round the sheds and stables in the garden here. If we're lucky, we'll find everything we need."

Saturday dawned a bright, blue February morning. Dragging open the swollen kitchen door, Helen was enchanted to find a clump of snowdrops in full bloom outside. "This place must have been quite lovely once," she said, as she set off down the overgrown garden path.

"Yes, it must." Alex looked at her. "But it'll be the site of a lovely shopping centre fairly soon. That's if our genial landlord has his way."

"If he gets planning permission."

"If he greases the right palms, plays golf with the District Surveyor, and knows a few of the blokes in Planning Office." They stopped outside a shed. "Okay, then," said Alex, "let's have a look in here."

"It's very dark inside." Helen edged her way into the gloom. "Look, what's that stuff up there? On those high shelves?"

"Pass me that old chair, and I'll find out."

Alex sorted through the rusty tins, discovering ancient cans of solidified gloss and clotted white emulsion. He reached for a big, blue tin. "Here's some Carradine's Bituminous!" he cried. He squinted at the label. "Ideal for the renovation and repair of garages, outhouses, asphalt and felted roofs—"

"Excellent!" said Helen.

"It's probably set rock solid." Alex shook the tin. "Hang about. It sounds as if it's liquid. Perhaps it'll be okay."

"That's great." Helen peered up into the dusty darkness. "I don't suppose there are any paintbrushes, or nails and hammers, too?"

"This woman only wants a miracle." Alex jumped down from the chair. "I'm afraid not, sunshine. We'll have to explore the rest of the estate."

So they went from tumbledown summerhouse to rotten, collapsing stable, from dark and spidery coalhole to dilapidated shed. They found piles and piles of miscellaneous rubbish, including a large consignment of Welsh slate, which somebody had once ordered but never got round to putting on the roof. They found coils of rope and various gardening tools, such as spades and forks and rakes. But they couldn't find anything in the way of hammers, nails or pieces of useful timber, suitable for mending holes in a kitchen roof.

"There's still that shed at the very bottom of the kitchen garden," said Helen, doubtfully.

"That'll be full of flower pots," said Alex. "There'll be broken glass from cold frames, watering cans and bits of string."

"I'll go and have a look round, anyway."

"Okay." Alex had found a bamboo cane, and was already stirring the tin of bitumen.

He assumed that Helen must have been attacked by a particularly large spider. One with tattoos on its knuckles, perhaps, and maybe a bit of body piercing, too. But, as he began to run towards the shed, the screams intensified, and Alex himself grew anxious. "It's okay," he cried, "calm down, I'm coming!"

But as he pushed the door of the shed wide open, the dreadful screaming stopped.

"Helen?" At first, he couldn't see her. But then, he realised she was in the corner by the window. Staring in horror, she was silent now. "Helen," repeated Alex, "Helen, what *is* it?"

In reply, she grabbed his hand, and clawed at it convulsively.

He pulled her close to him. "It's okay," he whispered, he hoped reassuringly. "Come on – what's the matter?"

"O-o-over there!" She pointed to the darkest, dustiest corner. "Oh God!" She buried her face against his chest.

It took a while for Alex to adapt, for his vision to learn to cope with the murky darkness. But then, as he stared and stared, he made out a bulky shape. A bundle of rags – old clothes. A denim jacket. A black leather boot. A boot which still had a human foot in it. Or rather, the remains of a human foot, for the bone which protruded above the cuff of the boot had been picked and nibbled clean. Even as Alex watched, a rat scuttled out from underneath the heap of whatever it was, gave him a dirty look, and vanished into the gloom.

Apart from a pungent mustiness, there was no smell to speak of, no odour of decay. Alex realised this must be because all the soft tissue must have long since been eaten. How long did it take, he wondered, for rats and other vermin to consume a human body? Two weeks, six months? A year?

Helen was clinging to him, sobbing like a frightened little child. "H-he must have come back here," she wailed. "He got into the car, he drove up Milton Road—"

"Come on, Helen." Alex couldn't begin to imagine it. "He'd lost a lot of blood. He couldn't walk—"

"The doctor stitched him up. He said he'd be all right, so they gave him a cup of tea, and let him go. Then he came back to get me." Helen covered her face. "He must have parked up near the old allotments. He made his way through all the grass and brambles—"

"Helen," Alex began. "I honestly don't think—"

But, even as he tried to reassure her, Alex knew it must

be true. His eyes were now accustomed to the gloom, and as he glanced towards the thing lying in the corner, he saw a wisp of fine, fair, curling hair. The bastard *had* been blond. He *had* been wearing a denim jacket, old blue jeans, black boots. Black Doc Martens, with orange-yellow laces, just like the mouldering, damp-spotted things the creature wore.

"What shall we do?" asked Helen.

"Let me think." Alex ran through the possibilities. Of course, they should call the police. But then the body would be taken away for forensic examination. They'd find the stab wound, they'd match this with a certain sort of ordinary domestic blade—

Or would they? If this were a television play, of course they would. But was it that easy, could it be that cut and dried, in real life?

"We have to get rid of him," said Helen, her tone flat and expressionless with shock.

"What?" muttered Alex, frowning. "What did you say?"

"We must bury him!" A note of hysteria had crept into her voice. Soon, Alex realised, she'd be screaming once again, and this time somebody passing by might hear her. "Alex, they'll arrest us! They'll charge us with murder, try us, find us guilty! They'll lock us up for the rest of our natural lives! Look, we must dig a grave. We must, we must—"

"Hush, sweetheart." Alex stroked her hair. "Just let me think, all right?"

"Alex!"

"Okay, okay." Alex kissed her forehead. "I saw some spades and mattocks in one of the other sheds. I'll go and fetch them."

"Please don't leave me!"

"You come with me, then."

So they left the place of horror and went to find some tools. Fearing that Helen might possibly faint or have some sort of attack if she had to go back into that charnel pit, Alex led her away from the kitchen garden and back towards the house.

"Where shall we dig?" she whispered, fearfully.

"Not outside, because somebody might see us." Alex thought for a moment. Then he made up his mind. "The floor of the scullery is only beaten earth. If we dig a hole in there, we can bury him. Then we'll lay some of those slates which we found in the stable on the floor."

So that was what they did. They spent all the rest of that day excavating the grave, piling the earth very neatly to one side, and separating the few large rocks and boulders from the general mass. "We'll weight him down with those," said Alex.

"When will we – will we—"

"Bury him?" Alex was sweating very profusely now. "Tonight," he muttered. "We must get it over and done with, out of the bloody way."

"I don't – I'm sorry, but I don't think I could touch him." Helen looked sick and ill. "I know it's pathetic. But I honestly don't—"

"That's okay. There's an old tarpaulin or something like it back in one of the stables. I'll wrap him up in that. Then, I'll bring him to the house."

"All by yourself?"

"He won't be very heavy." Alex tried to look as if he didn't mind. He failed abysmally. "Shall we have something to eat?" he said. "I'm starving."

"I couldn't eat a thing," said Helen, who was trying not to cry.

"Well, I must have a sandwich. Or a bowl of cereal, and a cup of tea."

So Alex ate his cornflakes, drank three cups of tea, then

went to find the sheet to shroud the body. He also found some ancient gardening gloves, and some instinct for his own self-preservation made him pull these on.

He went down to the potting shed, groped for the creature lying prone inside, and covered it with the cloth. Fortunately, this was quite enormous and easily large enough to cover the decaying body. Giving himself no time to think, reflect or reconsider, Alex rolled his grisly parcel into a lumpy oblong, tied each end with twine, then dragged it back to the house.

Helen opened the door. Alex manoeuvred his trophy through to the scullery, then rolled it into the grave.

"Do you think it's deep enough?" asked Helen, as she peered anxiously round the door.

"It'll just have to be." Alex fetched a rock. He dropped it into the pit. He fetched another, then a third, enjoying the dull crunch of dry bones being splintered, of Thomas Stenton's body being flattened. He dropped the biggest boulder on the skull.

Then they filled in the grave, and smoothed the surface of the soil. "We'll lay the slates tomorrow," muttered Alex, as he patted the last shovelful of earth completely flat and wondered what to do with the heap left over.

"Okay." Helen looked as if she'd run a marathon. "I must go and wash," she said. As she turned to leave the scullery, she glanced back towards Alex. "Thank you for all you've done today," she said.

They lay in each other's arms that night, afraid to be disconnected. Too tired to make love, they simply held each other until they fell asleep. The following day, they filled a succession of buckets with the surplus earth, then dumped it on the overgrown flower beds outside the kitchen door, carefully forking it in. They laid the blue-grey slates in the scullery. Afterwards, they were quite pleased with the results.

"It looks as if they've been there for years and years," said Alex, sweeping the last of the dust from the old Welsh slates.

"Yes, it does," agreed Helen. "Well done, you and me."

"Do you feel a bit happier now?" demanded Alex.

"I don't think I'll feel happy ever again." Helen brushed her hand across her eyes. "Oh, Alex! I never wanted him to die! I—"

"I know." Now Alex shrugged. "But we don't arrange these things."

"What about his parents? He was an only child. He was so handsome, he was very clever – he must have been their pride and joy! He—"

"Stop it." Alex took her by the shoulders, drew her to him. "We didn't ask him to come after you. To pester you, to terrify you half out of your senses, and then to attack me with a carving knife!"

"But—"

"He was asking for trouble, and you know it. He was obsessed by you. God, Helen! He might even have killed you, he—"

"But he couldn't do that now, because he's dead, because we killed him." Helen squirmed out of Alex's embrace. "I'm going up to bed," she murmured. "Alex?"

"What?"

"I'm saying this now, before we go upstairs, so there won't be any misunderstandings later. Alex, I–I don't think I want to sleep with you again."

"You want some time to yourself, you mean? Okay. I'll sleep down here tonight. I—"

"No, Alex. Listen – and try to understand." Helen looked away. "I'll be going up to Newcastle next month, to take up my permanent post. I–I shan't want you to visit me. In fact, I don't want to see you any more."

"But, Helen—"

"Think about it." Somehow, Helen managed to turn back to him, to meet his anxious gaze. "I appreciate all you've done for me. I'm grateful, I always shall be grateful, and I do mean that. But this – this *stuff* – it's just too difficult to deal with. We can't go on. We need to make new friends, to put all this behind us."

"Yes. Perhaps you're right." As Helen spoke, Alex realised he'd been thinking along somewhat similar lines himself. He still loved Helen dearly – but he knew they had to part. If they tried to continue their relationship, if they tried to move on – got married, perhaps, had children – the spectre of Thomas Stenton would be there, a malevolent shadow, always hovering, a ghost at the feast.

They were kind to each other, careful and polite, waiting for the hours, the days, the weeks to tick away. Alex had asked to remain in the south east, and he found his wish was granted. But he wasn't going to Basingstoke. He was staying at the local office, in Westingford itself.

The day after Helen left for Newcastle, Alex took the keys of the Merchant's House back to the landlord's office. He'd arranged to rent a room in Westingford.

"I reckon we'll have a supermarket on that site in six to seven months' time." The landlord, a bespoke-tailored, affluent human spider, sat at a huge desk, lurking in a web of telephones and wires.

"W-what will happen to the Merchant's House?" asked Alex, his heart missing several beats. He wondered if he dared dig up the body. But where could he put it? How would he transport it? When—

"I've been speaking to the Conservation people." The landlord grinned at him. "They agree the place is far beyond repair. It'll be condemned and then pulled down, in the next month or so."

"You can just do that, can you?" demanded Alex, who thought he might be sick.

"Oh, yes." The landlord grinned. "You have to know the people with the influence, that's all. But once a place has been condemned, as unfit for human habitation, it's fairly easy to get a demolition order."

"If you know all the right people," murmured Alex.

"Yes, exactly." The landlord stood up then. "Well, lad – it's been nice to talk to you. But as you can see, I'm a very busy man—"

So busy, in fact, that in his business dealings the landlord of the Merchant's House had overreached himself disastrously. The following month, in spite of heroic efforts to avert catastrophe, his firm went into voluntary liquidation.

Plans for the redevelopment of the site were promptly shelved. Alex decided there must be a God – and that this God was looking after him.

Chapter Five

It was very strange, thought Helen, as she unpacked the last of her fine bone china and arranged it on the shelves of her beloved Georgian dresser, how things always seemed to come full circle. She'd imagined she'd got away. But here she was, in the early April of 1996, almost twelve years older – but right back where she'd started, practically.

Of course, it wasn't *her* choice. When Pullen House Fine Wines had offered her husband Robin the lucrative post of area manager, for the whole of the Thames Valley, Helen had been appalled. She'd seriously considered trying to talk him out of it, especially when she'd realised he would be based in Westingford.

But then, if she had objected to the move, he'd have wanted to know why she was so much against it. Why did she want him to stay a four-store manager, in the cold north east? What did she have against Berkshire and Oxfordshire, and didn't she fancy Hampshire? After all, she was a southerner, born and bred. Her family came from Kent.

So, Helen had restricted herself to insisting they bought a house north of the river, just over the border into Oxfordshire, and as far away from Rettingham as she could reasonably be.

"I've heard the schools in Henley are much better than

those in Berkshire," she told Robin, as she admired the not particularly inspiring cottage upon which, she insisted, she had set her heart.

"I've heard they're much of a muchness," said Robin Harper. But he liked his wife to be happy, and he didn't – on the whole – tend to argue the toss with her, nor spend a great deal of his limited time in trying to fathom the mysteries of the female psyche. "But won't it be a nuisance, driving thirty miles to Westingford each day?"

"No problem, darling." Realising she'd won, Helen had smiled at him. "I'll only be working there three days a week, and I'll do most of my shopping here in Henley, I expect. There's a really splendid baker, and I saw a very good Waitrose in the High Street."

So, with a bit of luck, I'll never need to go near Rettingham again, she thought today, as she flicked the dust off her precious antique Meissen. She would blank the whole experience from her mind, she decided now, forget the place existed.

"Celia?" She called to her little daughter, who at seven years old had taken a very active part in the move down south, packing up her own toys and sorting out her baby clothes for the local Oxfam shop. She was at this moment checking over her precious Barbie dolls, and putting them all to bed. "Edward! Celia!" Helen cried. "Who's for milk and biscuits?"

The offer of food and drink always did the trick. "Me!" cried Celia, hurtling down the stairs.

"Me, too!" squealed her little brother Edward, hot on her heels and afraid to miss a thing.

They went into the kitchen, where the workmen had ripped out most of the original post-war fittings, leaving gaping holes and projecting copper pipes. But the fridge was working now, and the familiar kitchen table stood in the middle of the room.

"Do you like your bedrooms a little bit better now?" demanded Helen. She poured milk from a carton, then tore open the cellophane wrapping on a packet of chocolate biscuits.

"*I* like mine," said Celia, greedily slurping up her milk. "The Barbies like it, too."

"I like my room a bit. But Brolly thinks it's horrible." Edward pulled his monstrous gargoyle face, which on his cherubic features was sweet and charming. "Brolly says it smells."

"Oh, I'm sure it doesn't." Helen took Brolly and sat him on her lap. "What else don't you like about it?" she whispered in his ear.

"It's too high," said Edward, speaking for the bedraggled, knitted creature who was his special friend.

"That's only because you're such a little bear." Helen stroked Brolly's much-chewed, tattered ears. "When you're five, and as big as Edward here, the ceiling will seem quite low."

"He thinks the window's funny," muttered Edward.

"I see," said Helen. "Well – it's rather special, actually. If you sit on the window seat you can look up the lane, down the road, and right across the fields – all without getting up."

"I already told him that." Edward took a bite of chocolate biscuit. He fetched a huge, exaggerated sigh. "Well," he conceded, "I suppose it will have to do. For the time being, anyway."

"If Brolly knows *you* like the room," said Helen, "I'm sure that he'll begin to like it, too."

The following morning, the children were due to visit their new school. Celia was determined to be brave, and

Helen knew her daughter's stubborn pride would probably see her through.

Celia was fine. She came out at the end of the morning saying Thrushall County Primary was all right. There was a very nice girl called Ellie Nicholson, who'd shared her Monster Munch. Then she had offered Celia the use of her felt tip pens, including both the silver and the gold.

But Edward cried, and said he hated everything. He was never going back again to that horrible, nasty school. One of the boys had called him names, and a girl had said his hair was a funny colour.

"But it's a lovely colour," said Helen, smoothing Edward's copper curls. "It's just like your Granny Harper's used to be."

"I don't want to look like Granny!" Edward's lower lip began to tremble. So his father took him on his knee, and said if he'd be brave, and go to the horrible school in any case, Robin would take them to Chessington the following weekend.

Edward sniffed a bit, considered hard – but then said that he'd try. But it was very difficult, to be brave.

"So it's all working out quite nicely," Robin murmured, as he and Helen lay curled up in bed together later that same evening.

"I think so." Helen hooked one ankle over Robin's legs. "Edward's still a bit anxious about school."

"Yes, poor little chap. I heard him telling Brolly all about it." Robin turned to face his wife. "But fortunately, Brolly seems to think it'll be okay."

"Good old Brolly. I knew we could count on him." Helen kissed her husband on the nose. "By the way – I've found a lady who can pick the children up from school on Tuesdays. She's one of the other mums, and her two are about the same age as ours, so hopefully it'll work out very well. A man is calling round about the fences tomorrow afternoon, and I've got someone coming to look at the gutters first thing on Wednesday morning."

"Darling, you're so organised!" Robin grinned at her. "You pack so much into your working day. I expect you're very tired?"

"I'm not tired at all."

"But do you have a headache?"

"No, no headache."

"Jolly good. Come here, then." Robin took her in his arms. "We said, I seem to remember, that once we found ourselves a bigger house—"

"Yes, so we did." Helen quite liked the idea of another baby. So, as she and Robin went through their familiar routine, the midweek version of ordinary marital sex, with no special frills attached, she told herself that they'd be happy here. She felt it in her bones. Everything was going to be all right.

Robin settled into his new job, which he enjoyed. He'd always been good with people, was actually interested in their hopes, their fears, ambitions – or their lack of them. He'd soon identified the potential high achievers in the group of retail outlets for which he was responsible. He made sure that the chronic layabouts knew they were being watched.

In his spare time, he studied for his Master of Wine exams, he played with both his children, he tried to make his wife feel extra special – which, of course, she was – and he got himself elected onto the District Council. He'd always been very active in all aspects of local government, but one of the reasons he'd jumped at the chance to make this move down south was because he'd always wanted to be in parliament itself.

As a Tory MP, of course. As such, he reflected – perhaps immodestly – he'd be an absolute godsend to a party on its knees, unpopular at home and often ridiculed abroad, rocked by scandal, dogged by sleaze and mired in apathy.

For Robin Harper was a paragon. A respectable family man, who loved his wife, who adored his pretty children, who wasn't sleeping with his secretary, and who had never double-crossed or cheated anybody, in the course of his whole life. He had no dirty linen in his bathroom, or skeletons in his cupboard. His wife worked tirelessly for dozens of good causes, and was also a part time counsellor for Relate.

"What more could they ask?" demanded Robin, as Helen tied his new bow tie, then smoothed his dress shirt collar.

"Nothing," she replied. "You're just the man they need. When Frederick Jewell retires, they're bound to ask—"

"Well, let's not count our chickens." Robin glanced towards the full length bedroom mirror. "What do you think? Be honest!"

"I think you look both dignified and handsome." Helen kissed her husband on the mouth. "But then, I'm prejudiced."

"*I* think I'm getting fat." Robin frowned at the mirror. "I ought to stop eating pudding."

"You're just right. You're my lovely, cuddly bunny." Helen hugged him. "You'll have all those old ladies at the Chamber of Commerce banquet eating right out of your hand."

"God, I don't fancy that," said Robin, laughing. "How's Edward's cough tonight?"

"I'm afraid it seems to have settled on his chest. So I think I ought to stay at home this evening." Helen didn't mind, because she didn't much enjoy these civic dinners, where the food invariably gave her heartburn, and the company was often indigestible, too. "I wouldn't mind, if we could wave a magic wand, and have dear old Mrs Hampton babysitting—"

"But she's five hundred miles away, in Gateshead."

"Yes, exactly." Helen sighed. "I got him off to sleep, and he's had a second dose of Calpol. But the poor little thing's so restless that he's bound to wake up once, or several times. If he finds a total stranger in his room, he'll have the screaming habdabs."

"Yes, I know. Poor little Teddy." Robin kissed his wife. "Okay, then – I'll be off. I'll try not to be late."

Helen did some ironing, then went into Robin's study. She made a list of possible sponsors for a children's charity, for which she'd agreed to become a fundraiser. She wrote some begging letters to various companies. Then she switched on the television, hoping to catch the end of *News at Ten*.

She'd missed it by some minutes, and the local news was almost over, too. The very last frame, before the reporter handed the viewers back to the studio, was of Rettingham town centre. She recognised it at once, and a shiver of disquiet rippled icily down her spine.

She'd read in the local paper that there was some long term plan to build a bypass, or a ring-road, or something of the kind, around the ancient town. Well, she reflected, that didn't interest her. She didn't intend to go there.

The following morning, Edward's cough seemed better. But Brolly didn't think it would be a very good idea to go straight back to school. "Had we better give it one more day at home?" suggested Helen.

"I think so," said Edward, sagely.

So they dropped his sister off at Thrushall County Primary, and then drove into Henley to pick up some supplies. They took a leisurely stroll around the elegant new Waitrose, dawdled for ten minutes in the independent bookshop, where they bought a picture book for Edward, and then went into W H Smith. Here, Helen bought a *Daily Mail* and a *Tatler* for herself.

"Can we go home now?" Edward asked, as they came out into the sunshine.

"If you like." Helen took his hand in hers. "Or shall we go and see the swans? We could feed the ducks—"

"We'd better go home," said Edward. "Brolly will want his milk and biscuits soon."

So it wasn't until Edward was happily watching a programme about dolphins, and sharing his milk and chocolate buttons with Brolly, that Helen was sitting at the kitchen table, enjoying a cup of some very good Colombian filter coffee and reading her *Daily Mail*.

She turned the pages slowly. Reading her horoscope, she smiled and shook her head. She didn't think she really needed to brace herself for a sudden revelation. Or anyway, not today. She scanned the book reviews, then flicked to the fashion page. But as she did so, she happened to see the name.

"Mummy?" Edward had come into the kitchen. "Mummy, Brolly's spilled his milk. I think he needs a flannel. He's got some chocolate on his face, as well."

When Helen did not reply, Edward tugged at her sleeve. "Mummy?" he quavered, getting anxious now.

Helen scooped him up on to her lap. Burying her face against his narrow shoulder, she inhaled the warm and comforting essence of milky little child. She thought, if I just sit here very still, for about the next five minutes, when I look again it will have gone away.

Two, three minutes passed. Edward coughed politely. Then, he squirmed. "I want to get down now," he grumbled. "I want a chocolate biscuit."

"Give Mummy a little cuddle." Helen held him close, locking her arms around him so that he couldn't get away. "Darling?" she whispered, both her eyes shut tight.

"I want to get *down*!" Alarmed by her behaviour, Edward wriggled harder. So Helen let him go, and when she looked at that short paragraph again, of course the name was there. So small, so insignificant, it still blazed off the page.

"This will destroy me," Helen told herself. "It will also ruin everything for everyone I love."

Chapter Six

Helen spent the rest of that day in a daze. She made Edward scrambled eggs and Marmite toast for lunch, but didn't appear to notice when he refused to eat it and demanded a packet of Monster Munch instead.

So he got down from the table and went to help himself from the kitchen cupboard. He didn't really like any sort of flavoured savoury snack and ended up dropping most of it on to the kitchen floor.

"Mummy?" He pointed to the crumbs and mess.

"It doesn't matter, darling. If you're not very hungry, why don't you go and watch a video?"

So Edward wandered into the sitting room and sat there staring at the television and sucking Brolly's ear.

Helen glanced at her watch. Soon it would be time to fetch her daughter. She went to find her car keys, then called Edward.

"Mummy?" He looked at her. He knew there was something wrong. "Mummy, what's the matter?"

"I've got an awful headache." Helen tried to smile. "But I've taken some paracetamol, and I'll be better soon."

She drove to Thrushall Primary along the winding lanes. She found that she was late, and Celia was standing by the school entrance, all alone and looking very tearful.

"I'm sorry," she murmured, kissing her little daughter. "I'm not very well-organised today."

"Mummy has a headache," Edward told his sister. "She's had to take some para-para—"

"Paracetamol," said Celia, grandly. "Never mind," she told her mother. "When we get home, I'll make you a cup of tea."

Helen switched on the engine. Her eyes had filled with tears and she could hardly see to drive. How she was going to manage at Relate the following morning, she honestly didn't know.

She watched the early evening news with one child on her lap and the other at her knee, holding her breath in agonised fear and trembling, both longing for but dreading the awful moment when the round-up of that day's local events would inevitably begin.

The newsreader finally put her out of her anxious misery. It wasn't quite as bad as she'd expected. After standing there decaying, an eyesore for the past twenty years or more, the Merchant's House was going to be demolished.

The land around it was going to be developed. But the house itself – a wonderful example of Jacobean domestic architecture, said the chairman of the Berkshire and Hampshire Archaeological Trust – would be dismantled lath by lath and hand-made brick by brick, then re-erected on a special British Heritage site, which was just outside the town.

"That's the house they're going to make all nice and new again," said Celia, who had even stopped combing Starlight Barbie's hair in order to stare with interest at the screen. "Mrs Collins says we're going on a trip, to see how the men are putting it back together."

"I want to come," said Edward.

"You can't, it's not for babies." His sister looked up at Helen. "We're going to do a project about it soon."

"That'll be interesting." Helen thought she was going to

be sick. "Daddy's going to be quite late this evening," she told her children. "So perhaps you two could have your tea in here, all by yourselves."

"But what about you and Daddy?" demanded Edward.

"We'll have our tea later."

"In the dark?"

"They'll put the kitchen light on, you silly thing." Celia shook her curls. "I'd like banana sandwiches," she said.

"Have you had a hard day, sweetheart?" Robin asked her mildly, as he and Helen drank their after-dinner coffee, the children long since washed and brushed, snuggled into their pyjamas, then kissed and put to bed.

"What?" Helen blinked at him. Then she realised she'd been silent all the evening. "Sorry, darling. I was miles away."

Robin smiled. "I only asked if you'd had an awkward day."

"Well, I still haven't got to grips with the wretched oven. I've always been used to gas, so I don't understand the ins and outs of electricity." She forced a smile. "I'll send off for one of the manufacturer's handbooks. I'm sure I must be doing something wrong. That apple pie this evening was disgusting."

"I thought it was fine." Robin took her hands in his. "But apart from difficulties with apple pies, is everything okay?"

"Of course," said Helen. "W-why shouldn't it be?"

"No reason." Now Robin rubbed his tired eyes. "I think I need an early night," he said.

So Robin and Helen went to bed at ten. Following his habitual routine, Robin got undressed, emptied his pockets, and let his small change roll about all over his bedside table. He set the alarm on his personal organiser, got into bed, and then turned out the light. "Sleep tight, sweetheart," he yawned and closed his eyes.

But Helen simply lay there, open-eyed and fearful, hardly daring to wonder what the morning light might bring.

It would be all right, she told herself. It *had* to be all right. After all, why shouldn't it be? They wouldn't want to excavate beneath the Merchant's House. It wasn't as if they were looking for a corpse.

But what if they actually did turn up a body? There was nothing – nothing at all – to link Helen or Alex Colborn to the Merchant's House. There'd been no tenancy agreement, had there? They'd paid the rent in cash. Helen doubted if the landlord had ever known her name – and this, in any case, was different now.

All she had to do was sit and wait. Ride out the coming storm. In a month or two, a couple of tons of concrete would have covered Thomas Stenton, and entombed his bones for all eternity.

"But he didn't deserve to die!" To her horror, Helen realised she had spoken the words out loud.

"What was that you said?" Robin opened his eyes. He blinked, and stared at her "I wasn't asleep," he muttered.

"Of course you were." Helen hoped fervently that she was right. "It's okay," she whispered. "I was having a bad dream. Darling, go back to sleep."

To her immense relief, Robin turned over and did just that. But Helen lay awake for the rest of the summer night.

The following morning, Helen dropped the children off at school, then drove into Westingford. She travelled by a very circuitous route, which happened to take in Rettingham on the way.

Suppose I have an accident, she thought, as she manoeuvred her little Vauxhall through the mass of morning traffic.

Suppose someone runs into the back of me. How will I explain to Robin exactly what I was doing, on this particular road, at this time of the morning, when I ought already to be at work?

She gripped the steering wheel, her knuckles showing white. The traffic was heavy now, the cars were inching forward in first gear, and here was a big Mercedes trying to turn right out of a side road, into the stream of traffic going the other way.

Helen let it out. The driver behind her flashed his headlights angrily, then blared at her on his horn. Helen considered making a certain gesture, but then thought better of it. She was in trouble enough already. She inched a few feet forward once again.

She arrived in Rettingham at half past nine. After making a phone call from a public kiosk, to let her colleague know she'd had a few domestic difficulties that morning and was running a little late, she drove up Sydenham Street.

The site had now been almost completely levelled. Yellow diggers and dumper trucks ran backwards and forwards across what had once been the huge wilderness of garden around the Merchant's House.

The building itself was already half demolished and was receiving the expert ministrations of people in hard hats and workmen's denims. They were loading various lorries with bricks and timbers, each one carefully numbered, and logged by a teenaged girl on what was presumably the overall master plan.

Helen didn't get out of the car. She didn't dare to go and join the little group of onlookers and general layabouts who'd congregated on the opposite pavement and who were pointing and staring as the demolition people went about their work.

"You okay, my love?" The man who was tapping on

Helen's windscreen stared at her, concerned. "You don't look very well."

"I'm sorry?" Helen wound the window down. "What's the matter?"

"You feeling all right?"

"Yes, fine. Why do you ask?"

"You're looking a bit out of it, that's all. You're parked in the path of the dumper trucks, as well."

"I didn't realise that." Bravely, Helen smiled. "I'm on my way," she said.

Helen had no clients to see that day, so she caught up on a mass of paperwork. Whenever one of her colleagues spoke to her, she tried to be her usual bright, communicative self. The effort exhausted her, and she found it almost impossible to be patient with little Edward and to listen to Celia's unceasing chatter when she finally got home later on that day.

Robin came home to find her mixing soluble paracetamol. He stood and watched her drink it, then told her to sit down at the kitchen table.

He told her that in his opinion, she took on far too much. She looked after the children, she ran her various charities, she did the housework, all the gardening. "You should give up Relate," said Robin, sternly. "Or cut your hours, at least."

"Actually, I was thinking about that." Helen held the glass in a vice-like grip, trying to conceal the tremor in her hands. "Now the children are both at school, I ought to be earning something. I should contribute to the family exchequer. I—"

"That's not what I meant at all," interrupted Robin. He took her hands in his. "I earn enough to keep us all in – well, in reasonable comfort. If anything happened to me, you'd get the life insurance, a pension from the firm, another from the state. The children would still have Mum—"

"But—"

"But if *you* weren't around, it would be chaos."

So if I were sent to prison, thought Helen with a shudder, it wouldn't only be me who was made to suffer, but also—

She turned away from him. "It's chicken casserole tonight," she said to Robin. "We could have rice, potatoes or *fusilli*. So you choose."

Somehow, Helen got through the next few days. The days became a week, the week a month. Robin could see his wife was still on edge, but assumed it was because she was getting anxious about whether or not she might manage to conceive. He was sure she'd set her heart on having another baby.

But he hadn't noticed any little phials in the bathroom, so he didn't say anything. Helen had become so jittery when they were trying for Celia. The baby had been conceived within a year, but this had not prevented Helen from telling people who'd been trying for a baby for a decade that she knew exactly what they must be going through.

"You must have a bit of holiday coming up soon," he said, one day in early June. "Why don't we have a break? We could take the children out of school for a couple of days or so. We could all go to the seaside."

"I'm sorry, but I don't think I could manage to get away, not just at the moment. I'm very busy nowadays." Helen couldn't meet his gaze, so she stared down at her salad. She speared a radish on her fork, then chewed it vigorously.

She'd driven through Rettingham that very morning. The Merchant's House had all but disappeared from Sydenham Street, and was being resurrected on the site outside the town. When she'd called to collect the children after school, she'd learned that Celia's class was well into its project. The children had built a scale model of the place, and furnished it with Jacobean tables, chairs and tiny tester beds. They'd been to the new site, and even helped the people who were rebuilding the wretched place.

Soon, thought Helen. Soon, there'll be a raft of concrete over the whole area, and I can relax.

But then, on the day the very last bit of lath was taken away from the original site, an observant workman was walking across the muddy wastes when he happened to spot something glinting in the sun. He picked it up and took it to his foreman, who was known to be an *Antiques Roadshow* fan and something of a history buff himself. "Here, Gerry," he began, "just have a butcher's hook."

"Where did you find this, then?" Accepting the shiny metal artifact, the foreman peered at it. Rubbing the grime of centuries away, he shook his head, then frowned. "I don't believe it," he muttered, incredulous.

"What's up, mate?" The workman stared at him.

"This, my son, is a woman's golden bangle." The foreman grinned. "A very *ancient* golden bangle, too. Roman, by the look of it."

For one short second more, the foreman stood there, mesmerised, entranced. But then he came back to life. "Don't anybody move!" he bawled, across the mud and gravel. "You buggers over there – stay where you are!" He patted his jacket pockets. "Now, where's me soddin' mobile, for fuck's sake?"

He rang the local paper. The regional television station sent a camera crew. The early evening news reported that all work on the Sydenham Street Mall had been suspended. The County Archaeologist had been invited over, to have a better look.

* * *

Celia couldn't understand it. What had she done wrong? Her Mummy hardly ever frowned or shouted. On the contrary, she was always very pleased when Celia offered to clear away the dirty supper things, then load the dishwasher, whilst she herself took Edward up to bed.

It was hardly Celia's fault that a knife had slipped through the holes in the cutlery basket – that particular compartment had always had a little gap in it – and then got stuck between the racks and the revolving arm which sprayed the water on the plates. It wasn't because of Celia that the grinding noises had been followed by a nasty smell of burning, that all the lights in the house had then gone out.

But Mummy had come tearing into the kitchen, eyes ablaze with fury and screaming like a mad thing. She'd switched off the machine, jerked open the door to release the clouds of scalding steam, then shrieked at Celia to go to bed *at once*! No, she couldn't have a story! Celia could just put herself to bed, and stop being such a nuisance, did she hear?

So Celia had crept upstairs and into the gloomy bathroom. Trying not to cry, she cleaned her teeth, then washed her face with Edward's Snoopy flannel. She couldn't find her own, but she didn't dare call downstairs to ask this terrifying Mummy where it was.

When she looked into his bedroom, she saw that Edward was fast asleep, with Brolly in his arms. So Celia sidled along the landing down to her own room, where she slid beneath her duvet and screwed her eyes up tight.

She listened hard, hoping to hear the crunch of wheels on gravel for this would mean her Daddy had come home. But she was very tired and, in spite of being frightened and upset, very soon her eyes were closing. When Helen looked in half an hour later, her daughter was asleep.

* * *

Helen changed the fuses. The lights and domestic machinery came back on again. But she didn't want to speak to anyone, so when the phone rang fifteen minutes later, she let it burble on until the answering machine kicked in.

"Darling?" began Robin. "I suppose you're all in the bathroom, and didn't hear the phone. I'm afraid I'm going to be very late this evening. There's a problem at one of the shops. It looks like somebody's been fiddling the till and the bloody manager has called the police. I wish he'd told me first! Anyway, I'll be back as soon as possible. Love you all."

Helen bit her lip. Then she went into the kitchen, where she poured herself a glass of cooking sherry, which she sat and nursed in front of the *Nine O'clock News*.

There was bound to be something on the local round up, she supposed – and indeed there was. The studios had sent a crew to Rettingham that very afternoon. Here was the County Archaeologist, a pleasant-looking girl in jeans and a big, checked workman's shirt, agreeing that yes, this was a very exciting find. She'd spent the past few hours searching through the County Archives, and learned that there was evidence that Rettingham had been the site of a Roman *colonia*, a township for army veterans and their native British wives.

"Shit." Helen took another gulp of sherry, then she poured a glassful more. The bottle had been open for several weeks, so the liquid was oxidised and very sour. But the alcohol had the desired effect.

The camera panned across the barren mud flats. "We don't have unlimited funds at our disposal," the girl from County Hall was saying, her dark eyes very bright. "But since it seems that this may prove to be an important site, we're asking the developers if they'll agree to suspend their operations for a week or two, so that my team can do a small-scale survey. Then, of course, the work on the development will continue."

"So what exactly do you hope to find?" asked the handsome young reporter eagerly.

"Well – to be honest, we don't really know. But a seventeenth-century source suggests that there was once a Romano-British cemetery, not very far from here—"

"The discovery of a Roman artifact tends to support this view," cut in the reporter, beaming.

"Well, yes. Perhaps." The archaeologist smiled. "Hopefully, we'll soon have done our survey. Then, we'll see. I—"

But now Helen groped for the remote control and stabbed at the on/off button viciously. The television screen went black and blank. For one brief moment, she considered hurling her half empty glass at the bloody thing. But then, suddenly feeling very sick indeed and afraid that she might actually throw up, she lurched into the kitchen and hung over the butler's sink.

Soon she found she was sobbing uncontrollably. "I don't know how to deal with this," she wept, raking her damp, bedraggled hair away from her swollen face. "Oh, God – what shall I *do*?"

When Robin arrived home, Helen was in bed and feigning sleep. Dog tired himself, for it had been a hell of a bloody day, he took off his clothes and slipped in beside his wife.

The following morning he ignored the alarm and got up when the children and Helen did. "Hang on a moment," he said, as she reached for her dressing gown and slid her feet into her bedroom slippers, "I want to talk to you."

"Well, it'll have to wait." Helen glanced at her watch. "I must wake the children now. We're already running late."

"It doesn't matter if they miss Assembly just once in a

while." Robin caught Helen's arm and pulled her down beside him. "Now, tell me. What's the matter?"

"I–I don't know what you mean," said Helen, looking the other way.

"You don't? Then I'll explain." Robin still held her arm. "One, I know you're a nervous and – I suppose – a quite emotional person. You don't like things to be just sprung on you. So, before we made the decision to move down here, we did discuss it properly. In extensive detail, as I recall. You agreed I should take this job. But all the same, you've been like the proverbial cat on the proverbial hot bricks ever since we came down here."

"But Robin, I—"

"No, please let me finish. Two, when I was mucking out your car the other week, I happened to clock the mileage. You mustn't think I'm spying on you or anything like that, but I see you've been using the car a lot, at least just recently. But if you're only driving into Westingford, and going to pick up the children and the shopping, there's something wrong with the car, and we ought to get it checked."

"Okay, I'll take it to the local garage. Robin, I—"

"There's just one more thing." The pressure of Robin's hand on her bare arm intensified. "You haven't been sleeping well. You're tossing, turning and talking to yourself. Last night, when I came in, the kitchen stank of alcohol. Darling, you must tell me – do you have a problem? Perhaps there's something wrong at work?"

"No, there isn't."

"Then something is upsetting you at home."

"Why do you think that?" Helen stared at the wall. "It's like you said," she muttered. "I find it hard to make these big adjustments. I just can't cope with change."

"But, Helen—"

"I love this house, this village, all the people in it. The

children seem to be happy enough at school. You're doing well at work, and all my colleagues at Relate are very nice indeed. I've had to counsel some difficult people lately, I admit. But I'm properly trained, and I don't let it get to me. I just need time, that's all."

"Do you think you might be pregnant?"

"I know for a fact I'm not."

"Do you want another baby?"

"I'm not really sure." Now Helen shrugged. "I suppose I'm not that bothered, either way."

"If there was anything troubling you, you *would* tell me about it?"

"Yes, of course."

"Okay, interrogation over." Robin let her go. "I'll drive the sprogs to school. You get off to work. The weekend's coming up, so we'll do something as a family. Something nice and relaxing, so we can all unwind."

Helen saw the children and her husband off to school, then got into her car and drove to Rettingham. She parked in Sydenham Street and stared at the muddy site. Sure enough, there was that pretty dark-haired woman in the jeans and workman's shirt. She was wearing a hard hat today, and carrying a clipboard. She was directing a scruffy gaggle of a dozen other young people, who held notebooks, measuring tapes, mattocks and spades.

"How long before they find him?" It was a release, of sorts, to speak the words out loud.

Of course, she'd never told Robin about Tom Stenton, nor about Alex Colborn. She had never even mentioned them in passing, those former lovers who now seemed destined to become two permanent thorns in her shrinking flesh.

So where was Alex nowadays, she wondered, what could he be doing with his life? He must be married, she supposed.

Most probably, he had children of his own. Had *he* been watching the box, had he been reading the papers with the same near-catatonic terror, with the same growing sense of dread?

How long did fingerprints endure? For days, for weeks, for months, or even years? How long did denim and leather take to rot away? If only they hadn't wrapped him in that oilskin! If only—

"I'm sorry, darling, but I'm afraid you're going to have to move your car." A workman in jeans and a grubby flannel shirt peered through the open window, grinning appreciatively at Helen's pretty figure. "They're bringing some of them great big Outside Broadcast lorries the wrong way up the street."

"Mummy was horrible to us last night," Celia had told her father, as he kissed her, as he was about to leave her at the school gate.

"I'm sure she wasn't really." Having dropped Edward at the infants' entrance, Robin decided to walk Celia round to the juniors' block. "But anyway, tell me. What did Mummy say?"

"She shouted at me and told me to go to bed, but I didn't do *anything*." Celia's lower lip was trembling now. "I was frightened in the dark. I nearly cried."

"Mummy was probably a bit tired, that's all. I don't suppose she meant to shout at you." Robin gave his daughter a fleeting little hug. "Don't worry about it, sweetheart. When you come home from school today, Mummy will be her happy, smiley self."

"She won't be nasty and horrible anymore?" Celia looked unconvinced.

"Of course she won't," said Robin, cheerfully. But he was very worried, all the same.

As he drove into Westingford, he thought about his wife. She'd always been a nervous, anxious, jumpy sort of person. His racing thoroughbred, he'd always called her, his beautiful Helen, a complete and absolute contrast to himself, whose equine equivalent must be a Shetland pony. People must often wonder what a girl like her could possibly see in an ordinary bloke like him.

He'd get home early that evening, he decided, crises at work be damned. The suspicion had taken root, and it was growing, spreading, flowering in his mind. He knew she must have met another man.

Chapter Seven

"I don't think you should do anything," Helen told the thin-faced, weeping woman who sat across the desk from her, wringing a sodden tissue in her bony, trembling hands. "I know you're very worried, and it's usually a good idea to talk. But sometimes, it's much better to leave hurtful things unsaid."

"But I want to find out what he's actually done. If I know the worst, I might be able to come to terms with it." Mrs Sheldon began to sniff again. Soon, she'd be in floods. "I don't *want* to leave him," she continued. "But I can't go on like this, never knowing where he is or what he's doing—"

"He might think he's protecting you," said Helen.

"What?" Mrs Sheldon's red-rimmed eyes grew wide. "You mean, he thinks if I knew, I couldn't cope?"

"Exactly." Helen offered her the half full box of tissues yet again. "If you really love him and you're not prepared to leave him, if the children are doing well at school and seem happy enough at home, it might be an idea to let it go. He always comes back to you. He knows he'll be forgiven. Perhaps you should console yourself with that."

"Do you think *you* might?"

"I'm sorry?" Helen met her client's gaze.

"I suppose I shouldn't say this." Apologetically, Mrs Sheldon shook her head. "But if it was *your* husband who was playing around and making your life a misery, do you think *you* could forgive him? If he said he loved you, would that be enough?"

"It might be." Helen glanced at her watch and saw, to her intense relief, that the time was almost up. "But we'll need to discuss this in a little more depth, I think."

She opened the big diary on her desk. "So – just let me see – shall we say next Thursday?" She was desperate to get this woman out of the office, to scoop the litter of damp, discarded tissues into the bin.

"I don't know. Perhaps I'll ring you later on this week." Mrs Sheldon found her handbag. "I think you made a very good point today," she said, as she gathered up her things. "I mean, what the eye doesn't see, and all of that."

"We ought to talk again." Helen got up and walked towards the door. She opened it and saw her client out.

Last night she had considered telling Robin everything. But in the cold light of day, she realised it would be crazy to do that. How would it benefit Robin, how would it help *her*, for her husband to know exactly what she'd done?

They were invited to a Chamber of Commerce dinner that coming Wednesday. She would go, she now decided. She'd get dressed up, she'd sparkle, she'd make her husband proud of her. She'd put the past behind her, she would make herself forget the sordid details. Yes, they might find Thomas Stenton's body. But they couldn't prove a thing.

Robin's resolution to tackle his supposedly erring wife had wavered just a little. He had no proof of infidelity and he had no valid reason to suspect her, after all.

When he came home from work much later on that evening, he found his wife and children happily occupied. They were sitting at the kitchen table, cutting out paper shapes and sticking them on card. A collage of some sort was gradually taking shape and they were so absorbed in their cutting and their sticking that they didn't even hear him come in.

But, just then, Celia happened to glance up. "Daddy!" she squealed, her little face aglow. She launched herself at his well-pressed, pin-striped knees, and Edward followed suit.

"Hello, wombats." Robin scooped them into his arms and hugged them. He looked towards his wife. "Darling?" he began.

"Hello, my love. *You're* late." Helen was actually smiling. "Your dinner's almost ready."

Robin ate his *cassoulet* with one child on his lap, and another crayoning busily at his side. His wife poured him a glassful of the peppery, fruity red which he particularly enjoyed. He realised that, when all was said and done, there was nothing to worry about.

Robin took both the children up to bed. He came back down the stairs to find his wife reclining on the chesterfield, a glass of the peppery red held in her hand, her feet on a slubbed silk cushion. As he entered the room, she smiled, then made a space for him to sit beside her.

"Good day?" he asked, as he poured the rest of the Minervois into a glass of his own.

"Yes, actually it was fine." Helen – the old Helen, the warm and open, loving Helen – laid her head upon his shoulder. "I'm sorry, my love," she whispered.

"Come again?" Robin slid his arm around her waist. He pulled her close to him. "Sorry for what, exactly?"

"For being such a bitch." Then, Helen sighed. "Just recently, I've been snapping at the children all the time. I've been absolutely horrible to you. I—"

"It's as I say, you take on far too much." Now, Robin stroked her hair. "Darling, why don't you give up Relate? Do your charity work and run the home – then, if you find you have time on your hands occasionally, you could maybe find some other work round here."

"I could be a cashier at Waitrose, do you mean?"

"Of course not. Helen, please don't get all tensed up again." Robin continued stroking. His hand caressed her ears, her hair, her neck.

It was, thought Helen, as if she were a nervous little cat, a fidgety, fretful dog. That would be the next thing, she supposed – Robin would want a puppy, for the children. Some grinning, boisterous mongrel, it would be, some creature from the local Animal Rescue over at High Bank Farm. It would be almost comically keen to please, and even more determined to be loved. It would dig up all the bedding plants and throw up on the carpet, and everyone would say, "Oh, but he's *sweet*!"

"You could do some of your translating work, perhaps," suggested Robin, helpfully. "Or give French and German lessons to secondary school children."

"Although I'm just a little bit out of practice," murmured Helen, "and I don't—"

"You could soon brush up your Shakespeare. Or your Goethe, or Molière." Robin rubbed his eyes. "Sorry," he yawned. "I need an early night. What *is* the time, do you know?"

Helen glanced at her watch. "I make it just gone ten," she said. "Do you fancy a cup of coffee?"

"No, it'll stop me sleeping."

"There's some decaffeinated, if you prefer it."

"No, I hate that stuff." Robin stretched and yawned. "I'll catch the rest of the news, and then I think I'll go to bed."

Helen was about to move, to fetch herself some coffee. But then she decided to stay right where she was, here on the chesterfield, with her husband's arm around her waist.

This would be a test, she decided now. There was bound to be something about the site on *Southern View Today*. So, as the credits rolled, and as the silly, self-important music played, she steeled herself.

They made her wait and wait. "So, finally," said the anchorman at last, "we have a report from Rettingham, in Hampshire, where they're literally digging up the past – before they build for the future." The anchorman grinned at his own wit. "Earlier today, Fiona Smith and I went over there – and here's what we found."

It was all so horribly familiar. The camera panned across the littered wastes of pipes, of dotted mountains of cement and rocky hardcore, and groups of workmen half in and half out of various holes in the ground.

In one muddy corner, fairly near to where the Merchant's House had been, there was a grid of taped and numbered squares. As far as Helen could judge, this grid was ten, or maybe fifteen yards – but this was seeing with the eye of hope – from where the building itself had actually stood.

"So how long do you have, to make the find of the century?" The reporter grinned, and ogled the County Archaeologist, no doubt thinking she looked very tasty in her little white vest and sawn-off khaki shorts. "From speaking to the contractor over there, I understand they expect to lay the foundations on Friday week?"

"Yes, I'm afraid that's so. Apparently, we're on borrowed time already and they can't afford to hold up the construction work any more." Philosophically, the archaeologist shrugged. "But that gives us time to make a preliminary survey. To dig a couple of test pits, and to make a written record of what we've found."

"Have any more golden bangles come to light?"

"No. But we weren't expecting anything like that." The girl shrugged once again. "This land has been in cultivation for several centuries. So, even if we *are* digging on the site of a Roman *colonia*, I imagine any artifacts from that period in history have long ago been found." She grinned rather wryly. "I reckon they'll have been disposed of, too."

"So the discovery of the bangle here was a lucky stroke of fate? It was something our ancestors had overlooked – and that's our lot, as far as you can tell?"

"You could say that, of course." The County Archaeologist smiled politely. "But this site is very interesting," she said. "Today we've turned up some broken pottery, a corroded metal blade, and what might be a baby's teething ring. So our work on this site will certainly add a few extra dimensions to what we know of life in Roman Britain. Although I don't think we're in for anything sensational in the way of discoveries here."

"That's a shame," the reporter said. Of course, he would have much preferred to be reporting from a site which promised hoards of gold and silver, or caches of precious stones.

He turned back to the camera. "So there you have it," he concluded, grinning like a gargoyle. "But if anyone at home is interested in archaeology, and would like to take a closer look at the excavation here in Rettingham, you'd be very welcome to come along to the site, between about twelve and one tomorrow afternoon. A couple of friendly diggers will be on hand to show you round – if they haven't sloped off to the Dog and Duck, that is!"

Friday, Helen told herself. By Friday week, this nightmare will be over. Picking up the glasses, she got up from the sofa. She went into the kitchen. She dropped the empty bottle into the bag which was almost full of other jars and bottles to be taken for recycling. She locked the kitchen door, then laid the table for the family's breakfast.

"Friday," she repeated under her breath, as she set out the

Flopsy Bunnies cereal bowls, the Peter Rabbit mugs and the Jemima Puddleduck plates. "If I can just hang on, if I can stand it for another couple of days, then I'll be all right."

"I'm going up now," called Robin, from the dining room. "I think I'll have a nice, relaxing shower."

"I'll be with you in five minutes." Helen shook her head. She was extremely tired tonight, and a nice, relaxing shower usually made Robin randy. But that, she thought, would be another test. She needed to get some sleep, and so a little nice, relaxing, routine marital sex might be the very thing to get her nodding off.

She went upstairs, undressed, removed her make-up and then got into bed. Robin came in, a towel around his waist, a grin on his shaven face, and his hair sticking up in tufts like an unfledged bird's.

Helen smiled at him. "You don't need your pyjamas tonight," she said.

One warm, sweet-scented evening, later that same week, Alex Colborn was lying on the sofa. His eyes were closed. As the memories came flooding back again, he groaned. His companion croaked in sympathy, and unsheathed her razor claws.

His next door neighbour's cat had had enough of her owner's affectionate but extremely boisterous children and was contentedly asleep on Alex's chest. Feeling the vibration of his groan, she'd felt she should endorse it. She was the only cat which Alex had ever known whose voice was like a frog's with terminal laryngitis.

"Time for bed then, Ivy." Supporting the animal against his shoulder, and stroking her neat little head, he carried her over to the open kitchen window, then let her flop out on to the crumbling sill. She stretched, yawned delicately, then jumped down on to the yard. He closed the window after her, then went back into his cluttered living room.

Alex had bought this Victorian terraced cottage in Westingford's most sprawling, dingiest suburb at the absolute height of the Eighties property boom, and now it was worth a little less than two thirds of what he'd originally paid for it. In itself, it was quite a pleasant little home, a two up, two down, red brick artisan's house, in a district once entirely working class, but now part-gentrified and part-decayed.

He could have moved away. Since his last promotion, this time to deputy manager of the local office of the Benefits Agency, he could easily have stretched to a home in a far more genteel district. He could have gone to live on an executive estate, in a cul-de-sac called something like The Willows or Larchfield Drive.

But he found he simply couldn't be bothered to move. He spent his money on food and wine, he liked going to the races, where he always lost a fortune, and he took expensive, solitary foreign holidays. In the course of these, he usually met some desperate, single, thirty-something woman, also travelling alone, with whom he had mechanical but prophylactic sex. But when her letters came, suggesting they should meet again and continue the relationship on home ground, he always threw them straight into the bin. No one could replace the woman he had lost forever.

As he told his few close friends and anyone else who thought to ask, he liked it here in Westingford's terraced suburbs. This was where he felt at home and where he could relax. Here, nobody bothered him or asked him round to supper, where he might be paired off with a divorcee, and expected to hear all about her rotten marriage. He didn't have to wash his car, or spend all Sunday mowing an already shaven lawn. The lawns round here were weed patches which stank of prowling cats, or they were neatly concreted over.

Next door on his left there lived a noisy but charming family of turbaned, white-robed Sikhs. Mr and Mrs Singh were a somewhat tense and defeated pair, worn down by grinding toil and constant worry about their many children, who were growing up wild and headstrong in this cold and alien land.

They treated Alex like a priest or a respected family elder, asking his advice about nearly everything under the sun. They deferred to his noble judgement, and were almost embarrassingly grateful when this very important senior civil servant gentleman ever did them a little favour, helped one of them to fill in a form or write an important letter, or seemed happy to talk to them on equal terms.

But the three eldest Singh sisters, teenaged goddesses all, who looked like birds of paradise in their gorgeous outfits of red and gold and green, seemed to think he was a joke. They sniggered behind his back, smirked when he spoke to them, and then they'd flash their big, black almond eyes. They jangled their golden bangles, and their anklets winked and clanked, as they sashayed past each morning to their work at the local biscuit factory. Here, they made custard creams and Genuine Bonny Scotland Highland Shortbread.

On his right lived poor Anita Norman, a gaunt, exhausted-looking single mother, whose three small children constantly gave her hell. Her husband had run off with a West Indian, a generously-proportioned girl about half her lover's age. Anita had her eye on Alex as a possible second husband and ideal father substitute – according to the ever-speculative Mrs Singh.

How would they all react to this, he wondered. How would they deal with it if they were told that Alex Colborn, the lovely Mr Colborn who worked for the loathsome DSS, but who was never too busy to explain the rules, to investigate entitlement, who never behaved as if the money paid in benefits came out of his own pockets – even if it did – was a murderer? A fugitive from justice, and all the rest of it?

Alex picked up the *Westingford Telegraph*. He turned to page eleven once again. There she was, looking sickeningly pretty and almost offensively cheerful, arm in arm with her short-arse, balding, four-eyes of a husband at some Chamber of Commerce dinner.

Butter wouldn't have melted, he thought sourly. He read through the report again. "Mrs Helen Harper was also present," said the caption, "and she graciously thanked the Committee for its generous donation to the latest Aid for Africa appeal, for which she is the new local co-ordinator, and fundraiser-in-chief." Alex read the last few words out loud. He shook his head in absolute disbelief.

Helen Tremain – who would have thought it, eh? Helen Clare Tremain, wild child, sex bomb, undergraduate's wet dream, the Lady Macbeth of Rettingham and District, had metamorphosed into Mrs Helen Harper, the wife of a local tradesman, mother of Celia and – was it Edgar? No, Edward, it must be Edward, nobody called their children Edgar these days – and part-time marriage guidance counsellor. Not to mention collecting box supremo and local conscience-pricker *extraordinaire*. He would never have believed it if he hadn't seen it with his own two eyes.

Why was she married to that little runt, he asked himself, for the tenth, for the twentieth time. Helen had never been a conventional beauty but every man she met gave her the eye. Why had she not seduced a millionaire? She only had to look at a man to make him want to go to bed with her. Alex looked at the grainy photograph again. The man on Helen's left was staring at her as if he'd been hypnotised, and obviously fancied the virtuous Mrs Harper something rotten.

"Do you reckon she's been watching television lately?" Alex asked Ivy now. She had popped home, eaten her fish supper – ugh, she stank – then returned by way of the ground floor bathroom window. "Why did her husband decide to take a job in the Thames Valley – was it her idea, or his? Does she *know* what's going on in bloody Rettingham these days?"

Ivy looked at him. Then, she began to wash her delicate, shell-pink ears. She yawned expressively, then blinked, green-eyed as Helen had been, at him.

"Okay, I suppose you can stay here tonight." Alex picked Ivy up, then went upstairs.

He undressed, prowled naked around the room for a few minutes, and then got into bed. He'd do it, he decided. She *ought* to know, and she ought to be ready and willing to take on some of this responsibility. It wasn't fair, he reasoned, it wasn't right, that he should carry this burden all alone.

Now he'd finally decided what to do, he slept comparatively soundly all that night. He was lulled by Ivy, doing her celebrated impression of Davy Crockett's hat, purring contentedly upon his head.

"I'd like to speak to Mrs Harper, please." Alex had found the number of Relate quite easily – it was there in the telephone directory, no problem. He had his story already prepared.

"Hello? Helen Harper speaking," said a voice. "How may I help you?"

Her voice was just as he remembered it, sweet and soft and musical, and his heart turned over. "Helen Harper speaking," she repeated, when he did not reply.

"Hello, Helen." He gulped in some fresh air. "This is Alex."

"I'm sorry?"

"Alex Colborn! Look – I'm sure you must remember."

He decided not to beat about the bush. "I saw your picture in the local rag. I must say, I was surprised to find you'd come to live down here. Helen, do you know?"

"About the house, you mean?" She sounded as if she were choking, but at least she didn't pretend. "Y-yes, I know," she said.

"So what are we going to do about it, then?"

"It – it's not very easy to talk just now," she told him. "I—"

"You mean you're not alone?"

"Exactly."

"Helen, we must meet."

"I don't think that would be a good idea."

"Helen, I'm not *suggesting* this! I'm *telling* you, I need to see you soon, and if you make it difficult, I'll – God, I've been walking on eggshells for weeks, for months now, and if you think—"

But now he found he couldn't say any more. At the other end of the line, there was only silence. "Helen?" he whispered. "Helen, are you still there?"

"Y-yes, I'm here. Alex, where do you live?"

"In Westingford, of course."

"You never moved away?"

"No, I couldn't. I mean I didn't want – oh, never mind. Helen, are you free today?"

"Yes, I suppose so." She sighed, as if the fight had gone right out of her, and all she wanted was a bit of peace. "I'll meet you for coffee, shall I? Or for lunch, or something. Where do you suggest?"

"There's a place called – The Baker's Oven, I think it is. Or perhaps it's The Oven Door? Something like that, anyway. It's on the corner of Neville Street, opposite the Castle Steps."

"I know where you mean."

"I'll be there at one."

"Okay," said Helen.

"So you'll meet me inside?"

"I think that would be best."

Then the line went dead, and Alex was left staring down at the receiver. But at least he'd made a start, he told himself. At least she'd agreed to meet.

She was just as he remembered her, an attractive fair-haired woman of medium height and build, just a bit heavier now, her figure nicely rounded. She was actually spreading across the hips a little, but since she'd had two children, he decided to overlook it – and anyway, she still had a bosom and bottom which men would love to grope, and other women might envy. She was still, as an American might say, a 'piece of ass'.

Her hair was cut in a neat and shining bob, and didn't seem to be dyed. Her complexion was clear and healthy-looking, apparently quite innocent of make-up. But, on close inspection, he could see she was wearing lip gloss, a little discreet mascara and some softly smudged-in shadow. He also noticed the lines around her eyes.

The coffee shop was busy and very crowded, but its clientèle consisted of single people grabbing a quick sandwich, small groups of friends all chattering like starlings, and business colleagues making notes on filofaxes, stabbing electronic organisers, or barking crumbs into their mobile phones, as they drank their scalding coffee and talked with their mouths full of quiche or Danish pastry. No one paid Helen and Alex any attention. So they sat down in the darkest corner and waited to be served.

"How have you been?" asked Helen, pleasantly.

"How do you think?" growled Alex, who had no intention whatsoever of making any small talk. As Helen reached for the menu he met her gaze. “Does your husband know?” he asked. “I suppose you felt you had to confess to him?”

“Don’t be absurd.” Helen began to study the section headed Specials. “How would one introduce something like *that* into a conversation?”

Alex shrugged. “I just thought married couples told each other everything?”

“I can’t believe you ever imagined that.” Helen folded the menu and put it back on the table. “Alex, are *you* married?” she enquired.

“No, I’m not.”

“In a relationship?”

“No, not at present.” Alex decided he hated Helen then. He wanted to yell, of course I’m not in a bloody relationship, how could I sodding be, not that it’s any damned concern of yours! “What do you want for lunch?”

“I’ll just have an espresso.”

“One espresso, one decaffeinated, and a couple of cheese and bacon toasted sandwiches,” he told the waitress, who was hovering nearby. “One of us has to have something to eat,” he murmured. “They don’t like it if you just have a drink. Not at lunchtime, anyway.”

“It seems they intend to start work again on Friday,” began Helen, as the waitress laid paper serviettes and plastic cutlery.

“They *did* intend, you mean.” Alex took the new edition of the local tabloid from his jacket pocket. He opened it at page five. “Take a look at that,” he said.

Helen scanned rapidly. She blinked and frowned, as if she couldn’t – wouldn’t – believe her eyes. Her face lost all its colour, she looked almost grey-green. “W-who on earth is Mr Benjamin Palmer?” she managed to articulate, at last.

“A local businessman,” said Alex, who was comparatively relaxed. He’d had half an hour to digest this latest, ghastliest development. But Helen, of course, was shell-shocked. "He's in construction," Alex continued smoothly. "He and his partners are trying to buy a piece of land on the ring road. They want to build a hypermarket. Or maybe it's a discount shopping village."

"Whatever! Alex—"

"So I assume he's after a bit of – what's the word? 'Local goodwill', or 'credibility'? Anyway, he means to show what a noble-hearted, public-spirited sort of bloke he is. He's approached the Heritage people, and offered to put up the cash they need to prolong the Rettingham excavation for another week."

"But will the developers put up with more delays?"

"It looks as if they might." Once more Alex shrugged. "I don't suppose they'll lose very much in terms of time or money – and if that girl and her friends should dig up something *really* special, they'll be pleased as punch. Think of all the free publicity."

"I think I might be sick." Helen pushed her coffee to one side. "I'm sorry, but I need a bit of air."

She fled. Alex ran after her but was held up at the door. He realised they hadn't paid. "Thanks," he muttered, pushing a five pound note into a waitress's hand. "Table at the back, okay? The lady isn't well—"

He caught up with her in Peach Street. "Helen," he gasped, as he tried to grab her hand, "Helen, we ought—"

"Don't you bloody follow me!" Helen glared at him. "Go away!" she hissed, like an angry snake. "For God's sake, Alex! Go *now*!"

"Helen, listen, I'm not doing this to annoy you." Hoping to detain her for just a moment longer, Alex touched Helen's bare arm. She flinched as if he'd struck her. "I didn't use the office car park today," he continued, trying to meet her gaze. "My car's down here, as it happens, at the bottom of Mortimer Street. Come and sit down for a moment."

"I really don't think I should."

"But you look bloody awful! As if you're going to faint—"

"I shall be perfectly all right."

"Helen, just five minutes!" Alex willed her to say, yes, right, okay. "That's all I want!" he cried. "Five lousy, rotten minutes! If you can't even spare me that—"

"Please, Alex! Please, don't make a public scene." Helen's head was aching now. She could see flashing lights, and knew that any minute she would start a migraine – and she had two new clients to meet later that afternoon.

She realised Alex meant what he had said. "I'll come and sit in your wretched car," she told him. "But for five minutes only, understood?"

Robin Harper's office was in the business park on Westingford's small industrial estate. He didn't normally have any reason to drive through the congested city centre. But today, he wanted to go and see the manager of the store in the new precinct, so now he was cruising Westingford's dingy back streets, looking for a convenient place to park.

At first, he thought the woman he'd seen was just someone who looked a bit like his wife. But then, as he glanced in his rear view mirror, he saw that she was wearing the same blouse as Helen had put on that very morning.

Blue and white, with narrow stripes, it was almost a man's shirt, and Robin didn't like it. He really hated masculine clothes on women, especially those which hid their curves and contours, for although wild horses wouldn't have dragged this from him, he was a man who liked to see a shapely pair, pushing against a jumper or tiny crop-top. That sort of thing really brightened up his day.

Held up at a red light, he turned to look back at the dark blue Cavalier. The man who was sitting there beside his wife – for it *was* Helen in the car, he was almost sure of that – looked about thirty, maybe thirty-five. Quite nice-looking, dark-haired and broad-shouldered, he was obviously upset.

Then the lights changed again, so Robin was obliged to move along. He manoeuvred the company Mondeo into the outside lane, then had another quick look in his rear view mirror. The man had his head in his hands, but Helen herself sat upright, gazing serenely through the windscreen, presumably waiting for her client to get a grip again.

For surely it had to be a client, some poor sod whose wife had left him, whose life had come apart? Refusing to let himself so much as consider any alternative explanation, Robin gnawed his lip. Held up at another junction, he drummed his fingers on the steering wheel. Then, telling himself he'd sort it out tonight, he drove on to his meeting.

"Hello, darling." That evening, Robin Harper was home early. He walked into the kitchen smiling brightly, determined to be cheerful, to let his wife explain. "How was your day?" he asked her breezily.

"Fine," she replied, not even deigning to glance up at him.

But she didn't look as if it had been fine. There were shadows under her eyes, and her jaw was firmly set. Her mouth was shut like a trap in a thin, hard line, as if she were trying valiantly not to cry. When Robin spoke to her again, she still would not meet his gaze.

He noticed she had changed into a camisole and shorts. The camisole was silk and she had nothing on underneath, so when she moved her breasts swung heavily. He suddenly felt sick at the thought of clients eyeing her up, of other men staring fascinated at her prominent nipples. Perhaps men's shirts were better for the office, after all.

"Our meal's not quite ready yet," she murmured, stirring hard, her gaze still fixed upon her wretched saucepan. Then, leaving her cauldron bubbling away, she went over to the sink. "I'll make you a cup of tea or coffee, shall I?"

"Coffee would be great." He sat down at the table. He looked at her, and saw what he'd most feared. When Celia had broken something, when she'd lost her lunch box yet again, or when she'd been mean to her brother, she looked exactly as her mother did right now.

But perhaps there was some simple explanation. Perhaps, later on, she'd tell him all about it. At least she wasn't being offensively cheerful. She wasn't trying to brazen it out, to pretend there was nothing going on.

"I had a call from George Lloyd-Wright this morning," he informed her, as she placed a mug of coffee in front of him, then turned away again.

"George who?" She was peeling potatoes now, slowly, deliberately, giving it all she'd got. "Oh, the man who deals with the selection process, is that whom you mean?"

"Yes, that's right."

"So, what did he say?"

"They'd like me to meet the Committee some time next week."

"But – that's wonderful!" Suddenly, Helen turned to face her husband. Her whole expression was animated now. In fact, she looked quite delighted. "That's great, darling!" she exclaimed. "Well done!"

He shrugged in self-deprecation. He looked at her, considered asking her straight out, but then rejected the idea. "Do I have time for a shower?" he asked, instead.

"Yes, of course." She poured boiling water into a smaller pan. "I expect you need one. Well, I know I did, when

I came in from work! It's been so hot and sticky all today."

"Do you want to tell me anything?" he asked her later on that evening, as he came out of the bathroom, then sat down on the edge of the bed.

"I–I don't think so." For a moment Helen frowned. But then she forced a smile. "W-why do you ask?"

"I thought you seemed a bit preoccupied earlier on. I wondered if anything in particular had happened to you today?"

"No." Helen thumped her pillows. "In fact, I was extremely bored all this afternoon. I spent two hours on expenses claims, you see."

"You didn't have to see any difficult clients, then?"

"I didn't have to see any clients at all." Helen lay down, her face turned away from him. "Actually, Vanessa's reduced my caseload. So I can cut my hours, as you suggested."

"Oh." Robin felt as if he had just been kicked, or punched right in the kidneys. "If you ever do want to talk about your job," he said slowly, painfully, carefully, "if you ever feel the need to bend my ear, about anything at all, remember that I'm always willing to listen. I'm always here for you."

"Right." Now Helen swallowed hard. "Yes, I shall remember that," she said.

Chapter Eight

Over the next few days the local evening papers carried the full story of the dig. The visits of a well-known television personality, who lived in the vicinity and whose interest in archaeology was well-known, increased the media presence.

Soon even people who couldn't have distinguished between a potsherd and a pikestaff were taking it upon themselves to give their own opinions of the likelihood of finding hidden hoards of gold and silver, and of putting little Rettingham firmly on the global map. Several elderly people suddenly remembered their own grandparents had told them tales of buried treasure . . .

Seeking to give himself some fresh distraction from his own persistent worries, Robin encouraged Celia to take an interest in the excavations over at Rettingham. He even went to the local newspaper office to order some black and white photographs of the dig for his daughter to take to school.

A week after Robin had asked his wife if she wanted to talk, or to tell him anything, Helen came home from an Aid for Africa steering committee meeting to find these photographs spread all over the large pine kitchen table, and her children fascinated by what was going on.

"Mummy!" Celia beamed. "Come and see what Daddy's doing here!"

Daddy was helping Celia draw a picture of the Merchant's House, which he'd copied from one in the *Westingford*

Telegraph. Celia had a brand new set of chunky felt-tipped pens and she was busily colouring it in. "Now we've got all these pictures for our folder, me and Donna will have the bestest project book in the whole class," she told her mother, smiling proudly.

"Donna and I," corrected Helen, automatically. Steeling herself, she began to examine the photographs which Robin had brought home.

"It's turned into quite an extensive excavation," she observed, as she fought to prevent any inkling of despair from creeping into her voice. "This Mr Benjamin Palmer must have money to throw away."

"There's method in his madness," Robin told her. "He's hoping to convince the people of Rettingham that, far from being a greedy speculator, he's a decent sort of bloke."

Robin had echoed Alex Colborn so faithfully that Helen felt quite ill. "W-what have they found so far?" she managed to croak.

"A Roman wedding ring, a rusty sword blade, and a few old, broken teeth – which might be human, by the looks of things." Robin grinned, revealing his own sharp canines. "The County Archaeologist seems to think they've stumbled across an ancient burial site."

"A very old semmy – semmitry," added Celia, helpfully.

"Good God." Helen sat down, and tried to control her breathing. She couldn't believe that she was hearing this. "So what happens now?"

"They want to look at the whole of the area," said Robin, who was still grinning ghoulishly. "It's all in the evening paper. Here – do you want to see?"

"I'll look at it later." Helen wanted to scream. To howl like a madwoman, to wail and tear her hair. "Darling, I must have a shower," she said.

* * *

The torment went on and on. Each day the site at Rettingham yielded a little bit of this, a tiny piece of that. Glass beads, a few copper tokens, several low denomination Roman coins – shards of pottery, rusting nails, a couple of broken ribs – all made front page news in the *Rettingham Observer*.

But then, about a week after the intensive investigations had begun, the archeologists found a human skull, complete with teeth, which was provisionally dated as belonging to the first or second centuries BC. This made the front page of the *Guardian* and the *Daily Telegraph*, and Helen began to think she would soon go crazy.

She knew that Robin was giving her some rather puzzled, bewildered looks these days. He was well aware that something must be up. But she comforted herself with the assurance that, whatever he might suspect, he'd never guess the truth.

All she had to do was carry on as normal and it would all blow over.

Then, one afternoon, Alex rang her at home.

"*How did you get my number*?" She was so angry with him that she felt quite sick with rage.

"I rang Directory Enquiries, of course." Alex sounded at a loss, as well as extremely hurt. "I need to speak to you urgently," he said.

"Well, *I* don't think there's anything to say."

"No?" He paused for a moment. "Then you can't have seen the papers recently."

"Alex, I'm going now. I—"

"Just hang on a second," said Alex. "I went over to Rettingham this weekend," he continued, smoothly. "I spoke to one of the volunteers working on the excavation, and—"

"Alex, are you *mad*?" Helen was horrified. "He'll remember you now, you idiot! He'll—"

"But it's okay," interrupted Alex, as calm as Helen was agitated. "That's what I'm ringing to tell you. It's going to be all right. Last week, you see, they were using some sort of electrical scanner, all over the site, and—"

"Alex, what's this to me?"

"Just hang on a minute, and you'll see. Apparently, this instrument can locate and identify all the different sorts of materials buried on the site. To cut a long story short, they've now mapped out the probable boundaries of this so-called Roman burial ground. Helen, it's at least five hundred yards from where the house once stood, it's well away—"

"So they're not going to be digging anywhere near the foundations of the Merchant's House?"

"No, they're not." Alex sounded jubilant. "In fact, the builders will be pouring concrete all over the whole area, this very afternoon."

"But that's wonderful!" Helen felt as if an enormous burden had been lifted from her shoulders, as if she could float up to the clouds, like a helium balloon. "Oh, Alex," she almost wept, "that's bloody marvellous! Thank you for telling me!"

"I just thought you'd like to know," said Alex.

"You were absolutely right."

"That's great, then. Helen?"

"What?"

"Do you think we could meet some time? Only for a drink or a cup of coffee." Helen's guard was down, so Alex pursued his advantage. "Or for lunch, maybe?" he continued, boldly. "Just for old times' sake?"

"I don't think that would be a good idea," said Helen, firmly.

"Why ever not?" he exclaimed.

"Alex, I'm married! I have two children, I—"

"Oh, God," said Alex, groaning. "Please don't tell me you married some Neanderthal jealous bastard who'd beat you senseless for daring to have lunch with an old friend?"

"I'm married to a man who loves me and whom I love very much." Now, Helen realised she didn't want to see or hear anything of Alex Colborn. "I can't meet you for lunch," she told him, firmly. "In fact, I think it would be best if our paths never crossed again."

"Helen, for God's sake! I—"

"I must go now, Alex. Thank you very much for ringing me." Helen sought to soften the blow a little. "It was good of you to let me know what's happened, and I appreciate your kindness. But now I must say goodbye."

"Who was on the phone?" Home early for once, Robin walked into the kitchen just as Helen was replacing the receiver in its cradle.

"Just a member of the charity committee. We're having a stall at the village fair on Saturday. She wanted me to make a few chocolate cakes, or some of my toffee and pecan pies." Apple-cheeked and smiling, Helen turned to face her husband. "Don't worry, I haven't forgotten about tonight," she assured him, cheerfully.

"I should hope not, since it's quite important." Robin loosened his tie. "So what are you going to wear?"

"My navy linen suit, I think, with my cream silk top and a little gold jewellery."

"Don't wear that cream silk camisole," said Robin, thinking, I want them to fancy you, but I don't want those old bastards getting *too* excited. He searched for the right words. "It's a bit too revealing for something official like this. I'd suggest you wear your blue striped shirt, or an ordinary cotton blouse, and don't overdo the bangles and the beads."

Robin rubbed his tired eyes. He hadn't been sleeping at

all well recently, for Helen's tossing, turning and muttering had disturbed him, too. "Any tea in the pot?" he enquired, yawning.

"Yes, I've just made some," Helen told him. "Why don't you get a mug and help yourself?"

"Where are the children, then?"

"At Judy Drew's, for tea. She's going to bring them back about seven o'clock, then Mrs Laing from the village will babysit until we get home again." Helen smiled. "Well, my love – I think I'll go and have a nice warm bath, if that's okay with you. The dinner's in the oven, cooking itself – we'll be eating about six."

"Then I'll have ten minutes with the local rag." Robin sat down at the kitchen table. He poured himself some tea, then stirred in sugar, which he didn't normally take, but which he suddenly found he really needed.

As soon as Helen had gone upstairs, and he heard the water running into the bath, he picked up the telephone. Feeling as guilty as hell and hating himself for spying – but needing desperately to know why his wife had looked so pleased with herself, like the cat with the double cream – he punched in 1471. He listened carefully.

It was a Westingford number. One he didn't recognise at all. The women on the Aid for Africa committee all lived locally.

Taking out his pocket organiser, Robin carefully typed the number in. But of course he had memorised it by now.

"I don't think I like that." Passing her as he went into the bathroom, Robin glanced back towards his wife, who sat at her dressing table applying masacara. "The skirt's too short, and the top is much too tight. You'll give old George a heart attack if you turn up like that."

"Do you really think so?" Helen had decided she looked

quite fetching. Examining herself in the full-length wardrobe mirror, she had seen a smiling, pretty woman, in a dark blue linen suit. The skirt of this was a discreet three inches above her dimpled knees. The matching short-sleeved jacket fitted beautifully, emphasising her narrow waist. The tightly-fitting V-necked top which she wore beneath it moulded her slender figure to perfection. "I thought all those old blokes might like a little bit of cleavage. Or a flash of thigh."

"But *I'd* prefer my wife to look like a lady – not like a *fille de joie*." Robin pulled off his shirt. "I think your new green paisley skirt would be the very thing."

"But Robin, that's a horrible old rag. I only bought it for work, for when I need to blend into the background. It makes me look like my mother, or a Methodist minister's wife."

Helen smoothed her skirt. When she was sitting down, she realised, it *was* a bit revealing. But tonight she'd be wearing sensible, flesh-coloured tights, not sheer black stockings and suspenders – and the skirt itself wasn't really short, or not by today's lax standards, anyway.

"Go on, my love," she purred, as she kissed the air at him. "Let me seduce them for you."

"I want you to wear your paisley skirt," repeated Robin, shortly. He went into the bathroom, and he locked the door behind him.

He was nervous, she supposed. Poor Robin, she knew he really wanted this. He saw himself as one of the new breed, a desperately-needed, clean-cut family man, the sort of MP who would make it that much easier for the Conservatives to win the next election.

Frederick Gordon Jewell was retiring soon, after thirty years of blameless if unspectacular representation. Robin Harper meant to take his place.

Helen and Robin toyed with their supper, argued again about what Helen was going to wear, gave up and declared a truce – and then went out. As Helen sat beside him in the car, still in her linen suit and with her jacket folded neatly on her lap, but in a looser blouse instead of the contentious knitted top, she wondered why her husband was so scared.

"Don't worry, darling," she began, as they turned out of the lane and on to the main road. "You'll be fine, I'm sure."

Robin made no comment.

"They'll love you," she insisted, as he indicated left, following the signs towards the motorway.

Still Robin was silent.

So Helen let him cogitate, and hugged herself for the tenth, for the twentieth time, on account of the good news she'd heard that day.

The evening was not really a success. It wasn't even just all right. In fact, it was a disaster, and they drove home in frozen silence, neither daring to speak to the other for fear that something terrible, unforgiveable, might be said.

Helen sat rigid, both furious and bewildered, worrying a ragged fingernail right down to the painful quick. Robin's knuckles showed white on the steering wheel, and he changed gear with such angry, vicious violence that the poor car protested vehemently.

When they arrived home, they found Mrs Laing sitting quietly in the porch, enjoying the cool of the balmy summer evening. "Everything's fine," she told Helen, beaming happily. "Edward went off to bed like a little lamb, and Celia's done you a lovely coloured picture of that house they're doing their project about at school. I hope you and Mr Harper had a pleasant evening?"

"It was lovely, thank you." Helen didn't want Mrs Laing

to spread her gossip all over the village. "Now, can I run you home?"

"I could walk, I think." Mrs Laing smiled her appreciation. "It's only just down the road, and it's such a beautiful evening, I—"

"I'll drive you." Robin opened the passenger door of the saloon, and motioned to Mrs Laing to get inside. She shrugged, she pouted – but then, still simpering like a teenaged girl, she bowed to Robin's superior masculine judgement.

"That's a very pretty outfit that you're wearing," she told Helen, as she fumbled with her seatbelt. "It really suits you, with your nice, slim figure. I expect Mr Harper thinks so, too."

As Robin drove away, Helen covered her face with her hands. It was as much as she could do not to burst into floods of tears. Why, just *why* had Robin been so mean to her tonight? Why, when he'd obviously wanted to impress all those quite horrible old men, had he deliberately ridiculed his wife?

She could hear him now. "No, Helen doesn't work outside the home," he'd said. "But she manages to keep herself quite busy. She does a little charity work, she looks after our two children, and she's a brilliant cook. You should taste her pecan pie!"

"Pecan pie, you say?" That hideous Colonel Steerforth had grinned at her, then winked lasciviously. He'd eyed her up and down, stared pointedly at her breasts, then asked which charity it was that she supported, he was sure quite charmingly.

"Helen works with people whose relationships are on the rocks," said Robin. He shrugged, as if to imply, well – she needs to fill up her day, and she can't always be making pecan pies. "I suppose you could say she provides a kindly, sympathetic ear."

Then, before his wife could qualify this and explain that Relate was not *just* a listening post, Robin enlarged on Helen's scope and talents. "She also raises money for children's charities in the Third World," he said.

"Really?" An obese old woman, in high-necked nylon lace and an unsuitable dirndl skirt, revealed her yellow molars to the throng. "I collected for black babies once myself. This was when I was at school, a few years ago! We sold little pictures of Nigerian orphans, for threepence or sixpence each. The money went to the Roman Catholic Missions, to build churches in the bush, I think they said."

"*We* run highly-organised campaigns to provide communities with schools or health care programmes," began Helen. "We send out volunteers to work in the field and they train local people. We don't believe in making aid dependent on religious affiliation and we—"

"I'm sure it's a fascinating little hobby," cut in Colonel Steerforth, grinning, "and we'd all love to hear much more about it, perhaps some other time. Now, Mr Harper – what are your thoughts on this BSE fiasco, and all the fuss the local farmers seem to be determined to make about it? It's a bloody storm in a teacup, if you ask me."

So it had gone on, Robin not allowing Helen to get another word in, and cravenly agreeing with that ridiculous old man that BSE and New Variant CJD were indeed not worth any parliamentary time, but should be left to the medical boffins and the biochemical wallahs, who would surely sort it out, given time.

The Selection Committee wanted an obedient MP who would not rock any boats. The prospective candidate's wife was there to be seen and ogled – but not heard.

*   *   *

"What exactly have I done?" As Robin dropped his car keys on the kitchen table, Helen grabbed his arm. "Robin, you've ignored me all this evening, you're about to go to bed without even saying goodnight, and you seem to think that I should just accept this. Well, I don't accept it! Tell me what I have – what it is you think I've done."

But Robin merely shrugged.

"Robin!" Helen shook him. "For God's sake – speak to me."

"I don't think there's anything to say." Robin was trying to wriggle free, so Helen let him go. "I'm going to bed," he muttered.

"So am I." Helen removed one earring, then the other. "We'll talk in the morning, yes?"

"I'm afraid I have an early start tomorrow." Robin walked through to the entrance hall. Observing the white envelope lying on the mat, he stooped to pick it up. "Here," he said.

"What is it?"

"How should I know?" Robin frowned at her. "Go on, then – take it. It is addressed to you."

So Helen took the letter from his hand. It was addressed to Mrs Helen Harper, and had obviously been delivered that same evening. It was from Alex Colborn – Helen had recognised the writing straight away.

"Open it, then," said Robin.

"Oh, it's not important." Aware of her husband's suspicious gaze upon her, Helen blushed. "It'll be from Doreen Gray, about the cakes and pies for the summer fair."

"Why should she write to you?" Robin's eyes were slits. "You'll see her at the post office tomorrow, after all."

"Perhaps it's to do with something she particularly wants me to know this evening." Helen's face was on fire. “Go on up, my love,” she whispered. “I’ll see to things down here.”

“Open your letter, Helen,” said Robin, quietly – but also dangerously.

Chapter Nine

Helen realised that she had no choice. With Robin's suspicious gaze upon her, she clumsily tried to do as she was bidden. Tearing not only the envelope, but also the piece of paper which was inside it, she somehow managed this. Her fingers trembling, she smoothed the single sheet. Then, she scanned her letter.

"Well?" said Robin, coldly.

"Doreen wants me to make six lemon sponges, a tray of gingerbread, and four blackcurrant cheesecakes." Helen screwed up the little scrap of paper but she didn't lob it straight into the bin. Instead she kept it safely in her hand. "Okay?" she said.

"Okay," said Robin wearily. He began to walk upstairs.

"I'll be up soon," Helen called after him.

But when she did at last go upstairs to bed, there was no light on in the master bedroom. Instead, the golden glow was coming from under the spare room door.

"What on earth do you think you're doing?" she exclaimed, as she watched Robin put on his pyjamas, then get into the spare bed.

He didn't reply. Instead, he simply turned away from her, and clicked off the light.

"Robin?" began Helen. "Darling, please!"

"Go to bed now, Helen." Robin's voice was muffled by the pillow. "There's no need to shout," he muttered, sourly. "I may be bloody stupid, but I'm not deaf."

"But Robin, listen—"

"Helen, for God's sake!"

"All right, all right, I'm going." Helen didn't know how to handle this. So she took the line of least resistance, went across the landing to her room, and lay restless and sleepless most of the summer night.

She caught her husband just as he was about to leave the house at six the following morning. "Where are you going?" she hissed, as she beat him to the kitchen door and stood with her back against it.

"Get out of my way," he muttered.

"But I want to know where you're going!" she insisted, her voice rising, and her colour high.

"To work, of course." Refusing to make eye contact with his wife, Robin stared fixedly at the clock instead. "Somebody has to earn a living round here."

"Oh, Robin! What's got into you?" In an effort to calm him, and to steady herself as well, Helen placed her hands on her husband's shoulders. "Darling? What's the matter?"

Robin considered for a moment. Then he spoke, but very hesitantly. "What was that letter about?" he demanded, softly. "You know – the letter you received last night?"

"I told you, Doreen wants me to do some baking for the fair."

"Show me," whispered Robin.

"Show you Doreen's letter?"

"Yes, if you wouldn't mind."

"I–I put it down the waste disposal." Helen felt the blush creep up her neck. "Robin—"

"Get out of my way." Robin's tone was perfectly reasonable but there was a definite menace in his voice which Helen had never detected there before. So she did as she was told, and watched from the kitchen window as he put his briefcase in the back of the car, got in himself, then reversed out of the drive.

An hour later, the children were stirring and Helen realised that soon they would be up, demanding breakfast. They'd also want to know where Daddy had gone. As she set out their plates and cereal dishes, Helen told herself she had no choice. She simply had to see this whole thing through. Robin would get tired of sulking – might even explain what was actually bothering him. In any case, he would come round in the end.

"Where's Daddy's plate?" As Celia sprinkled far too much sugar on her soggy cornflakes, then added even more, she eyed her mother curiously. Suspiciously, perhaps? "Doesn't he want any breakfast?" she enquired.

"He had his before you two got up." Helen poured some chocolate milk into Edward's special cup. "He had to go to work early today."

"Why?" asked Edward, sleepily.

"I expect there were lots of things for him to do." Helen cut Edward's toast into little fingers, then spread the Marmite thinly, carefully. "Now remember, you're going home with Mrs Bright, and having tea with Sally and Joel today. I'll be fetching you at six o'clock."

Helen spent a miserable day, unable to concentrate on anything. Listening to a long-term client complaining about his wife, who obviously didn't understand him, she'd found she wanted to reach across the desk and grab him by his horrible, stringy throat. To shake him like a rabbit in a terrier's iron jaws. To cry, "Just listen, mate – if you think that *you*'ve got problems—"

Later, she picked up Celia and Edward, who didn't want to leave their new friends' house, for here there was a brand new home computer, unlimited Coke and popcorn, and satellite television permanently tuned in to all their favourite cartoons.

On the journey home, Celia was tetchy, irritable and cross, while Edward simply cried. "I think we need an early night," said Helen.

"You speak for yourself," snapped Celia, sounding just like Robin's mother.

"I want Brolly!" Edward wailed. He gulped and swallowed. "Mummy, I feel *sick*!"

By eight o'clock, the children had gone to bed, but Robin had not come home. By then, however, Helen had thought things through. She had at last made up her mind. She'd decided to explain what was going on.

She wouldn't tell Robin everything, of course, there was no need for him to know the whole disgusting story. But he did need – no, he did *deserve* – some sort of explanation. He was at least entitled to have that.

When Robin came in, he went straight up the stairs, to see the children and kiss them both goodnight. When he came down again, he went into his study, sat down at his desk and began to read the company's bi-annual report. No, he'd muttered, he didn't want any supper.

So Helen poured his favourite *coq au vin* straight down the waste disposal, and loaded the dishwasher. She switched it on, and then she followed him.

"Robin," she said, as she closed the door behind her, "I need to speak to you."

"I'm sorry, Helen, but I'm busy now."

"Robin, stop it!" Helen took three rapid steps towards him. "This is important!" she cried. "We need to talk, and I intend—"

"Please stop yelling," interrupted Robin, coldly. "You'll disturb the children."

"So *talk* to me, then. I want—"

"For God's sake, Helen!" Robin glared at her. But he put down the report. "Well?" he demanded.

"I want to explain to you about the letter." Helen sat down on a hard chair, her hands folded in front of her, her ankles crossed, her eyes meekly cast down. "I should have told you this last night, but I – the fact is, the letter wasn't from Doreen Gray."

"Yes," said Robin, "I somehow gathered that."

"Please, Robin!" Helen wished she'd never got into this. But now, she'd have to see it through. "It was from someone called Alex Colborn," she continued. "He and I once worked together – years ago, this is – at the Department of Health and Social Security, as they used to call it then. A few weeks ago we happened to bump into one another in Westingford town centre. He seemed delighted to see me once again. In fact, he asked me to go out with him for lunch."

"I see." Robin's expression was unreadable. "So why didn't you tell me at the time?"

"I don't know, to be honest." Helen sighed. "I suppose I thought you wouldn't understand."

"What do you mean, what wouldn't I understand?"

"Well, I thought perhaps you wouldn't want me to go out to lunch, not with another man."

"I don't see any reason why you shouldn't." Robin shrugged. "Provided you were in a public place, and – Helen, are you trying to tell me you're having an affair?"

"Of course not, I'd never *dream* of having an affair!" Helen was close to tears. "Robin, this man is a former colleague – a friend from university, in fact. He just wanted to talk about old times."

"I see." Then, Robin shrugged again. "But there's nothing else between you and this – this person?"

"No, Robin. Honestly, there's nothing at all."

"Okay," said Robin.

"You don't sound convinced."

"I'm surprised, that's all." Robin rolled a pencil backwards and forwards across his desk. Then he eyed Helen narrowly. "I knew you were lying last night," he said. "I wonder if I should believe you now?"

"I wish you would." Helen met his gaze and held it candidly. "I've told you everything."

"You have?" Robin shook his head. "So, do you intend to go and have lunch with this man?"

"No, I don't." Helen looked into Robin's eyes. "I used to get on well with him, at one time. But he's nothing to me now. I don't care if I never see him again."

Robin was very quiet for the next few days. But to Helen's enormous relief he didn't continue to be hostile. He returned to the marital bed and although he made no attempt to be conciliatory, to make love to his wife or even kiss her goodnight, he wasn't sullen or unpleasant now.

Helen decided she would count her blessings. "Take it one day at a time," she told herself. Just as she told her clients, in fact. One day, one week – one month at a time.

But there was still some business outstanding, and after considering the matter for a week or more – by which time the entire floor area of the Merchant's House had been covered by a foot thick raft of concrete – she decided to speak to Alex once again.

To explain to him, that was all. To thank him for his concern on her behalf, and to tell him that it wouldn't have worked out. It would be best for everyone if they didn't ever see each other again.

One Wednesday afternoon, Helen arrived home early, before the friend who'd agreed to meet Edward and Celia had brought them home from school. She put away her groceries and then she went upstairs to have a shower.

But the water was just lukewarm, so she switched on the immersion heater and sat down to wait the ten or twenty minutes for it to heat up again. She sorted through the linen basket, and then she filed her nails. Then, she picked up the phone.

"Alex?" He'd given her the number of his personal direct line, and she got through straight away. "It's Helen," she began. "Thank you so much for your letter."

"My pleasure." Alex sounded relaxed, light-hearted even, today. "It's wonderful to hear from you," he told her. "But, God – you've taken ages to reply!"

"I was trying to decide what I should say. Alex, are you alone?"

"Yes, my secretary's gone out. Helen, before you tell me it won't work—"

"Please, Alex," she interrupted. "Please, just listen. Now it's time for you to hear *me* out." Then, Helen explained to him.

Alex took a great deal of convincing, but eventually he seemed to understand. To accept that the break between them should be complete.

"So you mustn't ring," said Helen, anxiously.

"I shan't ring," Alex promised.

"You mustn't write to me."

"I shan't write." Heavily, Alex sighed. "But Helen, this – all this is going to be very hard for me. When we met again, I thought – well, I remembered how it used to be. I hoped—"

"Look, Alex – please don't make difficulties. You know I can't begin—"

"Helen, you must understand, I never stopped loving you." Alex was almost whispering to her now. "You can't have forgotten, surely? All those nights when we couldn't get enough of each other, when we certainly never slept! Do you remember when I touched you, when I kissed you—"

"Alex, stop it!"

"Then, afterwards, you would still be begging for it, but I could make you wait and wait and wait! It would be hours before we were satisfied! So is it like that for you and Mr Harper? Helen, I tell you now, I've never met anybody who could turn me on like you did. Who could do the things you did to me, and who—"

"I don't want to hear another word of this." Helen stared at the phone. "You promised," she whispered. "Alex, you promised me."

"Yes," he agreed. "I promised."

"Goodbye, then."

But Alex put the phone down first, without saying anything – least of all 'goodbye'.

Robin always made breakfast on Saturday mornings. He actually enjoyed mixing the muesli, making the toast and even setting the tray.

This particular Saturday, he picked up the post as usual and, whilst he waited for the kettle to boil, he opened a few of the letters – or rather, bills.

Gas, telephone and electricity – why was it that they always arrived together? He glanced at the telephone bill – and his heart almost stopped beating. For, there it was, the very last entry on the itemised statement, a call to Westingford 57743.

He went into his study, found his organiser, and checked. But he knew already that it must be that number.

He picked up the phone, and stabbed viciously at the keypad. A recorded message informed him that he was through to the local office of the Benefits Agency. That the office was closed today, but if the caller wished to ring again on Monday, between the hours of nine—

He replaced the receiver carefully, thoughtfully. Now, he

remembered the man in the car, the man who'd looked so upset. Distraught, even. Had that been Alex Colborn? Might he and Helen still be in regular contact, despite all that she had said?

Robin picked up the tray. He'd imagined he understood her, he thought, as he carried it upstairs. He felt sick as he realised he probably didn't know the very first thing about her.

She was ringing about her Family Allowance, or whatever they call it nowadays, said the voice of reason, as Robin pushed open the bedroom door, and saw the dear, familiar hump of her, asleep under the duvet. She might have been enquiring about a benefit entitlement, for a client or a friend.

But he didn't wish to consider that unlikely possibility. What was the bloody point? Instead, he wondered how he could leave his children, his precious, lovely children, to be brought up by a fornicator, a man who was not their father, who might abuse them, hurt them, beat them, even.

But he would have no choice. If he let Helen go on with this – this business, and he did nothing, how could he live with himself?

Chapter Ten

"Alex, there's someone to see you," said Gina brightly. She'd made her boss's own mid-morning coffee, and now she was searching in her cupboard for another mug, beaming in triumph as she finally found one. She plonked it on the tray. "He says he's an old friend."

"What's his name?" Alex was very busy. He was to be the office manager for the next six months, while his own boss was on secondment to another department, and he meant to make some fairly radical changes. He'd set aside that morning to write a couple of staff reports, and to plan some delicate reorganisation, which he hoped would not upset the unions – or at least, not very much. He certainly didn't want to be interrupted.

But it seemed this visitor had made a really big impression on Gina, and since she usually guarded Alex as zealously as any Cerberus, he couldn't be a total waste of time.

"I'll go and get a few more biscuits from the trolley, shall I?" Gina bustled about the office, tidying away stray papers, and plumping up the cushion on the visitor's easy chair. "It's a Mr Graham," she said. "He told me he was sure you would be very pleased to see him, and so since he was passing—"

"I thought I'd just call in." Having charmed his way past all the security staff and Alex's own secretary, Paul Graham sauntered into Alex's office, and sat down. "Well, me old mate?" he grinned. "Long time, no see. So tell me, how's it going?"

"Fine. It couldn't be better," lied Alex, standing up and holding out his hand. But he was seething, panicking and howling like a maniac inside.

He realised there was nothing for it but to affect an easy bonhomie. To offer his visitor coffee and biscuits, and invite him to be seated – which invitation Paul Graham accepted perfectly readily.

His guest, Alex noticed, was looking very well. He was obviously making his mark on life. After college, he'd worked as a sales representative for a pharmaceutical company, and become a saloon bar expert on the contraceptive pill. Nowadays, he worked for one of the high street clearing banks, and appeared not only to have survived a recent massive round of redundancies and so-called rationalisations, but also to have prospered.

Expensively dressed in what looked like a brand new designer suit, his hair cut like a well-known television presenter's and his complexion lightly tanned, he looked very pleased with himself and life in general.

Alex wondered what had brought him to the DSS. Might this be a purely social call? It was most unlikely, he decided, although he and Paul had never fallen out. They'd never even bothered to have a difference of opinion, for Paul accepted that Alex was a simple-minded pinko, and Alex knew Paul was a true blue capitalist lackey. But their lifestyles were so different that, intend as they might to meet up and have a drink, they saw each other most infrequently.

So, might some self-employed acquaintance need some in-depth benefits lowdown? Might Paul himself want something, had his wife lost her Child Benefit order book, or did his parents need Income Support?

But, "I'm not after anything," his visitor assured him,

dunking a digestive in his coffee, and appreciatively eyeing Gina's thighs, as she busied herself with some not very urgent filing, and Alex tried to think of some pointless errand on which to send her. "I've been meaning to give you a ring for ages, but – well, you know how time flies!"

"I do indeed," said Alex. "Look, it's great to see you, but—"

"I know, I know, you're busy. I won't keep you a minute." Reflectively, Paul shook his well-coiffed head. "The thing is, it's our wedding anniversary on the eighteenth of this month. Yeah, ten glorious years! So Diana's going to arrange a little party—"

"Oh, I see." Alex hated going to little parties, and he usually made excuses to avoid them. But today, he breathed a sigh of sweet relief. "So you've been sent out to round up merry revellers?"

"That's about the size of it." Paul took another biscuit, which he pushed into his face. "You'll be coming, won't you?"

"Well, perhaps. But you know I don't go in for—"

"You can bring any bird you happen to have in tow."

"Thank you very much."

"Great. I'll tell Diana you'll definitely be there." Paul grinned at his friend. "She likes you," he assured him.

"I like Diana, too." Alex picked up a pen. He reached for his personal diary. "The eighteenth, did you say?"

"I did." Now, Paul got up. "So, we'll expect you, yeah? In your best bib and tucker, and with a babe – the more decorative, the better."

"I'll have to see if Pamela Anderson's free."

"You do that."

"So what does Diana fancy?" Alex looked at his friend, who'd frowned – but then begun to grin. "No, stupid – for a present. I mean, is it your copper wedding? Or steel, or silk, or wood?"

"Oh, I get you." Paul shrugged helplessly. "I'm buggered if I know. Just bring a bottle, okay?"

"Okay."

"We'll see you there, then." Paul turned towards the door – but then turned back again. "I know what else I meant to ask you. Have you been following all that stuff about the excavation, over in Rettingham?"

"What?" Alex stared at him. So, this was a trick, a trap! His pen dug into the paper, and then skidded across the page. Aware that Gina's curious gaze was probably upon him, he fought for self-control. "Y-yes," he stammered, eventually, "I've noticed the odd article in the press."

"Fascinating stuff, wouldn't you say?" Then Paul winked expressively at Gina. "Old Alex and I, we used to live in the Merchant's House," he said.

"Hey, did you really? Cool!" Gina was amazed, impressed, entranced. "Alex? You never told me!"

"He's a secretive bastard, is our Alex." His grin as wide as the Blackwall Tunnel, Paul clapped his friend on the shoulder. "This is years ago, mind. When we were all still students. Or was it just after college? Yeah, when we first had jobs, that's right – God, my memory isn't what it should be!"

Still grinning, Paul shook his head. "You won't believe it – I mean, he's just a boring old bachelor these days – but Alex was a bit of a lad, back then. He was shacked up with this really gorgeous woman. Hannah, was it? Or Harriet?"

"It was Helen," muttered Alex, wishing Paul Graham would lie down and die.

"Helen of Troy, that's right." Gazing back down the lanes of memory, Paul looked wistful then. "She had legs up to her armpits and – well, I mustn't say it. You're not allowed to make remarks like that these days, you get yourself arrested.

But she was quite an eyeful, that young Helen. I wonder what became of her."

"She married a wine merchant," said Alex, before he could stop himself.

"She did?" Paul leered. "Lucky bloke!" he grinned. "I don't suppose you know if she still lives locally?"

"I haven't seen or heard of her for years." Alex got up. "I'll see you on the eighteenth," he said, briskly. "Look, we must have a drink some time. Perhaps next week, in the Fox and Hounds, we might—"

"This dig they've got going in Rettingham – have you been over to see it?" interrupted Paul.

"No, as a matter of fact I haven't," said Alex.

"Maybe we could go and give it the once-over some time?" Paul was at the door, his hand was on the handle, and he would never know how much his friend was longing to kick him into the lift shaft, or down three flights of stairs. "They reckon that Palmer bloke is thinking of pulling out," he continued, sagely.

"I beg your pardon?" said Alex, who felt sick.

"That developer chap who's financing the dig. He might come over all high and mighty, God's gift to Rettingham and all that sort of thing. But the word on the street is, he's not doing so well these days."

Paul paused on the landing. "I was wondering if you and I might try to drum up a bit of financial support? Some corporate sponsorship, for the excavation?"

"I don't have any influence with local businessmen." Alex pushed his hands into his pockets, where he balled them into fists. "It's been great to see you," he lied. "But I'm supposed to be in a meeting, and—"

"Yeah, so am I." Paul grinned again. "Right then, old mate. I'll be seeing you around."

* * *

"What a nice man," said Gina, when Alex walked back into his stuffy office, and slumped into his chair.

"What?" Alex glared at her.

"Your friend, I meant. He seemed a very nice man." Putting away her lip gloss, which she applied at least a dozen times a day, Gina opened a file. "Fancy you living in the Merchant's House! I mean, with those dead bodies all around you, and all those ghosts and things! It must have been well creepy!"

"But we didn't know about the cemetery then." Alex willed Gina to shut up, to go for lunch, or go and have a pee.

"They ought to make a film about it, my mate Alison was saying, when we were in the pub on Saturday night. They ought—"

"Gina, do you think you'll be able to get those letters done by lunchtime?" interrupted Alex testily.

"I've almost finished them." Gina consulted Alex's desk diary. "You're supposed to be in a meeting with the benefit supervisors at the moment," she informed him, in the patient tones of one whose own affairs are in perfect order, and who would like her boss to sort his life out, too. "It's tin, by the way," she added, "so you can get him a can of soup."

"I beg your pardon?" Alex stared at her.

"Just for a joke, I mean." Gina shook her head. "For your friend's tenth wedding anniversary. You ought to buy him something made of tin. Oh, never mind. Just go and have your meeting."

Chapter Eleven

After work that evening Alex drove over to Rettingham. He parked in a dingy side street by the canal, then walked across the town towards the site of the excavation.

Dusk was falling, and the soft, romantic twilight bathed the mediaeval streets of the old town in a warm, golden glow. When Alex reached the site, he found that the builders had long since finished for the day. Their yellow JCBs were all lined up in a locked compound, and the foreman's portacabin was in darkness.

Great, thick rolls of piping, wire and cable all lay sullen, waiting for the morning, or maybe for some opportunist thieves. Although there were plenty of big notices, warning trespassers of guard dogs and security men, posted up everywhere, no dogs or guards were in evidence tonight.

The archaeologists had all gone home to bed. Or maybe they had sloped off to the pub. But Alex wasn't there to see the Roman excavation, to join the groups of school children with clipboards and grubby worksheets, or the casual passers-by who hoped that today would see the discovery of a magnificent golden bracelet. Or a beautiful bronze mirror, or a hoard of silver plate.

As stealthily as a cat stalking a bird, Alex skirted the perimeter of the site. As far as he could make out, the place where the Merchant's House had stood was covered by a huge expanse of concrete, through which fat yellow pipes and bright blue cables protruded, apparently randomly. Nobody, it appeared, would be doing any excavating there!

The dig itself, moreover, had been enclosed by its very own chain link fence, supposedly courtesy of Mr Benjamin Palmer, and had its own portacabin and wooden sheds. It was at least a hundred metres from the site of the Merchant's House.

Alex walked back to his car with his shoulders hunched and his head bowed, apparently deep in thought. When he arrived back at the car, however, he couldn't find his keys, and he began to panic. But then he discovered he'd left them in the ignition. Very relieved, he grinned.

As he drove back to Westingford, he realised what a lot he had forgotten. He'd managed to blank out all the fear, the anger and the dread. These days, he felt nothing but pity for wretched Thomas Stenton, for the poor little devil whose only crime had been that he was too much in love with Helen Harper – Helen Tremain, as Alex still thought of her.

But Alex had been in love. Alex still was in love, and he knew he probably always would be.

He wondered why it should have come to this – why he was stuck in this particular rut, unable to go forward, to get on with his life. Helen was just a reasonably attractive woman, that was all. A personable English lady, who had once been a passably pretty girl.

As Paul had observed, she'd had good legs. She'd also had – she still had – big, green eyes, a slender figure and soft, fair hair. But she wasn't the Queen of Sheba. She wasn't Mata Hari, Cleopatra and some Hollywood screen goddess, all rolled into one.

'As if *that* matters,' said a voice, deep inside his head – and Alex had to admit it, physical appearance had very little to do with anything. One had only to read the newspapers, to look at the pictures of men or women who had inspired great passions. In whose names appalling crimes had been readily committed, the most terrible deeds done.

The women were sometimes absolute dogs – middle-aged and dumpy, double-chinned and pugnaciously heavy-jawed. The men were often fat and bald. When these people's adventures were retold on celluloid, their characters were played by stars who looked as if they'd come down from Mount Olympus, and even then their stories struggled to make even a particle of sense.

So Alex went home to his solitary supper, to a blameless evening of watching sport on satellite television, followed by an early bedtime.

"Shall I tell her, Ivy?" he asked the little cat, who'd scrambled through the bathroom window and now sat on the landing, washing her delicate ears. "She said she didn't want to see me. But I'm sure she didn't mean it. I think she feels it just as much as I do."

Ivy stared at him inscrutably.

"I'm sorry, but I don't think I'll be able to come to Diana's little party," Alex told Paul, as he rang him from the office, later on that week.

"But you must – she's got a salmon, and she's ordered a special cake! We've a firm of outside caterers doing the buffet, the place looks like a florist's shop, and she's even bought new curtains for the lounge!"

For a moment, Paul sounded genuinely disappointed. But then he recovered a little from his dismay. He even sniggered lewdly. "I reckon you've got some hot date," he said. "Don't tell me, let me guess. You've found yourself a bit of totty that you don't want to share."

Alex rose to the bait. "Look, Graham," he said, crossly. "If you really think—"

But Paul Graham was well into his stride. "Well, I can't

say I blame you," he continued, man to man. "Your bird might fancy me – and speaking of girls, that secretary of yours, I reckon she looks as if she'd go the distance! Do you have anything—"

"I'm going to be up in Preston, on a course," interrupted Alex, somewhat coldly.

"Yeah, right," leered Paul. "Well, you must come round for dinner some time."

"That would be very nice."

"Diana's got this friend, you see. She's divorced, of course – but then, they all are nowadays. I'm not saying we should blame her, mind. The husband was a bit of a rat, in fact. He played around with teenagers, and got one in the club.

"The little tart refused point blank to do the decent thing, so poor old Nick got lumbered with a child bride, and maintenance for Glenda and the boys, and didn't Glenda sting him! But she's really very nice when you get to know her, and she's had a rotten deal—"

"Yes, I'm sure." Alex had never had any time for this sort of conversation. So now he told Paul he had to go, because someone had just walked in.

He replaced the receiver thoughtfully. He hoped Paul wouldn't say anything to his wife, for if Alex didn't turn up at the party, he was sure he'd not be missed. But if Paul said that Alex couldn't make it, well-meaning and kindly Diana would be on the phone again this very evening, telling him she was so sorry he'd miss the party, and offering him a choice of dates for dinner.

Her friend, he was sure, would be a desperate woman. Thirty to thirty-five, she'd be bitter and angry or determinedly cheerful – but with that awful, bewildered misery in her eyes which said she was really anxious to have her faith in men restored. For her part, Diana no doubt told her friends that Alex was that rarest of unicorns, a heterosexual, quite good-looking man who hadn't found the girl with whom he wished to share his life, at least not yet.

After work, Alex took himself off to play a game of squash, got thrashed by the club professional, then drove home. He made himself some supper, gave Ivy some chicken from the night before, then sat down on the sofa with a plate on his lap and his feline visitor draped around his shoulders.

"What would I do without you, little sweetheart?" he asked the fat, vibrating scavenger whose left paw was even now snaking down towards his dinner.

He fed the animal a scrap of meat. "I'm going to live on a desert island," he told her. "I'm going to sell this house, then buy myself an ocean-going yacht and set sail into the sunset. Do you fancy coming along as the ship's cat?"

Ivy looked at him, then yawned in scorn.

"You think I wouldn't do it," Alex murmured. "Well, you're wrong. Other people have disappeared, and never been seen again. Who – apart from you – is going to miss me?"

Chapter Twelve

As Paul Graham had suspected, Alex Colborn had a date. He was going to the theatre with the wife of a chartered accountant, a bored and frustrated woman whose husband wasn't interested in her body any more. Afterwards, they would go back to her place – her husband was away – for energetic, non-committal sex. Then they would not see each other for a month or more, until one or other of them felt the need for therapy again.

Alex was having a bath when the telephone rang. Reluctant to get out of the hot water, or to disturb the cat, who was sitting washing herself on the pile of towels, he waited for the answering machine to do its stuff. When the phone went on ringing, he remembered, with some irritation, that he'd changed the tape last night. He'd probably forgotten to plug the thing back in.

It had to be the police. Nobody else would be so damned persistent, refusing to believe he wasn't in – and he was duty officer this week, on call if anybody broke into the office, to steal order books and giros.

"I'm coming," he grumbled, rising from the water like an unwilling Archimedes from his tub. Naked and dripping, he strode across the landing to the bedroom. "Hello?" he barked, annoyed. "Alex Colborn speaking."

"Alex?" The caller sounded as if she were crying. "Oh, Alex! Thank God I've found you!"

"Helen?" Astonished, he sat down on the bed. "I thought – I mean, you said I shouldn't call you. I—"

"I know what I s-said. Oh God, I'm sorry." Helen sobbed for a moment. But then, at last, she managed to get a grip. "We need to talk," she told him.

"Of course." More than anything, Alex wanted to be with her. He wanted to take her in his arms, he wanted to kiss her better. To hide away somewhere, and shut the wicked world outside. "Where would you like to meet?"

"It doesn't bloody matter *where!*" cried Helen. Miserably, she sniffed. "Do you have five minutes now? I mean, to talk?"

"I've all the time in the world," Alex replied. He reached for the duvet, then draped it around his shoulders. "Well?" he prompted.

When he eventually came off the line, he found the cat had come to sit beside him, and was licking his damp wrist. She was trying to dry him, he supposed. He scooped her into his arms, then buried his face in her soft, fragrant fur.

"What the fuck am I supposed to do?" he cried, as she purred and rubbed her face against his cheek. As her rough tongue lapped up his salty tears.

They met on the Riverside Walk, the very next afternoon. Alex was supposed to be chairing a management meeting, and Helen had clients to see. But this didn't stop them walking up and down together, for an hour or more.

He'd been shocked by the change in her. She'd lost a lot of weight. Her complexion looked most unhealthy, and she had purple shadows under her eyes. "I need to tell him!" she repeated, for the twentieth time.

"But tell him what, exactly?" Alex demanded, his patience sorely tried.

"Everything, I suppose. All about Tom. All about you

and me, and all the things we did together. About everything which happened in that house."

"You *do* mean everything?" demanded Alex.

"Yes, of course!" cried Helen, who then began to sob. "Oh, Alex!" she wept. "It's terrible at home, you have no idea how bad! He thinks I'm having an affair, but he won't actually say so."

Helen found a tissue. "When the children are around," she sniffed, "he pretends it's all okay. But the minute they're in bed or out of the way, he freezes solid. He won't say a word to me, won't touch me, won't even admit I'm there. I'd never thought anyone could actually look straight through a person as if they didn't exist. But Robin's got it down to a fine art. I think he's trying to drive me round the bend."

"Bastard." Alex ground his teeth in rage. "Leave him," he told her. "Come and live with me. You can bring the children—"

"Don't be absurd!" Helen stopped walking now. "He's only doing this because he loves me," she insisted. "It's all in his imagination, yes – but he sincerely believes that I've betrayed him, and ignoring me is the only way he can cope. Otherwise, he'd have to knock me into the middle of next week."

"I won't pretend I understand any of that." Alex scuffed the grass with his left foot. "Do you love *him*?" he asked.

"Yes," said Helen, simply. "I love Robin very much indeed."

"So if *he* had an affair—"

"I'd kill him. Then I'd kill her, too. I would – no question!"

"I see." Alex wondered if a person could actually die of what was usually called a broken heart. *He* hadn't, or not so far. But all the same . . .

"I want to tell him everything," said Helen, who now

continued walking, or rather pacing, towards the town. "If he knows exactly what happened then, and knows about you and me, he'll understand."

"You honestly think he might?" Alex grimaced sourly. "How many blokes has your husband done away with, would you say?"

"I beg your pardon?"

"How many people has your precious Robin killed?"

"Well, none. But—"

"Helen, think about it." Alex glanced behind him to make sure they weren't going to be overheard. "Think about what you would be telling him. When you were nineteen or twenty, you happened to have an inconvenient lover, of whom you were sick and tired, but who would not leave you alone. So when your latest boyfriend stabbed him, after a fight in the kitchen of the house which you both shared, you were relieved. Perhaps even delighted."

"Alex, it wasn't like that! I wasn't delighted, how can you say such things, I never—"

"Helen, please let me finish." Alex met her gaze. "The only problem was, the proper disposal of the body. But the new boyfriend came up trumps again. He dug a nice big hole in the scullery, and buried the bugger there."

"For God's sake, Alex! It wasn't like that at all! You *know* it wasn't, you—"

"However you choose to tell it, that *is* what actually happened." Alex stared out across the dark brown river, swollen with summer rain. "I can see your marriage has come up against a bit of turbulence. I suppose I sympathise. But do you imagine telling Robin that you were involved in a murder will make everything hunky-dory once again?"

"I—"

"Your husband could actually go to the police. I don't suppose you've even thought of that! We could end up spending the rest of our lives in prison. Do you really want to share your living accomodation with drug dealers and prostitutes and thieves? Do you want your children growing up ashamed of you, do you want—"

"I want Robin to believe I love him! I want him to know I'm not having an affair!"

"Then tell him so."

"He'd want some proof. He'd want—"

"So how does a person provide that kind of proof?"

"I don't know!" Helplessly, Helen shrugged. "But telling him about Tom Stenton would be a sort of start."

He realised she meant it. Helen actually meant to tell her husband everything, and Alex felt very cold. It was as if he were standing on a fault-line and a huge crack had appeared, which was growing wider. "Okay," he began, trying to sound calm, cool and objective, "you tell him about Tom Stenton and what we did to him. Then what happens?"

"He'll see why I've been upset just recently."

"But the fact that he got married to a woman who was involved in a particularly brutal murder, then in the burial of the victim's body – that won't actually bother him?"

"Alex, you *know* it wasn't like that!"

"Yes, of course I know. But who is going to believe me? You yourself supposed I had attacked him. That I—"

"But I was shocked." Helen looked away. "I know what he was like," she muttered. "I wouldn't have put it past him, to have pulled a knife on you. I accept it was self-defence."

"But, all the same, you weren't an actual witness. So, you don't *know* what happened that autumn evening." Alex looked at her. "Helen, just think about it. You make your confession to Robin, who understands that you weren't to blame for Thomas Stenton's death. You kiss and make up, and everything's fine again. But where does that leave me?"

"I'm sorry, what do you mean?"

"Your husband and you are friends again, okay? But then he says he can't let the matter rest. He persuades you that, whatever the circumstances of the crime in question, you can't just let a murderer walk free. So he goes to the police, who arrange to have the body dug up again. The pathologist finds the stab wound. Everything ties in with what you said, and I'm arrested."

"But—"

"Maybe you're arrested, too. The neighbours have a field day! That nice Mrs Harper, who'd have thought it? The children get bullied and picked on, and as for Robin – well, he can just forget about the next round of promotions at the office. In fact, he'll probably get the sack."

Alex warmed to his theme. "So anyway," he continued, "we're splashed all over the newspapers, and eventually one or both of us are charged and sent for trial." Now, Alex shrugged. "From then on, things could easily go either way."

"I suppose I hadn't really thought it through." Convulsively, Helen shuddered. "But do you honestly think it would come to that?"

"If your husband decided to blow the whistle on us, I really don't see how it could be avoided."

"Robin wouldn't want to hurt his wife, upset his children—"

"But he wouldn't give a tuppenny damn for *me*."

"Alex, stop it! You're frightening me now."

"What do you think all this is doing to me?"

"Oh, God." Then, Helen sighed. "I suppose I'd better not tell him anything."

"That's up to you." Alex wouldn't meet her gaze. "In some ways," he murmured, "it would have been a relief. If they had found him—"

"But they didn't." Helen squared her shoulders. "Perhaps that's a sort of sign. Perhaps we should say nothing."

"What will you do about Robin?"

"I don't know," said Helen, sadly. "It's funny – I spend half my life suggesting to people how they might mend or come to terms with broken relationships. But I have no idea how to mend my own."

"Physician, heal thyself."

"Exactly."

"Perhaps it will all blow over."

"I expect you're right." Helen managed a faint but bloodless smile. "Sometimes, he forgets. When he's playing with the children, perhaps, and finds he needs a pencil, so he asks me to get him one. I suppose, in the end, he'll forget what he was so worked up about."

"So you won't say anything?"

"Most probably not." Helen glanced at her watch. "I must get back to work," she murmured.

"So must I," said Alex.

"Alex?" began Helen.

"What?"

"Thank you for meeting me today."

"Oh, that's all right." Indifferently, Alex shrugged. "I really didn't have anything better to do."

"Goodbye, then."

"Goodbye, Helen. Look after yourself."

He watched her walk across the river bridge. He wondered if her heart was any lighter. Somehow, he doubted it. His own felt leaden with foreboding and dread, and he knew that soon he'd have to get away.

Chapter Thirteen

Alex took the keys round to Mrs Singh. He told her he was having a week off work. He wanted to do a spot of quiet fishing.

"So where will you be going, Mr Colborn?" asked Mrs Singh, as two of her pretty daughters eyed him speculatively, and sniggered whenever they managed to catch his eye. Their mother's muttered entreaties to behave like decent women, and to show this gentleman some respect, merely made them snigger all the more.

In the end, their mother lost all patience. "Go and get on with the supper!" she snapped, shooing them into the kitchen, then closing the door on them. "Well, Mr Colborn, I hope you will have a lovely holiday. Enjoy your little rest. You need this, certainly. You've been looking very under the weather of late."

"Really?" Alex was alarmed by this remark. "How do you mean?" he frowned.

"There are big, black circles under your eyes, and you never seem to smile at all these days. We never hear your music playing. You never whistle or sing." Maternally, Mrs Singh patted his arm. "So you go and have a few days of peace and quiet. See if you can catch a salmon! You'll need some milk and bread on Friday, yes?"

"Yes, please." Alex managed a sort of grin. "You're sure you don't mind keeping an eye on the house?"

"I've already told you, it's no problem." Mrs Singh looked up at him, and smiled. "I expect your girlfriend will come crying round to our place, while you are away!"

"I beg your pardon?" Alex was horrified. Who had seen him and Helen, on the Riverside Walk? Who had told Mrs Singh? They should have been more careful, he saw that now. They ought to have met in a pub. Out in the country.

"Such a greedy animal! Meera gave her a chicken leg last week, and you should have seen her gobble it up! It was as if she hadn't been fed for a month or more!"

"She's expecting any day," muttered Alex, weakly. "So she's eating for six or seven, I imagine."

"I hope she doesn't have them in our shed, just like she did the last time." Sighing, Mrs Singh shook her grey head. "The girls will go on and on and on, about keeping a kitten or two. But there's no way that my husband will have cats, not in our house. They make him cough and sneeze like anything! Well – isn't it time you were on your way?"

"Yes, I suppose it is. I'll see you all on Friday." Observing the youngest of his neighbour's daughters spying on him through a crack in the kitchen door, Alex gave the girl a cheery wave. "Bye for now, Anjali," he called – and was almost blown right out of the house by the gust of delighted giggles which erupted in reply.

Alex had never caught a salmon, but he did enjoy an occasional bit of ordinary coarse fishing. Sitting on the bank of a reservoir, wearing his silly hat, his padded gilet stuck all over with pins and lures and things, and with all the other gear scattered around him, he could drift into a daydream.

He loaded his equipment into the boot of the Cavalier, and by the time he set off he had almost convinced himself. He was looking forward to a week of rest and relaxation by the side of some flooded gravel pit or other. Then to swapping stories in the public bar at the end of the summer's day.

"Yeah, you look as if you could do with a holiday," Gina had told him briskly, when he'd mentioned that Mark Fraser, from the short term benefits section, would be acting up next week. "You've been behaving like you had the weight of the world on your shoulders for ages now."

Alex imagined the police interviewing Gina. Then speaking to his neighbours, colleagues, friends. Yes, they'd all agree, he *had* been acting very strangely. Yes, he'd been looking anxious recently. They'd assumed it was girlfriend trouble – it usually was in his case, after all! But, come to think of it, perhaps he had looked furtive. Or was it more sort of guilty? Yes, you *could* say that . . .

Stop it, he told himself, as he drove along the Henley road, then deeper into rural Oxfordshire. He'd stayed at the Lamb and Flag in Stanton Minster half a dozen times before. He wondered if the landlord there would notice any particular change in him.

Two or three days later, Robin Harper finished reading through the sales figures from the two flagship stores in the local area. He sat back in his chair and rubbed his tired eyes.

"Yeah, it's looking good," said Gareth Shaw, who was Robin's deputy and – in the opinion of several members of the Board – the man most likely to be chairman of the company one fine day. "We're definitely going places."

"What did you say?" growled Robin, who had not been really listening.

"The figures. This firm is finally getting its act together. We're eight per cent up on the market share." Gareth sat down, stretched his long legs and grinned. "Look, I don't want to pry," he said, "but what exactly's the matter with you these days?"

"Nothing's the bloody matter!" Robin cried. Then, somehow, he managed to force a grin. He knew perfectly well – had known for ages – that Gareth wanted his job. Not only that, but his deputy was a shark in human form, who could smell the blood almost before the victim was aware he had been wounded.

He was emphatically *not* the sort of bloke with whom a man could have a heart to heart down at the Dog and Duck. To whom one could say, I think the wife's been playing away from home. So do I let her have her fun, do I smack her in the mouth, divorce her – or what? "I've been overdoing the DIY a bit," said Robin. "I need an early night."

"Yeah, sure." Now Gareth grinned, displaying sharp, white, pointed teeth. "You need your sleep," he murmured, silkily. "You need to be on your toes in this game, right?" Meaning, you'd better watch your back, Mr Robin Harper. I'm coming up behind you fast – and I don't take prisoners, me.

That afternoon Robin sent Gareth over to nearby Coverham to harass the manager of the little shop in the precinct there. He gave his secretary some letters to do and told her he wasn't taking any calls for the next hour or so. He had some hard decisions to make, both about next year's lists and the future of a couple of stores.

So Sally left him to it, closing the door behind her after telling him she'd only bring him tea or coffee if he actually rang for it.

Robin waited until he heard the sound of Sally's nimble fingers tapping merrily away. This meant she had her headphones on, so wouldn't hear a single word he said. He picked up the phone. He punched in the number of Westingford DSS.

He'd rehearsed the conversation he would have with Alex Colborn a dozen, a hundred times. But now he was about to speak to the bastard, he felt his resolution waver and his mouth go dry. He wondered if he would be able to talk at all. If the telephonist would think she had a heavy breather on the line.

But when the switchboard finally answered, the girl replied to his croaked request in an extremely laid-back fashion. "Mr Colborn is on leave at present," she told him. "So I'll have to put you through to Mr Fraser – is that all right?"

Of course, Robin had not expected this. Whilst the line clicked and hummed, he tried to regroup his scattered thoughts. He'd only just managed to do this when a pleasant voice said, "Hello? Mark Fraser speaking. How may I help you?"

Robin replied that he was trying to contact Alex Colborn. It was a personal matter and nothing at all to do with the DSS. Then, taking a chance, he asked if Mr Fraser happened to know where Alex could be found.

"I'm afraid I can't help you there." Mark Fraser sounded genuinely apologetic. "But, if you like, I could leave a message on his answering machine at home. Or on his desk at the office here. He'll be back on Monday morning, anyway."

"Okay, I'll try to get hold of him on Monday." Robin was defeated. "Thank you for your time."

"No problem," said Mark Fraser. "What was the name again?"

But Robin had hung up on him. He reached for the telephone directory.

Colborn, Colborn, Colborn. There were dozens of them, it was one of those names which could be spelled in several different ways. There were Colbourns, Colbornes, Coleburns, as well as Colborns. But which one was the bastard who was knocking off his wife?

He decided to try a few numbers, and see what happened. On the ninth or tenth attempt, he had a stroke of luck. D. A. Colborn's answering machine informed him that Alex Colborn was not able to take his call at present. But in an emergency the caller should try ringing this Oxford number.

Robin scribbled it down. He wondered savagely if this was a hint to Helen, if the pair of them had made some secret tryst. He sat back in his chair and wondered what he should do next. Then he pressed the buzzer on his desk.

"I've put the kettle on. I'll be bringing your tea in just one moment," said Sally, cheerfully.

"Don't do that," said Robin, reaching behind him for his jacket. "I'm going out for while. If Head Office calls tell Frank he can get me on the mobile for the rest of today."

"Okay," said Sally. "Somebody's for the high-jump," she whispered to her lover Gareth Shaw, who was ringing her on *his* mobile. They often canoodled on an outside line, and held up Robin's calls. "Darling, of course I love you. Yes, my sweet – I'm wearing a black lace body, with black suspenders. Gareth, don't say things like that, not over the telephone! Look, I'll have to go."

She replaced the receiver just as Robin came striding through the office, in an evident hurry to be off somewhere.

This is quite ridiculous, thought Robin, as he reversed at speed out of the tiny car park, burned rubber through the town centre, then screeched off up the M4 motorway. I don't even know if this is the right man.

He put a call through to the offices of Westingford Relate, but Helen wasn't there. So he left a message to say that he would be late home tonight – not that Helen would care, he thought, his anger steadily mounting. His absence would give her time and space to daydream about her lover. To make plans to take Robin's beloved children away from him.

She'd know how to do that, of course. She wasn't a marriage guidance counsellor for nothing. She knew that mothers had all the rights, held all the bloody cards – and fathers could go and piss into the wind. He realised he was seeing the motorway through a red mist of rage.

He'd phoned the emergency number which Alex Colborn had thoughtfully left on his answering machine. This had turned out to be some pub in deepest Oxfordshire. Yes, the landlord had admitted, there was an Alex Colborn staying there. But he was out at present and the landlord didn't know when he'd be back. The bloke was probably fishing at the gravel pit, if that was any help.

Or rolling around in bed with Helen, thought Robin. Or screwing her in the long grass, or in some woodland glade. He saw his wife lying naked in the sunshine, a shadowy figure looming over her.

There was a sudden raucous screech of brakes. Robin had wandered halfway across a lane, and now an enormous lorry missed him by inches. The driver honked his horn and made an obscene gesture. Robin pulled himself together and drove on more carefully.

He realised he had not made a plan of action. Even as he drove through the pretty village of Stanton Minster, even as he pulled into the car park of the picturesque, half-timbered public house, he was still wondering just how he should play it. What should he do, what on earth was he going to say?

He walked into the cool dimness of the bar and asked for a large gin with lemon and tonic. "Do you have a Mr Colborn staying here?" he asked the barman.

"You're the bloke who rang an hour ago, is that correct?"

The landlord placed Robin's drink upon the counter. "There you go, sir. All the best. Alex?" he called, towards a group of drinkers mostly clad in the checked shirts and baggy khaki trousers which marked them out as fishermen. "They've caught up with you at last! This gentleman over here – he wants a word."

The man called Alex came walking towards the bar. Robin hadn't known what to expect – but, all the same, he wasn't prepared for this. For Alex Colborn was about six feet tall. He was strikingly good-looking, being dark-haired, dark-eyed – classically handsome. He was broad-shouldered and well-made.

Robin had always been sensitive about his own lack of inches. These days he was getting fat, as well. His hairline was receding inexorably. The fact that, in somewhat happier days, Helen had called him her teddy bear and her lovely cuddly bunny, didn't really compensate for any of these afflictions. He looked up at Alex Colborn in dismay.

"Hello?" The *Baywatch* superstud was actually smiling now and hesitantly extending his right hand. Mechanically, automatically, Robin took it, shook it, but almost at once he let it go again. "What can I do for you?" asked Alex Colborn.

"I–I'm Robin Harper," muttered Robin.

"Oh, I see." Alex looked at him for a moment. Yes, of course. This was the little fat bloke in the photograph. "Why don't we go for a stroll around the village?" he suggested.

"That might be a good idea," growled Robin.

"I told you they'd come and get you in the end, old son," observed the landlord, grinning, as the two of them walked through the open door.

"What exactly did he mean by that?" enquired Robin, coldly.

"Oh, nothing. He was just trying to make a joke," said Alex. "We turn left here, okay?"

They walked to the village pond and then began a slow and measured amble around its green perimeter. "Perhaps it would be best if you told me what you already know," said Alex, who by now was feeling very ill indeed.

"What I *know*?" Robin glared up at him. "That's just it! I don't know bloody anything! But ever since we moved down here, I've watched my wife going out of her mind. Or that's how it seems to me."

"But what do you think I have to do with it?"

"She told me that you and she were business colleagues once. This was years ago. But if that's *all* you were, why is she always ringing you, meeting you? Why is she like a cat on a hot tin roof, and why is she constantly lying to *me*?"

"How do you know she's lying to you?" Alex asked him gently.

"Because I – that's no damned concern of yours!" Robin felt so angry now that he wondered if he might take a swing at Colborn, enormous though the bastard was, compared to him. "I want to know what you mean to do," he muttered.

"Personally, I don't mean to do anything." Indifferently, or so he hoped it would seem to Robin, Alex shrugged. But inside he was a quaking, shapeless blob of helpless terror. He felt as if he were walking unprotected through the very middle of a minefield.

He looked at Robin, hoping to be given a clue – but nothing happened. "I–I think things should stay just as they are," he hazarded.

Robin glared at him. "You mean, you only want to screw my wife? You don't want her to leave me?"

"Good God, what are you saying?" Alex breathed more

easily. Quite obviously Helen hadn't said anything. Robin had seen them together, that was all. He'd tackled Helen about it – and been informed that Alex was an old acquaintance, from her DSS days. He'd let his imagination do its worst.

Poor little bloke, thought Alex. "There's nothing between me and Helen," he began. "We—"

"You expect me to believe that?" Still, Robin was glaring. "You must think I'm stupid!"

"But Helen hasn't told you everything." Alex looked steadily into the middle distance. "When we were at college together – this is long before she ever met you – Helen and I were lovers. We finished with each other just before she went to work in Newcastle. No, hang on. Please, let me finish!"

Alex rubbed his eyes. "The break was complete," he said. "We didn't write or phone, and until we happened to meet each other in Westingford one day, we hadn't seen or heard of one another since we split up. We—"

"You were pleased to see her again, I suppose?" interrupted Robin, coldly.

"I was glad to see her looking so well and happy, naturally."

"But then you decided that you and she might have a bit more mileage. So you thought you might begin—"

"No, you're wrong." Once more Alex shrugged. "I won't pretend I'm not still fond of Helen. When we split up – and it was Helen who gave *me* my marching orders, not the other way about – I was devastated. But when I asked how she had been, and she told me she was married and had two children, I was delighted for her."

"But, all the same, you thought you might be well in there. You thought—"

"Please," interrupted Alex, softly, mildly. "Please, Mr Harper, don't speak to me like that."

"Or you'll what?" demanded Robin, scowling belligerently.

Alex had never thought he'd pity Helen Harper's husband. But the poor man was in such a state that pity seemed the only possible reaction to being baited and got at in this way. "There is absolutely nothing between me and Helen," Alex said.

"Then why does she keep ringing you?" asked Robin.

"She's rung me twice," said Alex. "She wanted some advice."

"Advice about what?" demanded Robin, glaring.

"I think you ought to ask her."

"But I'm asking *you*." Then, however, with some obvious effort, Robin controlled himself. "Why aren't you married?" he asked. "I mean – there's nothing obviously wrong with you. You can't have been in prison or you wouldn't be so high up in the Civil Service. I imagine you must be solvent and I don't suppose you're gay."

Alex decided to overlook Robin's rudeness. "I suppose I've never met the right sort of woman," he began.

"You mean you still want my wife?"

"Mr Harper, I don't deny that I'm still very fond of Helen." Alex couldn't say, I love her to distraction. I always have, and I'm sure I always will. When I imagine her in bed with a little runt like you, slobbering all over her, mauling her and trying to make her come, I want to howl. "But she loves *you*," he said, instead.

"It looks like it," growled Robin bitterly.

"For God's sake, man – it's true!" Alex wanted to shake him, throttle him. "Please," he said, "go home. Tell Helen you've spoken to me. Admit you suspected her, that you were wrong, and tell her everything will be all right again."

"You need your head examined," muttered Robin. He turned on his heel and began to stride back towards the village pub. He was in the car and roaring off towards the motorway before Alex walked into the bar again.

Chapter Fourteen

He looks like Cary Grant, thought Robin, sourly. Cary Grant, with a touch of Gary Cooper. Or who was that tosser Helen and all her friends had been in love with, just before the family had moved from Newcastle to live in Oxfordshire? That tall, dark, arrogant-looking bastard, in the television series. What was *his* lousy name?

As a lorry overtook him, Robin scowled. He put his foot right down, chased it and passed it, flashing his lights and grinning as he sped by. So what if the lorry driver lost his rag? So what if he rammed the big saloon, then booted it into the central reservation? So what if they both ended up in a tangle of twisted, smoking metal? Helen would not care.

Robin had never known why Helen Tremain had married him. He'd assumed she was on the rebound from some broken love affair, but he had never dared to ask. Instead, he'd thanked his lucky stars that he was there to catch her as she fell.

Since Helen had become his wife, he'd never quite believed in his good fortune. He'd never have imagined a girl like Helen would have ended up as short, fat, stubby Robin Harper's bride.

But every woman needs to feel she's wanted, he supposed – and God, he had certainly wanted Helen! He'd have licked her boots if she had ever asked him. He'd have given up his whole family, never spoken to his friends, eaten sheep's eyes at every meal, whatever – if Helen had said that was the way she wanted things to be.

He wondered why she'd finished with Alex Colborn. Perhaps because he didn't have that edge? Because he didn't have enough aggression, enough ambition, enough bite? Robin had always been a go-getter, he'd be managing director of Pullen's one fine day, and he knew that he must earn far more than pretty boy Alex Colborn, who was just a pen-pusher.

Colborn might be six feet tall, but he was only a poxy civil servant. His phone number suggested he lived in a dead-beat part of town with all the students, the immigrants who hadn't made it into the middle classes and the single mothers on Income Support.

What sort of home would *he* be offering Helen and her children? A two up, two down, damp Victorian slum? How would neat, fastidious Helen Harper fancy that?

But, thought Robin, Colborn had the looks. He had the style. He had that easy, languid air, which an anxious, pushy, over-achieving nobody like Robin Harper could never hope to cultivate, never in a million years. The bastard had only to smile his sultry smile, and when he'd crooked his index finger Helen had come running.

Robin chased and overtook a gleaming, silver, top of the range Mercedes. It was driven by a man who wore a dark green chauffeur's uniform, and what looked like a Latin American dictator's braided hat. When *he* was managing director, Robin decided – no, when he was chairman of the Pullen group, the biggest and most successful retailer in the United Kingdom – *he'd* have some ponce in a peaked cap and gaiters, employed to chauffeur *him*.

Robin hadn't meant to go straight home. He'd intended to find a quiet pub, sit down in a gloomy corner, and then get very drunk. But the car seemed to know the way, and almost before he knew it, he had come off the motorway, off the busy main road, and was steadily bumping along the potholed track which led to the red-brick cottage upon which Helen had set her heart.

Now, of course, he knew why she'd wanted it. The house was very secluded, it was beautifully private. How many men had she had up here already while the children were at school? While she wasn't otherwise engaged in the business of telling other people how to run their lives?

"Daddy!" Celia had heard the car, and she ran out of the house. She came hurtling towards him, and as he got out of the driving seat, she flattened herself against his tailored knees.

"Hello, little wombat." He picked her up and hugged her, burying his face against her narrow shoulder, and breathing in the milky, delicious scent of little child.

Celia had always been his favourite. He loved little Edward dearly, it was true. But, whereas Celia was charismatic, affectionate and charming – a go-getter like himself – Edward was moody and very temperamental. Permanently anxious, he was far too easily reduced to tears. Like his mother in looks, with her fine eyes, good bones and slender frame, he was like her in character, too.

But, all the same, both children were so very precious to Robin that either of them could have had his kidneys, his heart, his lungs, his eyes, even his liver – the doctors could chop him up without anaesthetic, if ever the need arose, and he wouldn't turn a hair. So now, he decided firmly, he would never let Helen and bloody Colborn take away his children.

"What have you been doing today?" he asked, as he put Celia down again, but kept her warm, still babyish hand enclosed in his much bigger, stronger, hairier paw.

"We had a reading test, and I was top." Celia grinned up

at him. "I'm on the *Polly and Holly* Second Series Readers now. Then we all went into the hall and did a bit of singing. Then we had music and exercises, lying on the mats. Then we did topic work about Africa, and the things the African people make to sell."

"Gosh, what a busy day," said Robin, impressed.

"Yes," agreed his daughter. She nodded wisely. "But that's the way it goes. Daddy, we're doing a project. My class is making a great big book, it's all about our school, and we're going to send it to a village in the Gab – the Gania?"

"Ghana?" suggested Robin. "The Gambia?"

"Yes," said Celia.

"But which?" persisted Robin.

"I don't know." Celia shrugged as if to ask, does that really matter? "But the teacher in Africa is Miss Jackson's pen-friend."

"So Miss Jackson's bound to know her address." Robin let Celia lead him towards the house. He didn't especially want to see his wife, but he knew that of course he'd have to, sooner or later. Better get it over with, he thought. "Where's Mummy?" he enquired.

"She went to see Mrs Gray, about the fête." Celia took her father into the kitchen. "Edward's gone to bed," she continued. "Mrs Fraser's Sandra is looking after us. Mummy said I could stay up until she got back home. But if I was tired, she said Sandra could put me to bed."

"Or I could put you to bed?" suggested Robin.

"Oh?" Celia looked doubtful. "But will you read me a story?" she enquired.

"Yes, of course. We could have one big story, or two little ones – whichever you prefer. So now, do you want to go and find your nightie?"

"All right," said Celia. Apparently happy with Robin's generous offer, she scampered up the stairs.

Robin went into the sitting room. He said good evening to the babysitter, and told her that he had already eaten, thank you, so he wouldn't want any left-over shepherd's pie. He asked if the children had behaved themselves, was informed they'd been as good as gold, so he asked how much he owed her. He tipped her an extra pound or two, then sent her on her way.

"I want a bath!" cried Celia, who had taken off all her clothes, and was happily prancing and dancing around the landing, while admiring herself in the long, rectangular mirror hanging above the stairs.

"You'll catch your death," said her father, taking her firmly by the hand and leading her into the family bathroom. He turned on both the taps, poured a generous measure of Helen's favourite bath essence into the running water, and then whisked it to a foam.

Celia got into the bath. "It's cold," she pouted.

Robin turned on the hot tap.

Celia sat down, and promptly jumped back up again. "That's much too hot!" she squealed.

"Come on, it's just lukewarm." Robin held out her sponge. "All right, then. Get on with it. Start with your face and ears."

Celia grinned coquettishly, affecting a precocious, feminine helplessness. "I'm tired, Daddy. *You* wash me," she said.

So Robin did, soaping her pudgy little body, shampooing her hair, then using the shower to rinse her clean again. He wrapped her in a big, white towel and sat her on his lap to rub her dry.

She was going to look just like his mother, he thought, as he patted talc into her clear, translucent skin, as he tried in vain to smooth the lumpy tangles out of her soft, fine, ash-blonde hair. Inheriting her father's stocky build, and his very ordinary, undistinguished features, Celia would never be anyone's mysterious Dark Lady. She'd never kindle passionate desires. Instead, she'd grow up to be a pleasant, normal, ordinary woman. Robin himself would make quite sure of that.

He hugged his little daughter protectively. If Helen assumed she could just take them away, he thought, if she imagined she had simply to ask, and he would meekly let them go, she would find that she was very much mistaken. The idea that Alex Colborn might one day live in this house, might think he even had the right to wash Robin's own children, made Robin sick with rage.

Helen came back at midnight, hours after Robin had made himself a belated supper of two poached eggs on toast, and sunk a bottle of expensive burgundy. He knew it was foolish and paranoid, but as she came in he found that he was actually sniffing the air. He was almost sniffing Helen herself, for the taint of another man upon her body.

He forgot he wasn't speaking to her these days. "Where have you been?" he asked.

"To see Doreen." She was standing there so calm, so self-assured, that he found he wanted to shake her. To make her teeth rattle in her skull, like a pair of castanets. "Why don't you phone her, if you don't believe me?"

"Why shouldn't I believe you?"

"Oh, Robin!" Helen covered her face with both her hands. "Please, *please* don't start all that again!" she wailed.

"I wasn't aware I'd started anything." Robin was tired, he had a great many things to do the following day, and he hadn't the heart or stomach for a fight. "Perhaps you'd better explain."

"I'd sooner you forgot I ever said it." Helen went over

to the stove. She saw the congealing remains of shepherd's pie. "Robin, have you eaten?" she enquired.

"Yes." Robin yawned. "I'm tired," he muttered. "I'm going up to bed."

When Helen went upstairs, she found her husband sitting up in bed reading a magazine. "I thought you were tired," she said.

"I am – but we should talk." Robin narrowed his eyes at her. But when she began to unbutton her cotton blouse, he looked away again. "I think I'd prefer you to get undressed in the bathroom in future," he murmured. "If you don't mind, that is."

"But I thought you said you wanted to talk?" Helen frowned in puzzlement. "You—"

"All right, all right! We'll talk!" Robin glared at her. "I think – I've decided we ought to have a trial separation," he declared.

"What?" Helen stared at him. "I'm sorry, Robin, but *what* did you say?"

"You heard me." Robin scowled down at the duvet. "I think you ought to take the children, and go and stay with your parents down in Kent. For a couple of weeks, at least."

"Have you gone round the bend?" Helen sat down gingerly on the very edge of the bed. "It's the middle of term," she reminded him. "Celia has some important tests coming up in a fortnight's time. There are sports days, school fêtes, a PTA Quiz Evening – and I've put my name down to help at most of those. I can't just drop everything and take the children off to Kent! In any case, what will my parents say?"

"If you tell them you wanted to see them they'll be delighted. But what will they say if *I* tell them you're having an affair?"

"Robin!" Helen looked so shocked that Robin decided

she'd missed her true vocation. Tonight, she was giving a Royal Command performance. "How dare you!" she began, as if she were horrified and outraged. "Robin, how could you even *think*—"

"Helen, I'm not in the mood for histrionics." For one single, fleeting moment, he wanted to strangle her. To hurt her, to wound her, as she'd wounded him. "God," he cried, "I don't know how you've got the nerve! Of all the—"

"Mummy?" A frightened, pleading, barely audible little whisper, it penetrated the red fog of Robin's anger, and effectively silenced him. "Mummy, why's Daddy shouting?"

Helen turned to see her daughter standing in the doorway. Tousled and sleepy in her bright pink Barbie nightdress, she regarded them anxiously.

"Daddy wants you and me and Edward to go and have a little holiday." Drawing Celia into her embrace, Helen glared at the monster in her bed. "He wants us to go and stay with Granny and Grandad. Just for a week or two."

"But I can't, I've got my project!" Celia burst into stormy tears. Squirming out of her mother's embrace, she flung herself at Robin. "I don't want to go to Granny's house!" she wailed.

"But why not?" Comfortingly, Robin hugged her. "You like to see your Granny. You know you like to go—"

"I don't, I don't! It's boring, and I hate it!" Celia's eyes were bright with tears. "We have to be good, and quiet as little mice! If we shout or play loud games, Grandad tells us off! Granny says that Mummy was never, ever a naughty girl, and that she doesn't know who *we* take after—"

Robin met Helen's gaze. She looked away, embarrassed.

Celia stared at her mother, then her father. She sensed the tension between them. "Daddy?" she urged. "You know I've got to do my project! Why can't I stay with you?"

Chapter Fifteen

"It's all right, sweetheart. Nobody's going to make you go away." Taking Celia in his arms, and stroking her matted curls, Robin spoke as if he were soothing and reassuring a nervous animal.

"She's only half awake," he murmured, as Celia sighed, then subsided against his chest. Her thumb hooked itself round a corner of the duvet, then it found her mouth – and soon she was sucking and grunting contentedly.

"You might as well keep her here, then," Helen whispered. "Unless you feel like carrying her back to bed?"

"I think I'll leave her here," said Robin, well aware that his little daughter was sprawled across her mother's side of the bed.

So Helen spent the night in the spare room, trying – and failing miserably – to get a bit of sleep. Celia stayed with her father, until her snuffling, snorting and constant fidgeting grew too much for even him to bear, and he finally carried her back to her own little bed.

In the morning, she seemed to recall that there had been some sort of quarrel, during the hours of darkness. But it appeared she couldn't quite remember what had been going on.

"I had a very nasty dream last night," she said to Helen as she toyed with her breakfast cereal and watched her mother like a hawk.

"Did you?" Helen had heard her husband go out at six o'clock that morning. Good riddance, she had thought. Just now, she almost wished that he was never coming back. "I hope it wasn't about those hungry tigers in your book? Or lions, or grizzly bears?"

"It was about Daddy being all horrible." Celia regarded Helen narrowly. "He said he wanted us to go away."

"That was a funny dream." Helen managed a rictus of a smile. "I'm sure he'd never want anything like that."

"But – but where *are* we going?" demanded Edward, who had now stopped eating and was anxiously trying to follow all of this. "Mummy? Where—"

"We're going to school, that's where, so hurry up!" Helen took Celia in her arms, and hugged her. "You were imagining things," she whispered, softly. "You know your Daddy loves you. He wouldn't ever want you to go away!"

"Not until I'm a lady, anyway."

"Not even then, you silly little sausage." Helen found Edward's pencil case and lunch box. "Come on," she urged. "It's time we were on our way!"

But during the drive to school both children were unusually subdued and thoughtful and Helen knew that, if she'd gone back home and found her husband there, she would have cheerfully broken all his bones, including his stupid neck. How dared he drag the children into this! She had half a mind to ring him at the office, and scream abuse at him. When he came home tonight . . .

In the event, however, she didn't need to brain him with the fire irons. Robin came home in a calm and rational temper and, eventually, he and Helen made a sort of silent, reciprocal pact. They tried to be more cheerful. They tried to converse with one another, to be polite and pleasant.

But the strain must have been obvious for, far from

being reassured, the children now edged round them warily, aware that something must be wrong, that the peace was very fragile. Something was worrying Mummy and making Daddy very cross – but they were at a loss to discover exactly what this might be.

Both developed strategies for coping. Every day, straight after school, Edward took himself off down to the bottom of the garden for private conversations with his moth-eaten old bear. Celia, however, stayed in the house with Helen, trying to be good and helpful and being extremely careful what she said.

Robin slept in the spare room these days and of course, the children noticed, although they didn't actually comment. When Edward and Celia were around, their father made an effort. He spoke to Helen now and then, he tried to smile, and once or twice he even said how much he'd enjoyed his supper, that a pudding which Helen had made was very tasty.

But the moment both the children were in bed, it was as if a portcullis or drawbridge came clanking down. All pretence of normality quickly vanished. Helen felt she was sharing her home with a malevolent spectre, with a ghost who was watching everything she did – but who said nothing, even when addressed.

Finally, Helen felt she'd had enough. In the end, after thinking about it for a day or two, and after realising that if she were to turn up in Kent without her husband, there was bound to be an in-depth interrogation, she decided to ring her mother anyway.

She told Catherine Tremain that Robin was going on a four day management course, from this coming Thursday morning to Sunday evening. So she thought it might be nice to bring the children over, just for the weekend.

"Well, my love, you might have let me have bit more

warning!" Mrs Tremain adored her grandchildren. But these days her home was hardly infant-friendly, for antique porcelain figurines and expensive, sparkling crystal sat in pride of place on almost every extensively-polished surface, and a phalanx of silver frames invited sticky little fingers to leave their prints on each and every one.

"Please, Mummy!" Helen tried very hard, but in the end she failed to keep the tremor out of her voice. Soon, she knew, the tears would start to flow. "Please, I – we – we'd love to come and see you! We won't be any trouble—"

"We'd love to see you, too." But now Mrs Tremain was on the alert. "We'll have the Mortimers over some other time," she said. "Your father won't mind missing his Saturday golf, he only goes to the club to gossip these days, anyway. But darling, tell me – is anything the matter?"

"No, of course not." Helen almost collapsed on to a nearby dining chair. Pure, blessed relief was washing over her. "Nothing's wrong," she murmured. "So, we'll see you about eight or nine, on Friday evening – yes?"

"We'll both be looking forward to it." Mrs Tremain was frowning. She didn't like the sound of this at all. "Please drive carefully."

"Of course I shall." Helen managed a sort of barking laugh. "You know I always do."

There were things to buy, of course. Robin had always teased her about her extensive preparations for going away. He'd once observed that anyone watching Helen, sorting herself out for a day trip to the local safari park, might have been forgiven for thinking the family was about to leave for a fortnight on the Serengeti Plains.

So now, in order to stock up for her long weekend in Kent, she drove into Westingford to buy such useful travel aids as baby wipes, half a dozen brightly-coloured children's comics, a couple of new cassettes, and some of the chocolate-flavoured cereal which Edward loved, but which Mrs Tremain invariably forgot to buy.

Coming out of Boots, she collided with Alex Colborn, who was taking a short cut back to the office and thinking about a recent appeal against withdrawal of benefit, which the DSS had won. But, not satisfied with the local tribunal's reasonable decision, the claimant's solicitor was threatening to take his client's case as far as the House of Lords. This would be a waste of public money and of everybody's time.

So, for one short moment Alex didn't appreciate that he had walked straight into the person he most wished to see – but hadn't dared to contact, in case she accused him of breaking up her marriage. He didn't think he'd be able to handle that. "Sorry," he murmured automatically. But then he shook his head and blinked. He stared in disbelief. "My God," he began, "I didn't see—"

"I'm in a hurry!" When she realised it was Alex standing there, Helen had almost fainted. Then she tried to push past him, to disappear into the lunchtime throng. "I can't stop!" she insisted as he stayed there in her way.

"Please, don't go!" To detain her, he caught her sleeve. "Helen," he whispered, "we must talk. I know the situation is less worrying now – but we ought to make enquiries, don't you think? We need to find out if—"

"I told you, I'm in a hurry! I have a hundred things to do!" Shaking his hand away and glaring up at him, she clutched her lunchtime shopping to her bosom and strode off into the crowd.

Alex just stood there, staring after her, as if he'd been hypnotised.

* * *

"So there they were, standing outside Boots, hugging and kissing as bold as brass, and twice as natural!" Doreen Gray, the cake maker, was not a vindictive woman. But she did like a tasty morsel of new born, salacious gossip, and with her best friend Elizabeth Morgan egging her on, the words had spilled out of their own accord.

Well, almost of their own accord. Doreen wasn't getting in their way! The kissing bit was a rather deliberate fib, however, and Doreen felt her cheeks begin to glow. But it was very hot today . . .

"He was actually kissing her, then?" enquired Elizabeth, as she licked some cream off a pudgy index finger, and wondered about another dairy slice.

"Well, my dear – that was what it *looked* like." Doreen wasn't a professional liar. "He had his hand on her arm and was looking at her ever so lovey-dovey. His face was very close to hers and she was sort of gazing up at him – like in a poster for a film. You know the sort of thing."

"Just fancy that." Elizabeth shook her curly, greying head. "He was a nice-looking sort of chap, you said?"

"Yes, he was very attractive." Doreen sighed. "Mr Harper is a really lovely man, and that I can't deny. But he's no matinée idol, never has been, never will be. This other fellow looked just like a film star."

"I hope Mrs Harper understands what she's doing." Elizabeth plumped for a Danish pastry this time – no whipped cream, so it wasn't quite so sinful. "It's the children I really feel for, when this sort of thing goes on. Well, it can't make for a happy family life."

Robin wondered why Doreen Gray was being so nice to him, stopping him outside the Post Office that evening to ask after his health, and then engaging him in conversation when he went to pay the paper bill at the village shop. But this didn't start to worry him until she began to drop some heavy hints.

"Mrs Harper's going away for the weekend, then?" she enquired, as he stood at the counter in Thrushall Village Stores, while waiting to be served by Mrs Parker – whose radar was on instant red alert. "Colin Wright at the garage was saying she asked him to check her tyres, and they got chatting—"

"What?" Robin frowned at her. Then he remembered. "Yes," he agreed. "She – she's going to see her parents down in Kent."

Robin was very tired. He didn't want to talk to Doreen Gray. But it seemed she wanted to converse with him. "I know it's none of my business," she began, as he paid Mrs Parker for the *Westingford Evening Standard*, "but I've always felt it's best if things can be sorted out right at the very beginning. Before everything goes too far."

"Oh?" Robin frowned at her. "I'm sorry, but I don't think I understand—"

"No, of course. You're right. It's none of my business, really." Doreen simpered sweetly. "Anyway, if you're on your own this Sunday, I'll be doing my usual roast. So if you feel like popping round?"

"I'm afraid I'll be quite busy. I'm sorry, but—"

"No need to apologise." Doreen placed a plump hand on his arm. "I was saying to Elizabeth Morgan, earlier today – you and Mrs Harper, you're such a lovely couple, and you've fitted in so well here in the village. We'd hate to see anyone spoiling things for you."

Then, having dropped her lighted match into the gunpowder of Robin's own suspicions, Doreen picked up her carrier bag. She walked out of the shop, leaving Robin Harper staring after her and Mrs Parker twitching furiously.

* * *

Helen's last port of call that lunchtime had been at the local surgery, where she saw her GP. "You seem to be going through a rather difficult time," said Dr Bevan, after she'd given her patient a physical examination, given her the all clear, then listened to Helen's account of all her symptoms.

"I suppose I do too much," Helen concluded. "There's no other reason why I should feel this way. But I'm permanently tense and anxious these days."

"You're sleeping well, you say?" the doctor asked her, frowning. "You manage to eat three proper meals a day?"

"Oh, yes," lied Helen. "Yes, I'm always eating. In fact, I think I'm slightly overweight."

"No, you're just about right for your height and build. So don't go on a diet!" The doctor pursed her lips. "Apart from being so busy and feeling generally over-stretched, there's nothing else bothering you?"

"No, nothing."

"Well, I could give you something for the anxiety." The doctor reached for her prescription pad. "These particular drugs are beta-blockers – I expect you've heard of them. They'll soon make you feel less tense, but when this happens you mustn't stop taking them. Instead, come back and see me."

"Right." Helen accepted the prescription.

"Also, try to take some time off work." The doctor smiled. "You people at Relate offer a very valuable service. But you mustn't let your concern for other people and their problems begin to take over your own lives."

"No." Helen managed a feeble little grin. "It's a bit of an occupational hazard, that."

"Tell me about it." The doctor shook her head. "Come

back and see me in a fortnight's time. I'm sure you'll be feeling very much better then."

"I'm sure I shall," said Helen, agreeing almost mechanically. "I–I shan't become addicted, shall I?"

"No, don't worry." The doctor shook her head. "You'll need to come off the tablets gradually. But once you're feeling better, we can look at your situation once again, and then we can review the actual dosage. In the meantime, if you think of anything specific that's upsetting you—"

"Yes, I'll come back and see you. Thank you very much."

Helen began to take her tablets that very afternoon. When she got home that evening she felt sick and decided that she couldn't eat any supper.

"Robin?" Hesitantly, she tapped on his study door. Getting no answer, she opened it a crack, and then a little wider. She found him sitting by the window, staring at nothing in particular. "Robin, I'm about to start cooking supper. The children are having pizzas. Do you fancy ravioli and a mixed green salad?"

"I've already eaten," muttered Robin, refusing to look at her, to be caught out in a lie.

Helen backed out again. She closed the study door. Well, if he's not eating, he might lose a bit of weight, and that would be no bad thing, she reflected, uncharitably.

Chapter Sixteen

"You don't look very well." Mrs Tremain had ushered her guests inside, and now she was gazing into her daughter's eyes. She couldn't help but see the strain, anxiety and general wretchedness there. "I suppose it was busy?" she went on, but a little more tactfully this time. "I mean, on the motorway?"

"It was absolute murder, if you want to know." Helen gave a shudder. "I never want to drive on the South Circular again. Or not with these two in the back, at least."

"But we were *ever* so good!" cried Celia, looking up into her grandmother's kindly face, and tugging at her hand for some additional emphasis. "We didn't fight at all! Or say we were going to be sick! We didn't need the loo—"

"You were both very considerate indeed." Helen took her daughter's other hand. The sight of Celia's anxious little face was a reproach which Helen found she could hardly bear. So now she swept the child into her arms, and buried her face in her sweet-smelling curls. "But it was tiring, driving so far on my own, and at this time of night. That's all I meant to say."

"There's supper if you want it," said Mrs Tremain. She led the way to her large and welcoming kitchen. "I think we should give these two little people something nice to eat. Then, it will be time to go to bed."

* * *

"Where's Daddy gone?" asked Edward, as Helen tucked him up, then kissed her son goodnight.

"He's busy at work. I told you." As night time ritual demanded, Helen kissed Brolly as well. "He has to work all day tomorrow, too."

"Why does he have to work?" Celia had tried to understand. But she couldn't entirely grasp it, the fact that her father had to be at work on Saturday and Sunday, when he was usually at home with the family.

"It's a special sort of work," lied Helen glibly. "It's called a course. It's to teach him all sorts of things he doesn't know."

"Oh." Celia snuggled down. Pushing three stubby fingers into her mouth, a habit which Helen thought had died the death at least four years ago, she sucked them reflectively.

Helen left them dozing, and went to unpack her stuff. She'd been put in her old room, which she had slept in as a child, and not in the newly decorated guest room, which contained a large, soft double bed.

"The little ones asleep, then?" asked her father, offering Helen a glass of her favourite white Australian Chardonnay.

"Just nodding off." Helen took a grateful sip. "They always take a while to settle when they're not in their own beds." She managed a tired smile. "It's nice to be home," she said.

"It's very nice to have you here." George Tremain regarded his daughter closely. "There's nothing wrong, my dear? I mean, I don't intend to pry. But if there's something we should know—"

"Honestly, Daddy, you're even worse than Mum!" Helen forced another smile. "When I phoned, I told her everything – or at least, I thought I did! Robin's tied up all this weekend. He'll be busy all day, and probably half the night. So I thought it would be nice for us all if I popped over to see the two of you. You're always saying we don't come often enough."

"But you and Robin – I mean, you are okay?"

"Of course we are!" Helen wondered if she could manage a careless, girlish sort of laugh. She didn't think she dared risk it. "Look, Dad – if anything was wrong, you'd be the first to know, I promise you. If Robin and I were ever on the skids, we'd—"

But she got no further, for from the top of the stairs there came a terrible, anguished howl. "Daddy!" Celia wailed. Her sobs sounded as if they would choke her. "Daddy, I want my Daddy!"

"It's all right. She's having a bad dream. She's actually fast asleep." Recovering from her initial shock, now Helen raced upstairs, two, three or even four steps at a time. "It's okay, darling," she gasped, as she reached her daughter. "Don't worry, Mummy's here."

"I want my Daddy!" Celia sobbed. She glared at Helen, pushing her away. "Where's my Daddy?"

"Come on, my love, you're dreaming. We're all at Granny's house." Enfolding her daughter in her warm embrace, Helen manoeuvred Celia across the landing and back into bed.

"You were having a nasty dream," she told her daughter, who was shuddering and trembling violently, and had her mother in a stranglehold, tight around the neck.

"Where's Daddy?" Celia hid her face against the shoulder of Helen's blouse, smearing the silky material with saliva, tears and snot. "Why is he always shouting? Why—"

"He doesn't shout." Helen stroked Celia's hair. "You've been having bad dreams, that's all. I must stop giving you cheese on toast for tea. From now on, it will be Marmite soldiers—"

"Please, don't go away." Celia hung on like a baby orang-utan. "Mummy, stay with me!"

"Yes, of course – don't worry, sweetheart." Helen tucked her daughter in again. "I'll stay. At least," she added under her breath, "until you're fast asleep."

"What was all that about?" asked Mrs Tremain, as she came out of the kitchen carrying a laden supper tray.

"Just Celia having a nightmare," murmured Helen. "Here, let me take that."

"Too much excitement," said Mr Tremain, who was trying to be tactful.

"But they're settled now." Helen followed her mother back into the kitchen. "You know, I could really fancy a buttered crumpet. Or perhaps poached eggs on toast."

"I'll make you some. Come on, sit down. Your Dad can pour himself a cup of tea." Mrs Tremain switched on the toaster and opened the sliced bread. "So, what shall we do this weekend?" she continued, smiling brightly. "There's a very good steam engine exhibition over at Harlow Grange. Edward and your father would probably enjoy that."

"Yes, I'm sure they would." Helen cracked eggs into a pan of water. "Perhaps you and I could drop them off and then take Celia shopping? She needs new shoes and other bits and pieces."

"We'll go into Ashford, then." Mrs Tremain turned towards the old pine dresser. "There's some home made lemon curd up here, if you fancy it. Mrs Vernon brought me a jar round yesterday, and I find her things are usually very good."

Helen's mother twittered on, determined not to worry, and deciding that her daughter would most probably confide in her. But in her own good time.

Then the telephone rang. Helen jumped up, just like a startled rabbit.

"Your father will get that," said Mrs Tremain.

"Helen, my dear?" A mere two minutes later, George Tremain came ambling into the kitchen. "That was Robin," he told his daughter gruffly. "He said to tell you he's relieved to hear you've all arrived. He'd like you to give the children a kiss goodnight."

"But didn't he want to speak to me?"

"I told him you were having your supper." Mr Tremain looked sheepish. Robin had actually said there was no need to fetch his wife. "He said he'd give us a ring tomorrow night."

At first, Robin had missed her. Then he remembered why Helen had gone away – she hadn't been able to stand him any more. Well, he thought, he might have to get used to being all alone. Perhaps he'd buy a dog. Ever since he could remember, he'd wanted a springer spaniel.

But at least she was with her parents this weekend. There wouldn't be any funny business in front of that stuffy pair.

He would, he decided, spend Saturday morning mucking out his study. All those back issues of *The Vintner* could probably be dumped, in the recycling bins outside the local Safeway. The piles of letters, reports and other junk could then be sorted into keep, re-use as scrap, and chuck away.

Feeling both purposeful and self-consciously virtuous, Robin went into the kitchen to find a large, black plastic rubbish sack.

But by eleven o'clock tidying up his study had lost all its dubious charm. He ate a bit of lunch and then, still at a loose end, he finally decided to go into Westingford. He'd buy all the bits and pieces of timber, all the brackets and screws and stuff, which he would need to make his daughter a set of shelves for her ever-growing collection of Sindies, Barbies and other teenage dolls.

Robin bought the planks and brackets, looked at paints and varnishes and picked up a couple of explanatory leaflets. Then he left the car at Homebase and walked into the city centre, meaning to go to W H Smith.

He strode along the High Street, pretending he hadn't a care in all the world. But then, as he turned the corner into the Cornmarket, whom should he see but philandering Alex Colborn coming up the Abbey Garden steps.

For once, Robin's face was level with Alex's own. The two men stared at one another, each wondering if any sort of acknowledgement was going to be necessary.

Alex opened his mouth to speak. To make some innocuous remark, perhaps, about the lovely summer weather. But he chose to accompany his words with a polite if somewhat nervous little smile.

That smile was a huge mistake. Robin glared, drew back his fist – and one split second later, Alex was lying flat on his back at the bottom of the flight of steps.

Then, of course, people appeared from nowhere. A woman who announced she was a nurse was loosening the victim's collar and telling onlookers to stand well clear, to let this poor man breathe.

"What's happened, then?" demanded a mother with a pushchair, a baby and a grizzling little toddler.

"Some sort of fight, I think," said a middle-aged man.

"A pair of drunks, having a go at one another," declared a stout, fierce woman.

As if they'd been actually waiting here for something like this to happen, a small crowd collected all round Alex Colborn's prostrate – and quite possibly lifeless –

form. Getting out his mobile phone, one man rang for an ambulance. Another accosted a fortuitously passing policeman, who seemed to have materialised, as if by magic, like a genie from a lamp.

"This gentleman was mugged," declared a bird-like elderly lady. Glaring at Robin from the relative safety of the policeman's burly side, she favoured the supposed mugger with a fierce blue stare. "I saw it all!" she cried. "The gentleman was just walking up the steps, when that disgusting person there went up to him and punched him on the nose. Disgraceful, is what I call it! In broad daylight too! I can't think what the world is coming to—"

The policeman nodded sagely. He could see the nurse was ministering to Alex, so he opened his small, black notebook. "Your name, madam?" he began.

But just then there was a groan and a swelling murmur from behind her. Alex was coming round again and trying to sit up.

"It's okay," soothed the woman who had said she was a nurse. "You've had a nasty bump but I'm quite sure you haven't broken any bones. The ambulance is already on its way."

"I don't need an ambulance!" Alex coughed and choked, then spat a little bright red blood into the handkerchief which the nurse was considerately holding out for him. "I only slipped on the steps, and I don't want—"

"But that little fat man hit you!" The elderly lady stared. "He punched you in the face! I saw him do it!"

"Well, sir? How are you feeling now?" Effortlessly taking charge, the policeman hunkered down beside Alex Colborn – but kept his eye on Robin Harper, too. "That's a nasty little cut you have there, just inside your mouth."

"I caught it on the railing." Helped by the nurse, Alex had

managed to lever himself into a sitting position. "Officer, I don't want to make an issue out of this. I—"

"Do you and this gentleman happen to know each other?" The policeman nodded towards the so-called mugger, who stood there looking sullen.

"We're slightly acquainted, yes," admitted Alex. "We—"

But then, the wail of an ambulance was heard, and a moment later a couple of paramedics in green overalls and yellow plastic jackets came striding through the Cornmarket, looking for their patient.

"You'd better go to the General, sir, and let them check you over," said the policeman who could see that Alex was about to start protesting all over again.

So Alex made the best of it. He let the paramedics help him to his feet. He let them lead him to the waiting ambulance, and then he let them help him climb inside.

"Now, sir," said the constable, turning at last to Robin, whose only escape route was still blocked by an interested crowd. "I think you ought to tell me all about it. But first, give me your name and your address."

Robin obliged. He gave the policeman all his personal details, then admitted he'd punched his victim in the face. "What now?" he enquired, speaking of his own accord for the first time since he'd pushed Alex Colborn down the Abbey Garden steps.

"That will depend on the gentleman whom you appear to have assaulted." The policeman shrugged. "We'll be in touch. You may be asked to make a statement so I hope you weren't intending to leave the district?"

"I'm not going anywhere," muttered Robin. Then, realising he was free to go – at any rate, for the present – he walked away, in the general direction of the Homebase car park. Once there, he got into his car and drove home carefully.

* * *

"But I've told you, over and over again. It was an accident. Mr Harper didn't hit me. I just fell." Alex was sitting up in his hospital bed. Irritably, he stared down at the woven counterpane. "I don't wish to press charges, and I'd like—"

"We do have witnesses, you know." The policeman shook his head. "A certain Mrs Dorothy Jackson is prepared to swear on oath—"

"That she was imagining things?" Alex groaned. "She can't have seen what happened. When I tripped and fell down the steps, she wasn't even there."

"But you and Mr Robin Harper *do* know one another?" The bored detective constable who had taken Alex's statement checked through his notes again. "Well, sir?"

"We're slightly acquainted, yes." Alex scowled down at the bedspread. His jaw was throbbing painfully. His head was aching – that Harper bastard had a fist like a lump of lead – and all he wanted was to go to sleep. "But, all the same—"

"We have at least three witnesses who are ready to swear they saw Mr Harper punch you in the face. That this attack was unprovoked, and—"

"Oh, very well, then." Alex sighed. "I'm not going to go into any detail, right? But, some time ago, Mr Harper and I had a very insignificant little difference of opinion. Apparently, he's still annoyed with me. Look, I'm not actually *obliged* to press any formal charges, am I?"

"Well, no – not if you don't wish to do so." The detective constable closed his notebook, and put it in his pocket. "So it was a domestic, eh?"

"I beg your pardon?"

"Mr Harper is a married man, I take it?"

"Yes, that's right. But—"

"I don't suppose you happen to know his wife?"

"Well, as a matter of fact I do. But that has nothing—"

"You're looking much better now. Your colour's almost normal. I expect they'll let you go home in an hour or so." The detective stood up. "Okay, Mr Colborn. Thank you for your co-operation today. I dare say you and Mr Harper could arrange to have any future disagreements on your own private property?"

"Yes, I dare say," muttered Alex. He met the policeman's gaze. "What will happen to Mr Harper?"

"He'll just be bound over, I expect." The policeman shrugged. "There'll be a paragraph in the *Westingford Echo*. The neighbours will have a field day, his old woman will give him hell for about a fortnight – but then it'll all be water under the bridge."

"Oh." Alex thought about it. He realised just how much this would hurt Helen. "I don't suppose you could keep his name *out* of the paper, could you?"

"No, I couldn't do that." The policeman allowed himself a little smirk. "After all, it's not every Saturday that a respected member of the local Chamber of Commerce publicly thumps the bloke who's – how shall I put it – the bloke who fancies his lovely lady wife."

"But as I've told you already, he *didn't*—"

"I should try to forget all about it, if I were you." The policeman grinned at a passing nurse. "Thank you, Sister," he warbled, cheerfully. "This gentleman's all yours!"

"So what *did* happen?" enquired the nurse, half an hour later. She handed Alex a cup of tea and told him the various X-rays were all clear. The doctor had said he could go – when he felt ready, of course, he shouldn't feel that he was being rushed. So was there somebody she could call?

"I think I'll get a taxi." Alex chose to ignore her other question. "Thank you for being so kind."

"All part of the service." The nurse smiled knowingly. "The policeman said he was quite a little bloke. I mean, this chap who hit you. I suppose he must have taken you by surprise?"

"He did, a bit." Gingerly, Alex felt around his mouth. They'd had to put a few stitches inside this, and it still felt very tender. "Where are my shoes and the rest of my outdoor clothes?"

Chapter Seventeen

"I don't know about little Edward, but I'd have thought Celia should have grown out of this," said Mrs Tremain, as she gathered up the soggy sheets and piled them into a heap on the sunlit landing. She glanced back at the mattresses, which this morning both bore dark, damp, spreading stains. "Darling, I don't mean to nag. But if you'd only said you were having problems, we could have put rubber sheets on both the beds."

"I'm sorry." Feeling as if she were six years old again, and had been caught with her grubby hands in the biscuit barrel, Helen finished sponging the ugly stains. "I should have got them up and potted them when I came up to bed. They did have quite big drinks last thing, last night."

At breakfast, Celia was pretending it hadn't happened. But Edward was very upset and snuffled miserably into his Choccopops, stirring the soggy breakfast cereal round and round and round.

"Granny, I want *tea*!" he insisted, when his grandmother poured milk into a Peter Rabbit mug and passed it across to him. "You know I'm not a baby any more!"

"Yes, you are," snapped Celia. "You don't know any times tables. You're only on Book Two of the Magic Readers, and you can't do joined up writing. So you're just a silly little baby!"

Edward stared at her. Then his eyes grew very bright and he began to cry.

"Celia, that was mean," said Helen, finding a tissue and offering it to Edward.

He pushed her hand away.

"Come on, old man." His grandfather patted Edward's heaving shoulder. "Your sister didn't mean it. She was trying to make us laugh."

"Have a Marmite soldier," suggested Granny.

"Soldiers are for babies," murmured Celia, just loud enough for her little brother to hear.

"C-celia's a stinking bitch! She smells of pooh, and does it in her knickers!" sobbed poor Edward, as his grandparents stared in horror and his mother wondered about her choice of school.

The rest of Saturday was equally fraught. Celia was still wretchedly embarrassed by the mishaps of the night, and tried to cheer herself up by being both pettish and demanding.

None of the shoe shops had the style she wanted – or not in her particular width fitting anyway, and Helen refused to buy her shoes which she knew would pinch her daughter's little toes. So Celia demanded a Sunbeam Dancer Poseable Doll instead, and glared ferociously at her grandmother when Mrs Tremain exclaimed about the price.

"Daddy would let me have one," she observed. "*He*'s not mean – not like the two of you!"

Then Mrs Tremain remarked that in her own opinion, Celia had enough Sindies, Barbies and other dolls already. So why not have this nice little embroidery kit instead? Then Celia could learn how to do cross stitch and how to make a hem.

"I don't think so, Mummy." Helen steered her daughter towards the crayons and coloured pencils. "Darling, why don't we get you some new felt tips? Or a set of poster paints?"

Meeting his wife, daughter and grand-daughter at one o'clock precisely, Mr Tremain was sorry to report that Edward hadn't been interested in the steam engine fair. He'd really wanted to go to Nintendo World, and then to Burger Giant, for a Happy Teddy Brunch. But Helen didn't allow her children to eat much junk or processed food, so they all went along to the Army and Navy restaurant.

Here, Celia took all the bits of egg white out of her salad sandwiches, and then dropped them on the floor.

Edward, indulged for once and given chips, moved them around his plate for a good ten minutes, then complained that they were cold – and *why* could he not have tomato sauce?

"Because it's much too messy," said Mrs Tremain, who was wearing a lovely new cream-coloured blazer, and wanted it to stay that way – which, if her grandson were let loose with the ketchup bottle, it most probably would not.

"Eat up, old chap," encouraged Edward's grandfather, who was grinning jovially.

Edward stuck out his lower lip. Then, reaching for the shaker, he sprinkled sugar not on to his Strawberry Surprise, but all over his cold chips. Told off by his mother, he sulked for the rest of the afternoon.

"Well, they all have their off days," said Helen's mother, trying to make the best of it, but privately thinking that what those children needed most was a good clip round the ear.

"They do get over-tired," added her husband, who had taken no active part in raising Helen, for he'd been in the Merchant Navy when she was little and had only seen her once or twice a year.

* * *

That evening, Edward refused point blank to wear his towelling trainer pants to bed. Mrs Tremain couldn't find her rubber sheets. So Helen spread black bin-liners across the still-damp mattresses – whereupon both children complained about the nasty wrinkly plastic lying under their bottom sheets.

"It's only in case you have another accident," said Helen, who was tired and miserable and longing to go to bed.

"But I *didn't* have an accident," insisted Celia, boldly. "I spilled my glass of water on the bed – that's all *I* did!"

"So did I spill *my* water," grumbled Edward, his lower lip now wobbling dangerously.

"I see." Helen thought she might be getting a migraine. At any rate, her head was splitting and she couldn't face another argument. "Well," she said, "the thing is, Granny hasn't got any more dry sheets. So if we leave the plastic bags under these ones and you have any more little accidents with your water, it won't matter quite so much."

Celia saw right through the non-logic of that one straight away. But she knew when she was beaten so she snuggled down into her uncomfortable little bed, stuck three fingers into her mouth and closed her tired eyes.

"I don't want a kiss," muttered Edward, turning away and burying his face in Brolly's matted fur.

I wasn't going to give you one, thought Helen – but then felt very mean. None of this mess was her poor children's fault, when all was said and done.

Sunday turned out to be a slightly better day, or in any case it started well enough. Nobody spilled their glasses of water on their bottom sheets, and when Helen went to look for her children, she found them in their grandparents' big bed. They were larking around and burrowing under the soft pink hump of eiderdown while their grandfather pretended to think they were heffalumps or man-eating tigers who'd come in from the jungle in the night.

Later, after a peaceful and leisurely breakfast, Edward and Celia both said that they wanted to go to the village church with Granny. So Helen volunteered to cook the traditional Sunday lunch. But instead of simply roasting it, then serving it with the usual mint jelly, she smothered the leg of lamb with honey and rosemary, then studded it with little shards of garlic. And in place of the usual roast potatoes, she made *pommes dauphinoises*.

Her father was moved to pronounce the meal quite nice – which was high praise indeed, coming from him. He added that Helen's husband was a very lucky fellow.

"Did Robin phone?" asked Mrs Tremain, as she cut up Edward's meat, then tied a napkin round his neck.

"No, he didn't." Helen managed a reasonably careless shrug. "Well, I expect he's been extremely busy – and he'll be seeing us this evening, after all."

"*I* don't want to go home again," said Celia, who was trimming a minute piece of fat from a large slice of beautiful pink meat. "It's always much too noisy and shouty there."

"Well, *I* know who does the noising and the shouting," said her grandfather. He twinkled at her confidentially. "Do you remember all those heffalumps we found in our bed this morning? If they were to go to your house—"

"But it's Mummy who does the shouting!" Edward wasn't going to be told off again, especially for something he simply hadn't done. "She shouts and shouts at Daddy, and she calls him—"

"But sometimes Daddy yells at *her*," said Celia, candidly. "Granny, sometimes when Mummy goes to bed, my Daddy gets all angry, and he—"

"I think that's quite enough about yelling and shouting,"

said her grandmother, very firmly. She glanced all round the table. "Now, has everybody finished? Oh, but Edward, darling – surely you're not going to waste all that nice meat?"

"He doesn't like meat," said Celia.

"Well, that's the first I've heard of it," said her grandfather. "When he was a little chap—"

"He thinks it's smelly, don't you?" Celia looked at her brother. "He's going to be a vegetary – a vegetabalarian, when he's grown up."

"Don't forget, my darling." The car was loaded, the children were strapped into their special seats, and the story cassettes lay ready to be played. Mrs Tremain hugged her daughter close. "If there's anything you want to talk about, or if you just feel the need to get away—"

"We're always here." Her husband looked down at the mossy gravel drive. He wasn't any good at all at this emotional sort of thing.

But he loved his daughter dearly, and if she were going through a difficult time he was quite prepared to be her port in any sort of storm. If the truth were told, he'd never thought much of that tubby little Robin Harper fellow.

But it could have been much worse. What was the name of that young Scottish chap, the one with blue eyes and curly yellow hair? Even Helen's mother had gone overboard for him. There was no accounting for women's tastes, he reflected gloomily.

"Drive carefully," said Mrs Tremain.

"Ring us when you get home," put in her husband.

"Of course I shall." Helen fastened her seat belt. "Thank you both for a really nice weekend. You must come over and see us, very soon."

"Yes, we must fix a date." Mrs Tremain gave her daughter a comforting smile. "Now, don't forget – you ring us, or just turn up here, any time. Do give our love to Robin."

"Yes, all right." Helen kissed her mother. "Look after yourselves," she said. She wondered then if she were seeing her parents perhaps for the last time.

The journey home was uneventful. The children dozed through most of it and woke up only when they arrived in Henley.

"Mummy, are we there yet?" demanded Edward.

"Nearly," Helen told him. "It's only seven miles to Thrushall Green."

"Daddy!" Spotting her father walking in the garden, Celia unclipped her seat belt, opened the door and almost fell headlong out of her mother's car.

As Robin came towards her, she launched herself like a little rocket into his embrace. "Daddy, Daddy, we went to see Granny and Grandad! We had our lunch in the biggest, bestest shop in all the world! Edward poured sugar all over his chips!"

"I didn't!" cried Edward, glaring at his tactless, gobby sister. He wondered if he might cry. But then he, too, flung himself at his father's shins. "Brolly had a horrible time," he muttered, as he clutched at Robin's knee.

"Then I expect he'll be glad to be home again." Robin looked at Helen. "I've just put all the tea things out," he said.

The four of them walked into the house. "Journey all right?" asked Robin, as he filled the kettle and put it on the hob.

"Yes, it was okay." Helen took off her jacket. "No roadworks, accidents or anything. So how are you?"

"Oh, I'm all right." Robin sat down. The children had scampered off to talk to next door's ginger cat, whose territory included their own garden. "Okay, I'm telling you this so you don't hear it first from somebody in the village. The police were round here earlier. They—"

"The police?" repeated Helen. Suddenly, her face was drained of all its colour, and she sat down at the table heavily, as if her legs had given way beneath her. "Robin?" she whispered, looking terrified. "W-what did they want?"

"To speak to me, of course." Robin eyed her narrowly. "Helen, what's the matter?"

"Nothing." Helen tried to look unconcerned. "Well, go on. Go on."

"I went into Westingford on Saturday. I met your friend. You know the one I mean. I – I took a swing at him, and he fell over—"

"You hit Alex Colborn?" Helen found she wanted to laugh out loud. But of course, she wasn't amused, not in the slightest. An unholy devil's brew of relief, horror and astonishment now seethed and churned inside her, making her feel quite ill. "But why?" she managed to croak.

"I'll tell you later." For Robin had noticed Celia standing in the doorway, listening intently to every word he said. "I'll make us all some tea."

Alex thought his terrible headache would never go away. He'd been taking ibuprofen, paracetamol *and* codeine, but his body was still one shapeless blob of pain. His numerous bruises, cuts and and sprains were making themselves most uncomfortably felt.

He didn't want company. Even the presence of heavily pregnant Ivy, sitting on his lap and purring like a little generator, was almost more than he could easily bear.

He thought he'd go to bed. He'd only been up for an hour, but already today was proving to be far too much for him. But then the doorbell rang.

At first, Alex decided to ignore it. Then he thought it might be Mrs Singh, bringing him nourishing food and yet more motherly sympathy. Perhaps it could – it might – even be Helen, come to admire her husband's handiwork. Well, he reflected, there was plenty of it for her to see.

So, shunting Ivy off his lap and on to the littered sofa, Alex winced towards the door.

"Well, me old mate, you don't look very grand!" Somehow, Paul Graham had learned about the accident. Now, he'd called round to see his dear old pal. But only out of interest and friendly concern, he told himself, and certainly not out of ghoulish *Schadenfreude*, or even idle curiosity.

No, he had come here to visit the sick. To be a little ray of welcome sunshine. His wife had even sent a bunch of flowers. "Right then, who was this bloke?" he asked, straight out.

"A total stranger," Alex said. His attempted casual shrug became an anguished wince of pain. "Someone who'd had his benefit stopped, perhaps, who just happened to recognise me. So he decided to give me one."

"Well, that's not what *I* heard." Now, Paul Graham grinned. "I reckon Alex has been a naughty boy. You've been getting up to your old tricks again."

"What's that supposed to mean?"

"You've been seeing somebody else's bird. Her old man found out. I reckon it was that chartered accountant bloke." Paul Graham's grin grew even wider. "Or at any rate, that's the word down at the Dog and Duck."

"I see." Alex sat down again. He closed his aching eyes. "Well, I'm sorry to disappoint you," he began. "But there's not a grain of truth in any of that."

"No?" Unfazed, Paul Graham shrugged. He stared all round his friend's untidy sitting room. "I must say, it's a nice tip you've got here."

"It suits me," muttered Alex.

"Yeah, well. It takes all sorts." Fastidiously, Paul Graham sniffed the air. "The neighbours pop in and out, then, I suppose?"

"Yes, Mrs Singh has been extremely kind."

"I thought I could smell curry." Paul sat down. He cleared his throat, he cracked his knuckles, then looked at Alex pityingly. "Why do you still live in this hole?" he asked.

"I like it," Alex replied.

"I honestly can't think why." Paul Graham shook his head. "I know you were hard up once upon a time. Christ, old mate – we all had to count the pennies! I remember when eating out was a choice between a beer and a kebab, from Ari's greasy spoon, or the local Indian dump, where they served cat."

He grinned at the recollection. "God, what we used to do to our digestions! It's no wonder I get stomach ulcers these days. But look, old mate – you could afford to live just about anywhere you fancied nowadays. In one of those new Marlborough houses by the river – yeah? Or over on the Churchfields Park estate. A pal of mine, he knows the bloke in the sales office there—"

"I told you, I'm perfectly happy where I am." Alex began to struggle to his feet. "Well, it was very good of you to call. Give my love to Diana and tell her thank you for the flowers. But now I—"

"But you *are* going to press charges, aren't you?" interrupted Paul.

"I doubt it." Alex held on to the back of his chair. He was feeling very giddy and he thought he might be sick. "There wouldn't be any point," he muttered. "In any case, it would be very bad publicity for the office."

"How do you make that out?" Paul Graham looked quite genuinely shocked. "Look, old buddy. I can see you're not in a fit state to do anything at all right now. But when you're up and about again you'll feel quite differently, believe you me!"

"I don't think so. I—"

"Throw the book at the bugger, that's what I say. Get hold of the best solicitor in Westingford, bung him a grand and put him on the job. I know *I* bloody would!"

"I'll think about it," promised Alex, not because he would but because he wanted Paul Graham to go away.

"You mind you do." The visitor paused on the threshold. "You could come and stay with us," he suggested, then – and warming to his theme, he added, "yeah, why don't you come and stay at my place? Put your feet up, eh? Let somebody make a fuss of you, for once in your miserable life. Diana's always liked you, and she's a bloody brilliant cook—"

"I know, and thank you, but I'm all right here." Alex began to edge Paul Graham out of the front door. "Thanks very much for calling round. I do appreciate—"

"Yeah, okay, no problem." In one of the pockets of his designer jeans – grey leather, Alex noticed; he must be sweating like a pig in all this heat – Paul Graham found his car keys. He grinned again. "You know what *I* reckon?"

"No," said Alex. "What?"

"You're expecting the little woman any minute. Yeah, that's what it is, that's why you're desperate to get rid of me! Any second now, the little bird who's the reason for all this bit of how's-your-father is going to be popping round!"

"I'm sorry to disappoint you, but I'm afraid there'll be no birds of any sort coming round to visit me."

Eventually, Alex managed to get Paul Graham out of his little house. "Give my love to the family," he went on, as the visitor opened the door of his new saloon – after checking for scratches, naturally. In this sort of neighbourhood, you couldn't be too careful.

"Yeah, right. Cheers then, mate." From the safety of his gleaming, brand new motor, Paul Graham gave Alex a Queen Mother wave. "Mind how you go. I'll definitely be in touch."

"Blast his eyes, I hope the bugger crashes," muttered Alex to the ever constant Ivy, who was shedding hair and flea dirt on his jumper. He heard Paul accelerating up the narrow street, pause at the junction, then roar on his way.

Paul had always given the impression that he was a brainless idiot. His wife complained that he acted like a yob. But he certainly wasn't stupid. He'd ponder this development, just like he'd pondered essay subjects when they'd been at college. He'd worry the life out of Alex now – and he might, just might, stumble up against the truth.

Alex reached for the paracetamol. How much did one need to take, he wondered, before one could be certain? He didn't fancy waking up in hospital, having just had his stomach pumped. He didn't want to be counselled by the chaplain, or by some medical social worker who believed in God, and who would try to save his soul.

Death *would* be preferable to any of that.

Chapter Eighteen

"Jesus Christ Almighty, what the bugger is it *this* time?" The latest foreman to be working on the Rettingham Shopping Village site was not exactly happy. This new development in the town centre should have been several weeks ahead of schedule. The foreman had more men than he actually needed, he had the heavy plant and all the right machinery, and even the English weather had been kind.

But instead of being on schedule, he was at least five weeks behind and his bosses wanted to know the reason why. He glared at the electrician in charge. "Well?" he growled. "I tell you, this had better be good. Or I shall personally break your bleeding neck."

"It's them big cables, look. Them over there." The chief electrician took off his yellow hat, so he could wipe his sweating, furrowed forehead. He rubbed his gritty eyes and sighed. "I dunno who laid the buggers," he continued. "Especially them ones right next door to the last delivery bays. But I reckon the Rett'num Women's Institute could have done a better job than the tossers who put them partic'lar cables *there*."

"What's the matter with them, then?" enquired the foreman.

"They haven't been properly insulated, have they? You turn the power on, and any oil or water seepage coming close to *them*!" The electrician made an eloquent gesture, his fingers drawn across his stubbled throat. "Tossers," he repeated, savagely.

"So do they have to come up again?" the foreman asked. He already knew the answer, but he hoped the electrician might reconsider. If there were an extra grand or two in his pay packet this month – in cash, tax free, no awkward questions asked – he just might think of something, come up with another solution.

But the foreman's hopes were to be dashed. "Of course they bloody need to come up again!" The electrician looked at the foreman as if the latter were insane. "The sooner the better, too, if you ask me. Look, I'll want half a dozen of your best lads. Two of them Massey Fergusons, another JCB—"

"All right, all right, get on with it." The foreman groaned. "God, I dunno," he sighed. "First we get those naffing diggers, holding everybody up. Then that subsidence near the supermarket. Now it's the bleeding electricity. The whole site's bloody jinxed, if you ask me."

So the cement which had been poured all over the foundations of the Merchant's House was taken up again. In the process, the offending cables were destroyed. So new ones were uncoiled, and preparations made to lay them under the delivery bays again.

The men engaged in this hot, dirty job had been promised a generous bonus if they could get the work all finished by the end of the afternoon. So they went at it with a will and would have missed the body altogether had not a sharp-eyed medical student, ekeing out his grant as a summer labourer, spotted what looked like a human femur, projecting from a mass of broken concrete and dry, brown earth.

"Hey, hold on a minute!" The student bent to take a closer look. "Stop!" he cried, excitedly. He gestured towards the driver of the JCB. "Frank, stop digging *now*!"

"What you found, then, mate? Some buried treasure?" The driver grinned expectantly. He and the other men, who had been on the site since the work had started several months before, had never quite given up hope of finding a Celtic or Roman hoard.

So now, the men came crowding round the student, who was staring at the bone.

"Well, stone me," said a bricklayer.

"That human, is it?" asked a casual labourer.

"What the fuck's the matter?" The foreman, who had heard all the commotion and come running to sort it out – whatever *it* might be – gave the student a baleful look. "Mr Collins, sir? I warn you, if you're pissing me about, you'll be off this bleeding site so fast your feet won't touch—"

"No, Mr Greenwood – I think we've found a body!" The student, who knew the rules and regulations, was practically jumping up and down. "We can't do anything until the police arrive. We mustn't touch it, move it – anything."

The foreman took off his hard hat, and dashed it to the ground. He wanted to scream and yell and bloody throttle the fucking student. He was sorely tempted to tell the men to get on with the job. To leave the bones right where they were, to lay the bleeding, blasted replacement cables, and then to cover the whole lot up again. To tell Mr Simon Collins that if he had any objections, they would bury him as well.

"That's the last time I take on students," the foreman muttered, through his clenched and gritted teeth. He told everybody to down tools. To take yet another tea break. To wait for the local plods to come and have a butcher's hook.

"It's probably Queen bleedin' Boadicea," observed the chief electrician, a natural Job's comforter if ever there was one. "Now that whole bit of the site'll be off limits for months and months. We'll have all them archaeologist buggers back, having another poke around. Here, Barry – do you want to use my mobile?"

The foreman snatched it from him. Spitting and swearing, he punched in 999 – and the operator told him off, for this was not a real emergency. His language had to be heard to be believed and the operator disconnected him.

Fifteen minutes later the police arrived, three uniformed constables and a detective sergeant. Or a man who *said* he was a detective sergeant, but who looked like one of the workmen in his leather jacket, faded jeans and dirty, scuffed black boots.

Accompanying them was a flustered, thin-faced man, whom the sergeant casually introduced as Nigel. Then he added that Nigel was the new pathologist, and that this was his first job out in the field.

"Oh, great! Bloody fantastic!" snarled the foreman. "Let all the students and amateur wankers come! This Nigel knows his arse from his elbow, does he?"

"Well, let's hope so," grinned the detective sergeant. "So where's this body, then?"

The police had brought a lorry-load of shovels and a mile of incident tape. The whole area was neatly cordoned off and the three constables rolled up their sleeves. They put on wellingtons and overalls. Then, directed by the scruffy detective sergeant, they began to dig for victory.

"Who is it, then?" asked the foreman, when one of the policemen was relieved from his digging duties, and walked towards a terrapin hut to stand in a bit of shade. "Julius Caesar? Alfred the bloody Great?"

"Hardly." The policeman grinned. "It's a bloke, but he's only been down there a little while. About ten to fifteen years – or so the chap from Forensics reckons."

"You mean young Nigel?"

"Yeah, that's right."

"So how does he make that out?"

"From the state of the bones, of course." The policeman grinned. "Oh, and from looking at the clothes."

"The clothes?" The foreman frowned. "I'd have thought they would have all rotted clean away?"

"Man-made fabrics – nylon and polyester, and all that sort of thing – they almost never rot. This fellow was wrapped up in some sort of synthetic oilskin. So even his denim jacket's still in fairly decent nick. Look, I'm not telling you any of this—"

"No, of course you're not, we're talking about the weather." The foreman felt slightly sick. "So it's not a Roman soldier, then?"

"No chance, old son." Again, the policeman grinned. But then he sighed. "He was just a kid, judging by the look of him. He's got the most beautiful set of amalgam fillings you ever saw, so we'll soon have his particular name and number. Somebody's old Mum and Dad are going to get a nasty shock – and some other bugger's going to find out that he *didn't* manage to commit the perfect crime."

"Do you reckon there'll be others?" asked the foreman. "I mean, do we have a mass murderer on our hands?"

"Nigel thinks it'll only be the one." The policeman shrugged. "So now we'll go through the records, check the lists – we'll soon find out where this poor bugger came from, and who he was and stuff."

But it turned out to be not quite that straightforward. The pathologist's interim report suggested the body had been buried ten to fifteen years before – but that the burial had taken place a long time after the person's actual death.

There were no distinguishing features to aid formal identification, for all the soft tissue had either rotted away or been consumed by various bugs and vermin. The skull was crushed and at least a third of it was missing, so reconstruction would prove very tricky. An expert would be called in to work on this.

In the meantime, coverage in all the national dailies, the usual television appeals to the public and a search of the Force's own computerised files on Missing Persons all drew a total blank.

Paul Graham's job often took him away from home, and for the past week he had been at a conference in a big city in the north of England. When he came back from his business trip, however, the first thing his wife chose to ask him was, not how did he get on, but didn't *he* once used to live in the Merchant's House, over in Rettingham?

"Yeah, I did." Paul went to the cocktail cabinet, where he poured himself a generous double gin. "That's the house they dismantled earlier this summer. They rebuilt it in some theme park, didn't they?"

"Yes, that's right. But now they've found the body you buried there." Diana Graham liked a little joke. "So the game's up, old chap. If I were you, I'd go and turn yourself in at the local cop shop. You might get some remission for good behaviour if you confess *before* they come to get you."

Paul stared at her in horror. Obviously, he had no idea what she was talking about. He'd probably been watching the adult channel at the conference hotel, Diana decided. So he hadn't seen a single *News at Ten*.

Relenting, Diana explained what had been going on while her husband was away.

"My God!" Paul poured himself another gin. He drank it down in one. Then, good citizen that he was, he got on to the local police force, right away.

* * *

"You lived there during the summer and autumn of 1984, is that correct?" The detective inspector had been very interested in Paul Graham's story, and had come round to the house that very evening. "Tell me, sir – did you have the sole tenancy? Or were you sharing the Merchant's House with friends?"

"There was a mate of mine, and a couple of nice birds." Paul didn't like the way the policeman was looking at him now. He wondered if he'd done the sensible thing, inviting the plod into his inner sanctum. This bastard was obviously on the alert, and was trying to trip him up. "Look, Inspector," he began, "about this body they found – *I* never had anything to do with it!"

"No, sir – I'm sure you didn't." The inspector opened his notebook. "So tell me, what were the names of this mate and of the – ah – the two nice birds?"

"The bloke's called Alex Colborn. We were at university together. Alex lives in Westingford, he works for the DSS – salt of the earth, old Alex! As a matter of fact, I saw him only a week or so ago."

"Where exactly does Mr Colborn live?"

"In Paradise Road, I've never known the number. But it's a house with a black door, and it's the only bugger in the street which doesn't have net curtains."

"I'm sure we'll find it. Now, what about the ladies?"

"Their names were Helen Tremain and Julia Newman. Julia was mine. Well before your time," he added quickly, as Diana glared at him. "I dumped young Julia long before I first set eyes on you."

"So Helen Tremain was Mr Colborn's friend?"

"She was a bit more than his friend, if you really want to know the truth. Talk about a pair of ferrets, tied up in a sack! They were at it all day and half the bloody night. I dunno how old Alex stood the pace."

Paul stared into his glass as if he were looking into a misty crystal ball. "But she left him in the end," he muttered. "No, I dunno why. Poor bloke, I reckon he never got over it."

"How do you mean, exactly?"

"Well, he never married. He's never been engaged, or not as far as I'm aware. These days, he'll shag anything – you ask Diana here. The times we've had him round to dinner, introduced him to a bit of class, to somebody who's available – but no, he never takes you up on it. Instead, he runs around with other people's bloody wives."

"He's quite a busy chap, then." The inspector hadn't written any of this down. "He lives in Paradise Road, you say? Near the canal and the biscuit factory?"

"Yeah, in a dump in some old Victorian terrace – next door to some Pakistanis, and this scrawny tart who's always asking him to change her plugs. But she's not his type. He always liked a bit of meat, old Alex—"

"I see." The policeman nodded. "You don't happen to know the whereabouts of Miss Newman or Miss Tremain?"

"No. Sorry, mate – I don't." Paul Graham shrugged. "I expect they're both married by now. A couple of tasty birds like that. It stands to reason, doesn't it?"

"Yes, I suppose it does." The policeman stood up. "Well, sir – thank you for all your help tonight. I expect we'll be in touch."

"Right." Paul stood up, as well. "I dare say you'll be calling on old Alex?"

"Yes, sir, I expect we will. Why do you ask?"

"He got beaten up a week or two ago. I reckon it was some bird's husband, but Alex says it was this bloke who'd had his benefit stopped—"

"Yes, I remember now." The policeman nodded. "So it's *that* Mr Colborn."

"Yeah. So look, he's still off work, I think. When I was

with him last, he was a bit of a bloody mess – this fellow must have really laid into him. So go easy on him, won't you? I mean, he had nothing to do with any of this."

"You'd put money on it, would you, sir?"

"I would." Paul drew himself up, to his full six foot two. He looked the grinning copper in the eye. "I'd trust old Alex with my life, Inspector, with my money and my life."

Alex went back to work. He knew he was still in a state of shock, and sometimes he wondered if he would ever function normally again.

But since he had good reason to be reclusive, having two black eyes and lots of yellowing bruises, and since he was always reserved and taciturn, he managed to go about his daily business without his colleagues noticing anything particularly amiss.

Gina was very kind and tried to help. She told him he shouldn't be at work, not yet – he ought to be at home, recovering. She made him endless cups of soup and went out to buy him sandwiches and the *Daily Telegraph*. She'd probably have done his washing and ironing if he'd actually asked her, for Gina was a natural mother. She was engaged to a local builder, and intended to have a family of ten.

Alex thanked her for her kindness, and let her cluck around him. He read the *Telegraph*. In the evenings, he sat and watched the *News at Ten*. He'd seen the special reports on the local round-ups, heard the appeals to the public for their help, so he assumed Helen must have seen and heard them too.

His hand was being forced. At first, he'd thought he might sit tight and wait. But then he decided the time had finally come. He took the following morning off, ringing Gina to say he had a bit of a headache and would come in a little later, probably at mid-day.

He phoned Helen at home. If her husband answered the phone, he decided, as the line connected, he would just hang up.

"Hello?" said Helen, almost immediately.

"Hello," said Alex softly.

"Oh, God." Helen sounded horrified. "Alex, I'm sorry, but I can't speak to you," she told him, straight away.

"You must." Alex willed her not to cut him off. "Your husband – I assume he's gone to work?"

"Yes, he left an hour ago. But, Alex—"

"Listen to me." Alex paused for a moment, searching for the right words. The words which would make Helen take the risk and throw in her lot with him.

He'd always known he'd get her, in the end. He hadn't worked out how, or anyway not in any detail, for he'd never thought he'd have this golden opportunity. But now, he held all the cards and he meant to play them – brilliantly.

"The man you're living with is insane," he told her. "He attacked me, Helen! He just came up to me, and thumped me—"

"I know what he did."

"You're not safe with him. Helen, you and your children are in danger! You must come away with me."

"I don't think so," Helen said. But she went on listening.

"I have plenty of money," Alex told her. "I have a brand new passport, and I can get passports for you and for the children, if you don't already have some of your own. I'll come and fetch you from your house, we'll go—"

"Alex, this is absurd!" Helen sounded as if she were choking. "God in heaven, think about it! We can't just disappear!"

"Of course we can! That's what I'm trying to say! We'll go, we'll vanish—"

"It's impossible, Alex."

"Actually, Helen, it's not." Now, Alex cleared his throat. "I work for the DSS, remember? So I get to know these things. But have *you* any idea how many people go missing, every year? How many are never seen or even heard of, ever again?"

"Alex, this is pointless—"

"Helen, we're talking hundreds, maybe thousands! They can't *all* drown themselves in gravel pits. Or jump off Beachy Head!"

"All the same, they'd find us. Alex, I know they would!"

"Then what do you suggest? That we wait to be arrested? We'll be tried, convicted, and then thrown into jail!"

"They'll never be able to prove that it was us." Helen wished she could believe what she'd just said. "Besides, if we run away, it will make it all look so obvious!"

"On the contrary," said Alex. "People will merely suppose that you were leaving a brutal husband."

But now Alex heard Helen's sharp intake of breath, and realised he had made a big mistake. He tried back-pedalling. "Helen," he whispered, "tell me – what do you intend to do?"

"I think we should both stay where we are, and wait. We should say nothing at all, to anyone."

"So what if this phone is tapped?" asked Alex. "Helen, had you actually thought of that?"

"Don't be ridiculous!" But Helen sounded worried all the same. "Look, Alex," she whispered, as if by lowering her voice she could prevent any other listener from overhearing, "this will all blow over. It's bound to, in the end. For heaven's sake – they haven't even identified him yet! Perhaps they never will."

"I'm coming over to see you."

"Alex, you mustn't! Listen, you can't—"

"This afternoon, about half one, okay? I'll leave my car parked in the village, and walk up to your house. Helen, I did it for you, and you can't pretend it simply never happened! We must think, and plan. We must decide what we should do."

Chapter Nineteen

But Alex never arrived at Helen's house. A crisis blew up at work, and he had had to go into the office to sort the whole thing out. Later – too much later – he realised that his deputy, or even a section supervisor, could have done what was necessary. Gina herself could easily have answered the Minister's urgent letter – which turned out not to be urgent, after all.

But, at the time, he'd thought he had no option. It would have been foolhardy to refuse this sudden summons, to say sorry he couldn't make it. It would have looked as if he were scared of something – and that could have been his downfall.

Helen watched the clock until it was almost ten past two. All through that awful morning she'd turned various schemes and plans and possibilities over and over and over in her mind.

She supposed she wasn't surprised it had come to this. She was lucky to have had ten years of grace. She'd been blessed with two adorable, healthy children, and she was fortunate indeed to have had such a happy marriage. But now, she realised, the game was up. That life of doing school runs, good works and voluntary service in her own little community, that was all behind her.

Since that snippet in the local paper, reporting Robin's

scrap with Alex Colborn, the neighbours had been on tenterhooks, agog for the next instalment of the drama. Robin was a sort of local hero, especially to old women like Doreen Gray. Helen supposed that *she*, by contrast, must be the local Whore of Babylon.

But did she really have to leave her children? She went over it once again. Alex had said he'd take them, but she wasn't sure if he had really meant it. But now, she decided, that was something he'd have to understand. The children came with her, they were a package.

Suppose she went to collect them – now – from school? She could still meet up with Alex, somewhere, somehow. The four of them could be at Heathrow Airport, and on a plane, long before Robin had left work for the day.

They could go anywhere, she reasoned. Anywhere in all the world. Well – almost anywhere. Alex would become her husband and she would be his wife. They'd be father and mother to Celia and to Edward – who might even take his name.

Sitting down at her dressing table, she looked at herself in the glass. Her reflection stared impassively back at her.

"But you don't *want* Alex," she said, out loud. "You never really did. Okay, he was very attractive. He's still very attractive! You could sleep with him, have sex with him, no problem. But Robin is your husband. *He's* the man you love."

Helen stared at herself, at her impartial, talking head. "But he doesn't deserve to be married to a murderess," she whispered. "Leave him, let him go, and let him find a decent woman. He's young, and he's not the type to mope or pine his life away. Let him realise his suspicions were justified, and then he'll soon get over *you*."

So, Helen convinced herself. She went and fetched a suitcase from the cupboard under the stairs. She threw in underclothing, jumpers, nightwear. Then some basic toiletries, and a complete change of clothing, for the children and herself.

She found her passport – fortunately, the children were on her passport, not on their father's – and she put it in the pocket at the side. Then, she went downstairs and fetched her handbag. She counted her ready money. She found she had almost ninety pounds in cash, for she'd collected the Child Benefit yesterday. Well, that was quite enough to be going on with, and there were banks at all the airports, anyway.

She looked at the clock again. She was supposed to be at the office now, counselling the bewildered and distressed. Why didn't Alex come?

In the end, she could bear the suspense of it no longer. Going back upstairs again, she rang Alex at home. She listened to the answering machine warble the recorded message. She rang again, but this time she asked Alex aloud to please, please, *please* pick up the wretched phone!

But there was no response. So then, far too wound up to think about the possible consequences of such a reckless action, she rang him at the office. "May I speak to Alex Colborn, please?" she asked the woman, who finally answered Alex's personal phone.

"I'm afraid Mr Colborn's very tied up at present," said Gina, smoothly. Helen had called Alex on his personal direct line, on a number to which the general public should have had no access. But somebody with a benefit complaint did occasionally get through and it was one of Gina's duties politely to redirect them. "May I know who's calling, please?" she asked.

"This is – my name's Helen Harper. I mean, Helen Tremain." Helen had no idea why she had given her maiden name. But then, she supposed, she wouldn't be using Robin's any more. "I – I'd like him to call me at home, please, if he would."

"Yes, of course – just let me get a pen." Gina reached for her note pad. "So could you—"

"It's okay," interrupted Helen. "He already has my number. D-do you know how long he's likely to be busy?"

"I'm afraid I couldn't tell you. You see, he has the police with him just now."

"The *police*?" Helen felt her legs give way beneath her. She sat down on the bed with a sudden thump. "Th-thank you," she managed to stammer, before dropping the receiver on the floor.

So, what she'd feared had actually happened. They'd been found out at last. The telephone had been tapped, and all their conversations taped, most probably to be played again in court.

Presumably the police were on their way to get her now. At any minute a squad car would come squealing through the village, then down the rutted lane.

Helen didn't know how long she sat there, immobile, poleaxed, frightened half to death. But when she glanced at the bedside clock, she was surprised to see that nearly an hour had passed, that it was almost half past three.

The children would have come out of school nearly twenty minutes ago. They'd be waiting for her at the gates, getting really anxious now – crying perhaps, and wondering what on earth had happened to Mummy.

But surely one of the teachers would be able to sort that out, thought Helen, as she found her car keys, then ran lightly down the stairs. It could hardly be an unusual occurrence, a parent being held up for some reason and a child or children being left high and dry. Most probably another mother would offer to run them home.

To run them home. Perhaps they were coming down the drive this minute! Helen realised she would have to get a move on.

But she reversed out of the drive quite unobserved, and she didn't meet anybody in the lane. She drove into Westingford and parked the car in the nearest multi-storey. Then, she went straight to the police station, in nearby Oxford Road.

She'd never been inside a police station before, and the all-pervasive smell of disinfectant, the sight of the pinboards overloaded with pamphlets, notices and various coloured posters, and the duty sergeant chatting with another uniformed officer, who was sitting on his desk, unnerved her a little.

"Yes, madam?" Looking up and noticing her at last, the sergeant grinned. "What may I do for you?"

I've come to confess to a murder, Helen thought, then almost giggled – or groaned, she didn't know quite which, for the enormity of all this was horrifying. She managed to pull herself together. She squared her shoulders bravely.

"I – er – would it be possible to speak to somebody? I mean, in private?" she asked, at last. Or rather whispered, fearfully.

"Well – yes. Of course." The police sergeant looked Helen up and down. She didn't *look* as if she'd just been raped or beaten up. But you could never be sure.

He picked up the internal phone. "If you'll just take a seat for a moment," he said to her politely, "I'll ask one of our WPCs to come and talk to you."

Hastily summoned from a business meeting, Robin arrived at Thrushall County Primary to find his daughter Celia in hysterics. Edward was weeping silent, anguished tears and the Head of the Juniors was sitting in her study looking tight-lipped and accusing. As well she might, for Celia had just been very sick, and Edward had made a huge and spreading puddle upon her parquet floor.

But it seemed that Mrs Fisher had been kind to his poor children – Celia told him afterwards that she had given them milk and let them choose from the special toffees kept in the yellow tin – and Robin was very grateful, at least for that.

"But where's my Mummy?" Celia wailed, as Robin strapped her into the brand new company BMW – he'd taken delivery only yesterday – then offered her a paper tissue, and told her to have a jolly good old blow.

"I expect she must have got held up, with one of her special clients." Robin attempted a reassuring smile. "You know, one of those people she talks to when they're feeling sorry for themselves. Or perhaps her car broke down when she was on her way to fetch you."

Silently cursing Helen for not letting the school know exactly what had happened – for God's sake, the woman *did* have a mobile phone – Robin slid a plastic bag under Edward's soggy shorts. Then he strapped him in too.

"Don't cry, my pet," he soothed, for Celia was beginning to sniff once more. "We'll soon be home again. Then everything will be all right. You'll see."

"It doesn't tally with anything that Mr Colborn told us." The detective sergeant, who had spent almost all of that hot summer afternoon making routine enquiries, and only twenty minutes actually talking to Alex Colborn, frowned at the WPC. *She* had just heard Helen Harper's account of what had happened at the Merchant's House, one evening eleven years ago. "Well, Carol?" he enquired. "Does this woman look as if she's mad?"

"No, sergeant. Not at all." WPC Carol Reilly shrugged. "But she *is* very upset, and she's adamant that she wants to make a statement. She kept saying over and over again that none of it was Alex Colborn's fault. That this Thomas Stenton chap was in every way to blame."

"Thomas Stenton being our friend down in the mortuary, right?"

"Yes, that's right. Well, Mrs Harper reckons he was a former boyfriend, who was insanely jealous of her new relationship with this man Alex Colborn. One day, he called at the house where Mrs Harper and Mr Colborn were then living, and attacked Mr Colborn with a kitchen knife."

"Yeah, right," said DS Sanderson. "Okay, don't tell me, let me write the script. First, there was an argument. Then things got a little bit out of hand. There was a scuffle, somebody grabbed the breadknife which happened to be lying on the table—"

"Look, I know it sounds as if it's something she got out of a novel. But that's exactly what the lady said. In the confusion, Mr Stenton was accidentally stabbed, somewhere in the upper body. He fainted but they thought he'd live, so they took him to a surgery and dumped him on the steps. They rang the bell and then they legged it sharpish."

"But then he came back to haunt them. I mean, as a mouldy corpse."

"They found his body, yes. They realised they might be accused of murder and they panicked. So they dug a grave and buried him beneath the foundations of the Merchant's House."

"So what do *you* reckon?" The detective sergeant fancied Carol Reilly. He valued her judgement, too. "Menopausal, is she?"

"Hardly," said the WPC. "She's only thirty odd."

"So is this just attention seeking? Might she be anorexic? Or that other thing?"

"Bulimic?"

"If you say so. Or has she escaped from somewhere?"

"None of those." WPC Reilly shook her head. "I'm just going to get her another cup of tea. Look, Tony – I know it all sounds ever so far-fetched. But *I* think we should take her seriously."

Chapter Twenty

"So are you going to charge me with murder, then?" Helen asked the scuffed and soundproofed wall. She realised she had no idea of the correct procedure. Her understanding of how the police force actually worked was very limited, and the little she did know had been gleaned from newspaper reports, detective fiction, and various television cop shows.

She assumed that, now she had confessed, they would formally caution her. They'd take her written statement, get her to sign the wretched thing, then bang her up for the night in some malodorous, echoing cell. One already occupied by an alcoholic vagrant. Or a heroin addict, possibly.

Unless she could get bail? What were the conditions, and how did a person organise getting bail? Helen had no idea.

She bit her lower lip. She'd really done it now, and she wasn't sure if this had been a very good idea. That WPC had been extremely kind but, from the way she'd looked at her, Helen could see the policewoman had thought she was seriously unbalanced.

But perhaps the young policewoman had a point? Perhaps they would section her under the Mental Health Act? Perhaps they were observing her through a video link? Perhaps they were listening to her now, muttering to herself and calmly talking to the wall?

"All right, Mrs Harper?" began WPC Reilly, returning to the interview room with a packet of ginger biscuits and a cup of stewed, brown tea. "Helen, love? You look a bit out of it. Do you feel okay?"

"What?" Startled out of her reverie and embarrassed to realise she *had* been overheard as she was talking to herself, Helen blinked and stared. "Y-yes," she muttered. "Yes, I'm fine."

She accepted the polystyrene cup and sipped its lukewarm contents gratefully. "What happens now?" she enquired.

"Detective Sergeant Sanderson would like to talk to you."

"In here?" asked Helen, glancing round the stark and cheerless room.

"Yes, that's right." WPC Carol Reilly sat down at the table. "We have all the facilities here, you see. I mean, for taping the interview, and stuff. So – okay – before we start, do you want to go to the loo, or anything?"

"No, thank you," said Helen, meekly. "I'm all right."

"I expect you'd like to ring your husband," the policewoman continued.

"My husband?" As she'd talked to the WPC, Helen had been transported back eleven years or more, to the time when she and Alex had been lovers, conspirators, murderers. A pair of almost laughably clichéd partners in violent crime. She'd almost forgotten that Robin had ever existed.

But now, with a sudden jolt, she was brought back to the present day. "I hope he remembered to fetch the children," she whispered helplessly.

"*I* could ring him, if that's what you'd prefer?" offered the WPC.

But Helen did not speak.

Carol Reilly shook her head and sighed. She couldn't make this woman out at all. If Alex Colborn *had* killed

Thomas Stenton, why was Helen Harper so very anxious to take the blame? If everything had happened as Helen had said, it was hardly *her* fault that a rejected lover had come round, to confront his rival, or successor. If he'd got himself assaulted in the process.

She tried again. "Mrs Harper? Helen, listen – do you want to use the phone?"

"You ring Robin." Helen looked down at her bitten finger nails. "But tell him everything's been sorted out, that it's all under control. He doesn't need to come rushing over here."

But twenty minutes later Robin was at the police station, wild-haired, wild-eyed and almost incoherent as he harangued the duty sergeant on the desk.

"Just hang on a minute, sir," said the unflappable station sergeant. "Someone will be coming to see you shortly. If you'd like to take a seat?"

Robin glared at him. He wished he had a cigarette, but he'd given up smoking seven years ago, when Celia was born. Instead, he glowered and muttered and paced the reception area floor.

For of course, he'd found the half-packed suitcase, lying on the bed. He'd found the boxes of tablets in the dressing table drawer, he had read the leaflet warning the patient of various unforeseen adverse reactions and possible side effects.

"Mr Harper?" Carol Reilly smiled at him. "Please, don't look so worried. If you'd like to come this way?"

Robin followed her down the corridor.

He was shown into a room, where Helen sat at an empty table, reducing a packet of biscuits to a pile of golden crumbs. When he entered she didn't look up or even seem to notice he'd come in.

"Leo Foster's on his way," he told her, sitting down beside her and trying, but in vain, to take her hand in his. "He said you're to say nothing more to the police until he gets here. You ought to know—"

"But I've told them everything." Indifferently, Helen shrugged. She would not look at Robin, but stared down at the grubby table top. "Do you want me to tell *you*?"

"Yes!" cried Robin. But then he shook his head. "No, not yet," he muttered. "Oh, God – what's going on?"

"Mr Harper, please. Try not to upset yourself." Again Carol Reilly smiled, and in any other circumstances Robin would have said she'd made his day. "Now, would you like a cup of tea or coffee?"

"I wouldn't mind a double scotch." His bloodshot eyes, wild stare and bone-white face made Robin look as if he'd been to hell and back. "Helen, listen – have they cautioned you?"

"No," said Helen. Again she shrugged. "Well – I suppose they might have done. But if they have, I'm afraid I don't remember."

"Mrs Harper hasn't been cautioned," said Carol Reilly.

Robin turned to look at her. "Do you think we could have a few minutes by ourselves?" he asked, politely, although inside he was in turmoil, in a nightmare.

"Yes, of course." WPC Reilly nodded. "Mr Harper, your wife was concerned about the children—"

"They're being cared for by a neighbour." Robin met Carol Reilly's gaze, willing her to sympathise, to try to understand. For of course, whatever Helen had told the police, whatever nonsense she'd confessed, it had to be some wild, insane delusion. Some fabrication dreamed up by a disturbed and anxious woman, who was not in her right mind.

"My wife's being treated for anxiety," he told the WPC.

"The doctor warned her that the tablets might have certain side effects. So if she's said—"

"I'll get you a cup of tea," said Carol Reilly, interrupting Robin gently, but also very firmly. "I'll have to leave the door ajar, okay?"

"Okay," said Robin. "Helen?"

"Perhaps we'd better wait for Mr Foster," murmured Helen. So she and Robin sat there, like a pair of living statues, waiting, waiting.

When Robin's solicitor arrived, he was greeted like an old friend by the station sergeant, then taken straight in to see his waiting client.

"Mrs Harper? I don't believe we've met." Leo Foster offered Helen his hand. He didn't seem at all put out when she did not take it. "Robin, old man – I'm sorry for the delay. We had a bit of a bun fight at the office. A client's husband threatening to beat old Henry up, would you believe it? A very nasty business! I couldn't get away."

"At least you're here now," said Robin, looking relieved but anxious all the same. "Look, will this be an informal interview? Or will they want to tape all Helen says?"

"They'll tape – it's standard practice, has been since the nineteen-eighties." Leo Foster looked at Helen. He tried and failed to meet her listless, downcast gaze. "Mrs Harper," he began, "you're looking rather worried—"

Helen did not comment.

"Okay," said Leo Foster, "whatever they ask you – if you're not sure if you should answer, just hang fire for a moment, and have a think about it. Or you can ask me. You can always say—"

But then, Detective Sergeant Sanderson came into the interview room. He greeted Leo Foster man to man, nodded at Robin, and then told Helen that she should take her time. There wasn't any hurry.

He explained what was going to happen. Then, the tape recorder was switched on and the interview began.

Meanwhile, Alex Colborn had been collected in a squad car and driven to the station. Here he was asked if he would like to contact his solicitor before he spoke to Detective Inspector Harris.

"What's this about?" asked Alex. "If it's to do with the Merchant's House, I saw an officer earlier today. I've already told him all I know."

Alex was informed there'd been an interesting new development. Although he wasn't obliged to speak to the police, his co-operation would be much appreciated. So if Mr Colborn could spare half an hour, DI Harris was anxious to hear anything he might have to say.

"But what did Alex tell them?" demanded Helen, who had been told she was free to go. Flanked by her husband and solicitor, she walked into the neon-lit brightness of the station lobby. "Mr Foster, can't you ask them, has Alex been arrested? Have they charged him?"

"It's okay, Helen." Leo Foster was used to dealing with hysterical women. "Let Robin take you home, put you to bed. All this won't seem so frightening in the morning."

Helen was about to argue. To protest, to insist she had a right a know, to demand to see the officer in charge.

But then, she realised, she might make matters even worse for Alex. So she let herself be led away, towards the open door. To just a few more hours of freedom.

"You understand you mustn't leave the district?" DS Sanderson had asked her, when he'd switched off the tape recorder, and met her gaze across the desk. He'd turned to

Robin then. "Mr Harper? I'm sure you understand that we might wish to talk to Helen here again?"

"I'm sure my client will do everything in her power to co-operate with the police," Leo Foster assured the sergeant smoothly.

"I'm sure she will," said DS Sanderson. "Mrs Harper? We might wish to speak to you any time, either here or at your home. Do you understand?"

"I understand," said Helen.

"Come on, let's get you back to Thrushall Green." Robin had slid his arm beneath Helen's elbow.

He would not remember that half-packed suitcase, he decided, as they walked towards the car, which of course had a couple of parking tickets now. He would not even think about Alex Colborn, or what the bastard did or didn't do to Thomas Stenton in the kitchen of the Merchant's House such a long time ago.

As for what Colborn and Helen appeared to have done with the fellow's body – Robin couldn't deal with that, not yet. That was just like something from a nightmare. For heaven's sake – real people simply didn't *do* that sort of thing!

But whatever she might or might not have done, thought Robin, Helen was still his wife. She was the mother of his children. The woman whom, in spite of everything, he still loved to distraction – and that was all that mattered.

"So what did he tell you?" asked the detective sergeant, as his boss came out of the interview room across the narrow passage, yawned, then told a passing constable to go and fetch him a couple of bacon sandwiches. Oh, and a mug of tea. "What did our Mr Colborn have to say?"

"Not a lot." The detective inspector shrugged, and then he sighed. "I get the feeling he's protecting the lovely Mrs

Harper. The bugger certainly carries a torch for her. But I don't know if the lady still has a soft spot for him?"

"I didn't get that impression." DS Sanderson shook his head. "She was quite up-front about the fact that they'd been lovers once. But she also insisted that when she left the Merchant's House, it was all over. History. *Finito*."

"But, all the same, she might have been more heavily involved? Perhaps she killed this Stenton bloke herself? Cheers, Michael." The detective inspector bit into his greasy bacon sandwich. "But Colborn's been spinning us this yarn about taking Stenton to a surgery."

"Yes, sir – Mrs Harper mentioned that."

"They went in Mr Stenton's car." The DI spoke through a mouthful of bacon fat and soggy crumbs. "He reckons that after this alleged kerfuffle, he and Mrs Harper put young Stenton into his own vehicle, and drove him to the nearest surgery. They rang the bell, then scarpered."

"Yeah, that tallies."

"Colborn says he's prepared to swear that when they dumped him, Stenton was still alive."

"Well, that should be easy enough to check with the surgery."

"I'll send young Benson round there. But I reckon it can wait until the morning." The detective inspector wiped his mouth. "I'm going to let Alex Colborn go," he said.

"Right," agreed the detective sergeant, nodding.

"But we'll keep an eye on him."

"We could have him for obstruction, anyway."

"He's a very plausible bastard." The detective inspector shook his greying head. "I suppose we ought to contact Mr Stenton's aged parents – if they're still alive."

"I'll get on to it tomorrow, first thing." The detective sergeant rubbed his tired eyes. "It would be nice," he mused, "if they *weren't* telling us a lorry load of porkies.

It would look damned good on the records, if we could get this business all cleared up. The targets for this month—"

"Don't you talk to me about bloody targets," growled the inspector, scowling. "I didn't join the Force to massage figures! To satisfy some bugger sitting in Whitehall, who only cares if it looks all right on paper. If he can reassure Joe Public, and pacify the bleeding electorate."

Told he was free to go but that he should not leave the district, and must make himself available should the police wish to speak to him again the following day, Alex went home by taxi.

He sat there in a daze. He'd been so shocked by Helen's behaviour – by her betrayal, as he couldn't help but think of it, as the full implications of what she'd done were all brought home to him – that he wanted to scream, to howl.

He wondered what on earth had made her do it. Perhaps it was his fault? Perhaps he'd pushed her a bit too hard, just a little bit too far? But then, she was a woman. It was amazing, he supposed, that she'd kept their secret for so long, that she'd never even told her fat, bald husband.

Alex paid the taxi driver, then went into his house. He could hear the squeaking and purring as he walked up the unlit staircase.

He went into his bedroom and switched on the overhead light. It was just as he had thought. While he was otherwise engaged, down at the local cop shop, Ivy had given birth to a fine litter of six or maybe seven squirming kittens on Alex's unmade bed.

He crouched to stroke the cat's small head. "I'll go and get you a bit of chicken," he whispered, as Ivy rubbed her face against his hand. "You'll have your paws full, looking after all this lot."

What would Ivy do, Alex wondered, if – or rather *when*

– he was sent to prison? What would happen to her helpless kittens? Anita would just drown them or put them out for the dustmen in a sack. "I'll have to take you with me, puss," he said.

Chapter Twenty-One

"They're both asleep at last," said Doreen Gray. She looked at Helen with big, round, curious eyes. Her mouth hung open slightly, as if she were all ready to be astonished. Or at least surprised.

Inwardly, Robin groaned. The woman wanted – and indeed was entitled to – at least *some* explanation. "Helen's had a difficult day," he began, as he ushered his shell-shocked, blank-faced, exhausted wife inside. "Yes, you go on up to bed," he continued, as Helen stood there dithering, at the bottom of the stairs. "All right, Doreen? Got your stuff? I'll just run you home."

So Doreen Gray picked up her bag. "Goodnight then, Mrs Harper," she began. "I hope you'll soon feel better. If you need—"

But Helen was already half way up the stairs. She didn't look back, and Doreen understood that her friendly good wishes had fallen upon deaf ears. Robin was holding out her coat to her – and so, defeated, she meekly slipped her arms into the sleeves.

"Mrs Harper's been under rather a lot of presssure lately," she said, as they drove off up the lane. "Or at any rate, that's how it seems to me."

"What did you say?" asked Robin. "Sorry, Doreen. I was looking out for rabbits. I hate to run anything over. But the stupid creatures *will* sit in the road!"

"My George says run them over, and teach their friends a lesson they won't forget. If you don't actually squash them, they make quite a decent pie." For a moment, Doreen Gray appeared to be side-tracked. But then, she remembered she was owed an explanation. "The children were as good as gold," she added. "I mean, all things considered."

"I'm sure we're very grateful for all you've done tonight." Robin turned into the village's main street. He pulled up outside Doreen's blue front door. "It looks as if George has gone to bed," he murmured.

"Yes, I expect he has. After all, it's very late." Doreen gave Robin a very old-fashioned look. "Well, we mustn't sit here gossiping. I know there's no harm doing, as they say. But there's always foolish people as will talk."

So saying, she clutched her big beige raincoat to her generous bosom, opened the car door, and stepped out into the soft, summer night.

"Thank you again for helping out," called Robin.

"The pleasure's all mine, I'm sure," muttered Doreen, crossly. She'd rung Elizabeth from the Harpers' house, and the two of them had spent almost an hour in scurrilous gossip and idle speculation. But now what could she tell her friend when they met for elevenses the following day?

Helen was sitting on the bed when Robin came up the stairs. The suitcase and all its contents were now nowhere to be seen.

"Where shall I start?" she whispered, as Robin sat down next to her.

"At the beginning, I think," said Robin, softly. He slipped a comforting arm around her shoulders. "I know I've heard it once, but I'm still not really clear about everything. So start when you went to Rettingham first, okay?"

Helen began to talk. Robin listened, interrupting only

very occasionally. He wanted to know things which the police had not thought particularly – or indeed at all – important. "This Thomas Stenton," he said, gently. "When did you first meet him?"

"At London University," said Helen.

"He was your first lover, right?"

"I suppose you could say that." Indifferently, Helen shrugged. "Although lover isn't the actual word *I'd* choose. He fucked me, scared me, manipulated me—"

"How exactly did he scare you? I thought you told the police that he was only a little bloke?"

"He *was* quite small – compared to Alex, he was just a midget – but he was bigger than me." Once more Helen shrugged. "When I first met Tom, I thought he was a really lovely person. He was funny, clever, quite good-looking – pretty, really, I suppose you'd say. He had big blue eyes and freckles. Golden curls—"

"He sounds repulsive," Robin couldn't help himself but say. "He sounds—"

"No, he was very attractive. All the girls in my year fancied him." Helen bit her lip. "But he was spiteful, too. He liked to hurt me – I think it made him feel he was in control. If he was feeling bad about anything, he'd punch me, kick me, slap me around a bit—"

"Bastard," growled Robin, softly

"But – well – I know I often used to annoy him." Helen sighed. "Sometimes I did it quite deliberately. I'd borrow his car, for instance, and go out for a drink or a meal with another man. At a party, I'd snog someone else, or dance with him all night. So when Tom beat me up, I sometimes felt that I deserved it. As I've since discovered women often do."

Helen shook her head. "It's so bloody childish, isn't it? Goading someone until they actually thump you?"

"I've never really thought about it." Robin shrugged. "But you must have come to your senses in the end. Why didn't you leave the bugger?"

"Robin, I did! At least, I *tried* to leave him. But he always came after me. He'd make a scene, say over and over that he couldn't live without me. That if I left him, his life wouldn't be worth living."

"So when you had the chance to get it together with big, strong Alex Colborn—"

"Yes, exactly." Helen hung her head. "Tom used me, and I used Alex. Disgusting, isn't it?"

"In the circumstances, perhaps it's also perfectly understandable." Although Robin didn't feel he understood, at least not yet.

But what mattered most was that his wife was finally confiding in him. She was leaning on him, letting him carry some weight. "So you came to Rettingham," he said. "You and three others rented the Merchant's House. Well – what happened next?"

Helen shrugged. "Tom found out where I'd gone. Actually, my bloody mother told him."

"Typical," muttered Robin.

"No, Robin – that's not fair." Helen laid her head upon his shoulder. "Tom could be very charming when he put his mind to it. My mother was quite bowled over when I took him home once for a long weekend. But, anyway—"

"Sorry. I won't interrupt again." Robin held his wife safe in his arms. He wondered now how long he'd be allowed to keep her with him. When they arrested her – as he imagined they were almost bound to do, and quite soon, probably – would they let him try to raise some bail?

He mentally reviewed his own financial situation. The house could be re-mortgaged, he could take out a personal loan, and then perhaps her parents would chip in.

He stroked her soft, fair hair. Helen talked, sometimes repeating things she'd said to the detective sergeant, sometimes telling him something completely new. But she never contradicted herself, she never faltered or seemed to pause for thought, and search as he might for flaws and inconsistencies, Robin couldn't find a single one.

So he knew she must be telling the simple truth. That this was something which had haunted her, with which she'd lived for years. He couldn't help but admire her bravery.

"There, I've finished. I've told you everything." Helen felt so relieved she was light-headed. The secret of the Merchant's House had oppressed her to the extent that, now she was rid of its enormous weight, she felt as if she were made of gossamer. As if she could float away. "Robin?" she whispered. "Now, you know it all."

"You swear this is the truth?" Robin met her gaze and held it, as if he were daring her to look away. "I mean, it all sounds so far fetched. So unlike you! So, so—"

"It's true." Helen looked down at her finger nails. She supposed they'd grow again some day, perhaps when she was finally sent to prison. "Tom and I were – I don't know – we were sexually involved, does that make sense? After I left him, I went to live with Alex. I suppose I was involved with him as well, although I can't remember *how* I felt, these days! You must think I was a horrible little tart?"

Robin said nothing. But he didn't let Helen go, much less push her away.

"That night," she said, "when Tom called at the Merchant's House, the night he went for Alex—"

"Or so the bastard says."

"Tom attacked Alex, I'm quite sure of it." Helen looked up again. "Robin, you never knew Tom. He was so devious, so underhand—"

"Okay, so there was a struggle, fight – whatever – and Thomas Stenton came off much the worse. You and Colborn bundled him into his car, and drove him to the nearest surgery. You rang the bell, and then you dumped him there. That *is* what happened, is it?"

"That's it," whispered Helen.

"The police are bound to check this out."

"I *know*!" Finding a tissue which was crumpled up her sleeve, Helen dabbed at her eyes. "The doctor's records will support our story. The surgery must have taken him in, they must have sewn him up, they—"

"What happened to the car?" interrupted Robin.

"What car?" frowned Helen.

"Stenton's blasted car, of course!" cried Robin. He grimaced in disgust. "What colour was the upholstery, do you remember that? The seats and carpet must have been all bloodied – would anyone passing by have noticed it? How long was the car outside the surgery? Who saw it that same night? Who might have seen—"

"God knows!" cried Helen, covering her face. "I didn't even think of the rotten car! We left the keys in the ignition, as I seem to recall. Perhaps somebody pinched it."

"Okay." Robin was tired to death, he was extremely hungry, and he felt he was in the middle of a nightmare. But he still ploughed gamely on. "So Stenton got himself patched up—"

"So we suppose."

"Yes, okay – whatever. Then, at some point – perhaps it was later that same evening, or perhaps it was several weeks or months before he was up and getting about again – he went back to look for you. He went to the Merchant's House again. Helen, when you found the body, was there – was there any blood on Stenton's clothes?"

"I didn't look." Helen shuddered. "I went into the shed.

The first thing that I noticed was his foot – or what was left of it. There were bones, white bones, and bits of torn blue denim where the rats had been chewing at it, trying to get at him. I started screaming, I suppose. Alex came running, and – actually, Robin, I can't remember what exactly happened after that."

"The body was wrapped in an oilskin," prompted Robin.

"Yes, that's right, it was." Helen rubbed her eyes. "Alex must have found it in an outhouse, or in the woodshed. He was absolutely marvellous, you know. He kept his head, and saw to all of that."

"What a tower of strength!" said Robin, coldly. "What I don't understand is, why you didn't just call the police?"

"The *police*?" Now, Helen stared at him, in horrified amazement. "But we'd have been arrested! We—"

"Not necessarily." Then Robin shrugged. "They'd have had no reason to think the two of you were guilty of anything. You reckon Colborn stabbed him. Well, that would only have damaged some soft tissue – unless he'd been unlucky enough to graze a bit of bone. In any case, it might have been impossible to discover the cause of death. Especially since the body was so decayed."

"We panicked, I suppose." Helen shook her head. "He wasn't very robust," she continued, as tears filled her eyes. "I don't think he could have come back that same night."

"But when he did come, he must have climbed the fence, made his way across the garden, and then gone into a shed." Robin looked at his wife. "So why did he do that?"

"To hide, or find a weapon of some kind?" Helen was at a loss. "To spy on us, perhaps? To make sure Alex and I hadn't moved on, that we were still living there?"

"Perhaps," said Robin. "But then what?"

"He must have gone to sleep or something. Or perhaps

he fainted. He did have a serious heart condition – or so he always reckoned. He'd certainly had several operations when he was a little child and they had left some really awful scars. It always made me nervous of upsetting him. I thought that if I hit him back—"

"He might drop dead?" Robin shrugged, as if to say, would that have been such a terrible tragedy? "So you reckon he had some sort of heart attack?"

"Well, yes – perhaps. Robin, it was very cold that winter. Maybe he collapsed. Then he became unconscious, and then he froze to death one winter night."

"Poor bastard," muttered Robin, almost sympathetically.

"Poor little Tom." Then, Helen shook her head. "My mother really liked him. She was very cross when I said we'd broken up. His parents were her sort of people, and I think she had visions – well, so what? Why should I have ruined *my* whole life?"

"Why indeed," said Robin. One of his legs had gone to sleep, and now he was trying to struggle to his feet. "I need a shot of caffeine," he told Helen. "I think I'll go and put the kettle on."

"Why didn't you tell me any of this before?" asked Robin, very softly. He placed a steaming mug of tea on Helen's bedside table.

"I couldn't have told you anything like that," said Helen, looking away from him. She bit her lower lip. "Look, Robin – I'd spent years and years just trying to forget it, trying to blank the whole thing from my mind. By the time I met you, I'd almost managed to convince myself that it was all a dream." Helen took a sip of scalding tea. "You'd never have believed me, anyway."

"Yes, I *would*!" Robin took her hand again. "Helen, I *do* believe you!"

"I feel so very much better, now that it's all come out." But Helen looked wretched then. "Alex will never understand, you know. He'll never, ever forgive me."

"I don't quite see what *Alex* needs to understand, or what he must forgive." Gently, Robin kneaded Helen's fingers. "Alex isn't injured, is he? Alex isn't dead."

"No." Helen met her husband's gaze. "Do you think I might get life?"

"Oh, for heaven's sake!" cried Robin. He was genuinely astonished. "I don't see that *you* had anything to do with any of it! You weren't even there when the stabbing itself took place. You found the body, but you didn't bury it. I don't see why you should carry the bloody can!"

"I was an accessory after the fact." Helen worried her well-chewed lower lip. She turned away from him. "Oh, God! I expect you really hate me now!"

"Helen, as if I could!" Touching her cheek, Robin turned her round to face him. "I'll do everything I can," he promised, softly. "You'll have the best solicitors, the best QC, the very best advice that money can buy. That's if they ever charge you with anything, and Leo Foster seems to think that's extremely unlikely."

"People have been given twenty years for less. The women's prisons are full of people who simply watched or waited, while their lovers or husbands committed terrible crimes."

"*You* did not conspire to commit a crime. You didn't wield the knife. The very most they could charge you with is something like unlawful concealment of a human body." Robin resumed his kneading of Helen's fingers. "Anyway, love – we're both in this together. That is, unless—"

"Unless what?" frowned Helen.

"Tell me, honestly. Do you love Alex Colborn?"

"I don't and never did love poor old Alex." Miserably, Helen shrugged. "I was desperate to get away from Tom. He'd threatened to kill me more than once, and in the end I believed he might get round to doing just that. Alex was big and strong and available. He offered some protection, I suppose."

"But I suppose you *liked* him?"

"I found him quite attractive, certainly." Helen looked deep into her husband's eyes. "But I was never in love with Alex Colborn. It hurt me more than I can say, when I realised you thought – when I remembered what *we'd* had together. When I saw you thought I really might prefer him."

"But he's a good-looking bloke." Then, Robin sighed. "When I first met you," he began, "when you said that you'd go out with me, I thought good God, I must be bloody dreaming. You weren't the sort of girl that I'd gone around with, do you see? I couldn't believe it when you actually seemed to fancy me."

"Oh, Robin!" Helen stared at him. "Why shouldn't I fancy you?"

"You were so beautiful. Christ, you're lovely still." Robin ran a hand through his short, thinning, greying hair. "I know what people think about us. Lucky bastard, they all say, how did a short-arsed little nerd like him pull a classy bird like that?

"Then there's your family. Your parents have always looked at me as if I were something the dog did on the carpet. Your Dad still speaks to me like a bloody brigadier addressing a gormless batman."

"Robin, Daddy speaks to almost *everyone* like that!" Helen stroked her husband's stubby fingers. "My parents love you!" she cried, urgently. "Honestly, they do! They were quite disappointed when you didn't come, that horrible weekend."

"I see," said Robin. He didn't look convinced. But then he shrugged, and yawned. "I think we ought to get our heads down now," he told his wife. "We'll probably have quite a busy day tomorrow."

"But won't you be going to work?"

"No, I don't think so." Robin fished in his jacket's inside pocket. "I received a summons this morning," he told Helen. "I have to appear at Westingford Magistrates Court, at two o'clock on the fourteenth of next month, to answer a charge of causing an affray. Leo says that if I'm lucky, I'll be fined fifty quid and costs. Then I'll be bound over to keep the peace. *I* shall soon have a proper criminal record."

"Oh, Robin." Helen touched her husband's hand again. "I'm sorry," she whispered softly.

"All water under the bridge." Robin caught at her fingers. "So was it true what you said about bloody Colborn?" he demanded. "You never loved him? You don't want him now, and you never will?"

"That's absolutely right," said Helen, softly.

"I love you," said Robin. "I love you more than anything."

"I love you, too." Helen kissed him, opening his mouth with her own. "This might be the very last time," she whispered.

"No chance," said Robin, bravely. His hand stroked Helen's breast. "I've missed you, love," he told her.

They did not sleep that night.

"Stenton, Stenton, Stenton – yeah, right – here the bugger is!" The policeman sitting at the computer keyboard moved the mouse, then clicked the button to open another window. "Thomas William Stenton, 12 10 62. Born in Edinburgh, moved to London 1979. Last known address is 36, Marmion Terrace, Inverlochiel, Strathclyde."

"Has he got any form?" enquired the tired detective sergeant, who was looking over the constable's right shoulder.

"Yeah, he's got two convictions, actually. One for dangerous driving – fined three hundred quid, licence endorsed. One for threatening behaviour, fined again and then bound over. That was in May 1982."

"Right." Now the detective sergeant sighed. "When you've found Mum and Dad, will you let me know? Then some poor bugger can go round, and give them a nice surprise."

Robin had got up and was wandering all around the house by half past six the following morning. Helen soon joined him, and together they prowled from kitchen to study. They went into the sitting room, where Helen touched and looked and tried to remember – where she painted a living picture, deep inside her head.

"I might never see it again," she said, as she stroked an old Staffordshire spaniel.

"You do talk nonsense," muttered Robin.

They made themselves some breakfast, and then took this up to bed. They knew it might be their last chance to do such boring things as spill their coffee on the sheets, or get smears of marmalade on their pillow cases.

Celia came in to find her parents still in bed, not speaking to each other, but snuggled up very close. So she got in beside them, and then squirmed down between them. Then Edward came in, and they all had a hug.

"You were late yesterday," said Edward, whispering in his mother's ear. "Brolly was really worried about you!"

"I was worried as well," said Celia. "So I hope it won't be happening again."

"I'm sorry," said Helen. She hugged both children tight. "Robin, I think we ought—"

But then, the telephone rang.

"Hello?" said Robin. "Oh – hello, Mr Harris. Yes, Helen is just here. We'll be there by nine fifteen, no problem."

"Who is Mr Harris?" asked Celia sharply.

"A gentleman Mummy and I need to go and see. So come along, you wombats." Robin shovelled both children off the bed. "Have your breakfast, then get off to school."

"*I* don't want to go to school today." Edward looked quite mulish. "I want to stay here with Mummy."

"Mummy has to go out." Robin stroked Edward's hair. "But she'll see you later."

"Where's Mummy going today?" asked Celia, frowning.

"To Westingford, my darling. She's got lots of work she needs to do this morning." Robin gave Celia a special hug. "But she'll be home before bedtime," he told her, his fingers crossed, and his smile reassuring.

"You *will* come back, Mummy?" Edward looked at her, anxious and needing a definite, firm promise.

"Yes, I'll come back," his mother said. Of course, she could not say when this might be.

"Robin, are you like this at work?" asked Helen, as they finally drove off down the lane.

"At work?" Robin frowned at her. "How exactly do you mean?"

"Well, are you as masterful? As focused, and as determined? Do you make firm decisions? Do you always see things through?"

"Well, I always try." Again, Robin glanced at his wife. "What's that got to do with what is going on today?"

"I'm just glad you're with me, is what I meant. I'm glad you're on my side."

"Where's Mummy going?" asked Celia, who was all

ears and eyes. "Mummy, why's Daddy coming to school with us?"

"Don't worry, sweetheart," said Robin. "Mummy's going to Westingford. I'm giving her a lift. It'll all be okay."

So the children were dropped off at school, and Robin and Helen drove towards the town. Robin seemed anxious to get to their destination, and took a series of short cuts which ensured they arrived there at least ten minutes early.

"Be brave," he said, as he paid for a whole day's parking. He locked the car, then took his wife's hand firmly in his own.

"So you're *not* going in to work?" said Helen.

"What?" He stared at her, incredulous. It was as though she'd asked if he were thinking of flying to the moon. "*I'm* coming with you!"

"To hand me over into custody?"

"Oh, darling!" Robin gave Helen's fingers a comforting squeeze. "I'm coming to the police station with you. Then I'm going to sit in on what is going on today – that is, if they'll let me. Then I'm going to take you home again."

"I think they'll throw the book at me today."

"We'll see," said Robin. He forced a cheerful grin. "Come on, sunshine. Best foot forward, and all that. Don't lie down until you're actually dead."

"Yes, Mr Harper, of course you can stay with us. That is, if Mrs Harper has no objection?"

"I'd like my husband to be here," said Helen.

So Detective Inspector Harris indicated a hard chair, and Robin sat down on it. "We've just had a call from Mrs Harper's solicitor, as it happens," went on the Detective Inspector, pleasantly. "He's been held up in the traffic, or so he says. But he'll be here in about ten minutes' time. Mrs

Harper, please don't look so worried. Shall I ask somebody to get you a cup of tea?"

"No, thank you," murmured Helen, thinking, so *he*'s going to be the nice cop. Where's the nasty one?

She realised Leo Foster must have put his foot down hard because two minutes later he walked into the interview room. Red-faced and breathless, he nevertheless seemed more than ready to start the business of the day.

"What's happened to Mr Colborn?" Helen dared to ask, as the inspector arranged his papers, then flexed his fingers and yawned languidly.

"Mr Colborn will be coming in some time later." The detective inspector looked at Helen's lawyer. "Mr Foster? I assume it's okay with you if we begin?"

"Go ahead," said Leo Foster, nodding genially.

So Detective Inspector Harris slotted a new tape into the cassette recorder and Helen was asked to go through it all again, this time from start to finish. Then to sign a declaration saying that her statement had been made of her own free will.

"Thank you, Mrs Harper." The policeman smiled, and rubbed his lantern jaws. "You've been most co-operative. Indeed, you've been very helpful. I should go home now, if I were you. We'll be in touch if we need you again today. So please stay close to a telephone, in case—"

But then, someone tapped sharply on the door.

"Come in," growled the inspector.

"Sir?" The young police constable, who opened the door just wide enough to poke his head inside, was looking very pleased with himself indeed. "Mr Colborn's just come in," he said, "and there's a call for you from an Inspector Arden in Strathclyde."

"I'll take it in my office." The detective inspector grinned at the uniformed man. "I'll be five minutes," he promised.

"Kevin? Go and get these people some coffee, will you? Or a cup of tea."

"But why are they being so nice to me?" asked Helen when both policemen had gone away, leaving the door wide open.

"They're softening you up." Leo Foster heaved a patient sigh. "I've spoken to Robert Jackson," he told Robin. "I phoned his clerk in chambers to ask the great man to call me back, but Mr Jackson happened to be there."

"What did he say?" asked Robin.

"He'll be very happy to act for Mrs Harper. But Jackson's one of the best, so I warn you now. It'll be a hefty fee."

"That's okay," said Robin, bravely.

Helen said nothing at all.

Five minutes, ten minutes, fifteen minutes ticked by. The coffee they'd been brought sat on the tray, cooling down, untasted. Then the inspector came back in again.

He had a piece of paper in his hand. "Thomas William Stenton," he began, looking straight at Helen. "Born twelfth of October, 1962. Five feet six, fair hair, slim build – that's the gentleman whose body you and Mr Colborn found and buried, beneath the foundations of the Merchant's House, in the early spring of 1985?"

"That's correct," said Helen.

"You told us Mr Stenton and you were lovers?"

"Yes." Helen looked down at her hands. "Detective Inspector," she whispered, "I promise you I've told you everything. Do we actually *need* to go over and over and over—"

"I've just been speaking to Mr Stenton's mother," interrupted the policeman. "She said she remembers you with great affection, and she asked me to give you her very warmest wishes. Or was it her kind regards?"

The inspector frowned down at his piece of paper. "But,

anyway – Mrs Stenton told me that Thomas William Stenton was admitted to the Strathclyde Royal Infirmary, for a long-awaited heart-lung transplant, early yesterday."

Chapter Twenty-Two

"They're softening you up," Leo Foster had told her just a few minutes ago. But nothing and no one had prepared her for this, and she stared at the policeman in stark, blank amazement, as if she had been hypnotised.

Recovering a little, she looked down at the desk. She fixed her eyes on a dirty mark just to the right of the inspector's file. Why, Helen wondered, were they doing this? Why were they playing this game? She'd told them the whole story. She had not lied to them. So why were they lying to her?

"Mr Harris," began Leo Foster politely, "do you think I might talk to Mrs Harper in private? Five minutes is all I need."

"No problem, Mr Foster." The detective inspector grinned. He opened the door again. "I need to have a word with Tony Sanderson, anyway."

When the inspector had gone away, Robin took Helen's frozen hands in his. He rubbed them hard as if he were trying to bring her back to life, and indeed she looked as pale as a living corpse. "I don't know what they think they're doing now," he muttered, sourly, "but this isn't bloody fair. What do they hope to gain by it?"

"God knows," said Leo Foster. He met Helen's frightened eyes. "Listen," he said, "whatever you do, don't alter your story now. You haven't confessed to any crime, and you mustn't let them think—"

"What about burying the little bastard's body?" interrupted Robin tersely. "Or burying *a* body, anyway?"

"Oh, that's nothing." Leo Foster shrugged. "Well, compared with murder, unlawful killing, malicious wounding – anything like that – it's relatively insignificant. So sit tight and say you've nothing to add to your original statement, while we wait to see what they'll come up with next."

"I wish I could speak to Alex," whispered Helen.

"I expect they're talking to Mr Colborn now." Leo Foster folded his arms and sighed. "God, I could do with a proper cup of tea! Ceylon, Earl Grey or some decent Lapsang! Even a pot of Assam would do the trick."

A quarter of an hour ticked slowly by. Then it was half an hour, and then an hour, and Detective Inspector Harris still had not returned. "But what are they doing?" whispered Helen, as if she were fearful of being overheard, caught in an act of treason, perhaps, or of conspiracy.

"I expect they're trying to catch Mr Colborn out." Idly, Leo Foster rolled a pencil across the desk. "When they've done so, they'll come back in here to talk to you."

"But I've already told them everything!" Helen's brow was furrowed, and she looked ready to burst into angry tears. "They know it all!" she cried, "and if they think—"

"Well, I suppose they want the actual truth." Leo Foster shrugged. "So, Helen, if you *do* decide to change your tune, please think very carefully about what you wish to say."

"Mr Foster, I have no intention of changing anything. In fact—"

But at that moment, Detective Inspector Harris came back in. At his side was a small, fat, balding man who carried a folder under his right arm. He smelled of pungent chemicals and strong industrial soap. "This is Dr Gordon Brady," said Detective Inspector Harris. "He's our pathologist. Mrs

Harper, Mr Harper, and Mr Foster, whom I'm sure you must already know."

"Hello, Leo." The forensic pathologist nodded to Helen's solicitor. He placed his folder on the desk, then sat down in the detective inspector's chair. "I assume you'll have no objection if I ask your client a few straightforward questions?"

"I don't mind at all – provided of course you don't expect her to answer any of them." Enigmatically, Leo Foster smiled. "Why don't you just tell her – and me – what this is all about?"

"Go ahead," said Detective Inspector Harris.

So the pathologist opened his file and took out a report, the pages of which he fanned across the desk. There were also some photographs, at which Helen could not actually bring herself to look.

"I don't mind admitting that my colleague Dr Nigel Smith and I had just a bit of trouble with this fellow." The pathologist pushed his glasses on to his nose. He glanced through various typed and scribbled notes. "I was at a conference when the body was discovered. Then I went away on holiday. So yesterday was my first chance to give this chap a through going-over."

"Come on, Gordon," said the detective inspector. "We haven't got all day."

"So what do we have here?" said the pathologist who, in spite of the policeman's obvious impatience, remained calm and unruffled. "Well, the body of a young person, between twenty-five and thirty years of age. The soft tissue is almost entirely missing, and the bones are badly damaged or decayed."

Helen thought she was going to be sick.

"It is obvious that the person is or was of the male sex." Dr Brady sighed. "But further clarification was, at first, extremely problematic. This person had been wearing very ordinary chainstore clothing. A denim jacket, washed blue jeans, heavy black leather boots. The standard uniform, in fact, of many young people, everywhere today.

"There were no documents or relevant papers in any of the pockets. We failed to come up with anything by way of dental records. So we were in a quandary, to say the very least."

"That is, until Mrs Harper here decided to pay us a visit." Detective Inspector Harris looked at Helen. He folded his brawny arms. "Helen?" he whispered, softly.

"Mr Harris?" Steadily, Helen met his gaze.

"Do you wish to add anything to what you've already told us about certain events which you say took place eleven years ago?"

"No, I don't." Helen turned to the pathologist. "Do you want me to see your pictures?" she enquired.

"You're welcome to look at the pictures, certainly. But I don't think you *need* to see them." Dr Brady glanced down at his notes. "The pelvis was badly damaged," he observed. "The upper body was crushed, and all the ribs were cracked or broken. The skull was smashed, as if by a heavy blow to the side of the head."

"When we dug the grave," said Helen, "we found some big, round boulders. When we buried the body, Alex decided to weight it down with stones." She realised she'd forgotten about that. But now it came back to her, the sound of bones breaking and splintering, as Alex dropped those heavy boulders into the shallow pit. "We—"

"But one thing we have established now," interrupted Dr Brady, "is that the person had sustained quite a range of fairly serious injuries, while he was still alive. For instance, his nose had been broken twice, at least. His arms had both been fractured. I suppose he might have been a wrestler once. Or a devotee, perhaps, of one of the more aggressive martial arts."

Helen shook her head. "But that's ridiculous," she whispered. "Tom had never—"

"This fellow was heavily made, with very well-marked features and large bones. I'd say he died between the ages of twenty-five and nine – or just possibly in his early thirties. We have yet to establish the cause of death. But we're running various tests, and we are confident that this will soon be done. My personal suspicion is that this death was accidental – quite possibly drug-related, as so many of them seem to be today."

"Do go on," said Leo Foster, sitting back in his chair. He grinned at the inspector. "All this is really fascinating stuff."

"David?" Gordon Brady looked up at the policeman.

"Be my guest," he said.

"What follows is pure speculation," continued Dr Brady. "I'm sure a fine detective like Inspector Harris here would never dream of making such wild guesses – but from the worn condition of his clothes and boots, I would imagine this fellow was a vagrant. His hair – or what remained of it – was filthy, and there was some suspicion of body lice. These infest the seams and creases of natural fibre clothing.

"So, he was on the tramp, perhaps from Westingford to London, where he might have been intending to spend the winter. He came across the Merchant's House, which seemed to be derelict. He saw there were several outbuildings which offered reasonable shelter. He decided to doss down in one, perhaps for just one night. But, as we know, he died there."

Helen looked astonished.

Detective Inspector Harris merely shrugged.

Leo Foster tried to look as though he had thought as much.

"So this must let Helen off the hook." Robin Harper's voice cut into the silence like a hot blade through butter. He would have said much more, if Leo Foster had not caught his eye and given him a warning look.

"Mr Harris?" began Leo Foster, smoothly.

"Mrs Harper is free to go." The detective inspector loosened his crumpled tie. "But we shall certainly wish to speak to her again. There might be other charges. So I'd appreciate it if she didn't go off on her summer holidays for at least a couple of weeks."

"We understand," said Robin. "Helen, darling – are you ready? Then let's get out of here."

As Helen and Robin walked into the lobby, they saw Alex Colborn talking to a uniformed policeman. Alex was coming towards them, walking down a flight of stairs. But when he saw Helen and her husband, he stopped dead.

He was looking very pale. In fact, he seemed quite ill. Helen could see his features were very haggard, and that his eyes were dull. He looked like a man who had lost something particularly precious, who knew he had no hope of ever recovering it again.

The policeman spoke to him, apparently jollying him along. So Alex had no choice but to start moving. Coming up to Helen, he nodded curtly. For a single, fleeting moment their eyes met, but then Alex frowned and looked away again. Then he walked past her and through the double doors into the street.

Leo Foster ushered Helen towards the sergeant's desk. "He'll get over it," he murmured, sympathetically.

Helen did not comment. She had seen the look in Alex Colborn's haunted eyes. He'd known, he'd always known! He'd not only deliberately deceived her, but had also meant to go on deceiving her. Even, presumably, when they'd built a whole new life together.

Helen had been prepared to lose her husband. For Alex Colborn's sake – to please a scheming liar – she had risked her future happiness and the happiness of her beloved children, because of a total stranger.

Robin was close behind her. He took his wife by the arm and led her towards the double doors. "Come on, love," he whispered. "Let's get out of this awful place."

The three of them sat in Robin's car and grinned at one another. Or at least, the two men did. Helen still seemed shell-shocked.

"They made an absolute pig's ear of that!" Leo Foster was quietly jubilant. "Mrs Harper, I must congratulate you. I think you were magnificent today."

"Whatever do you mean?" Helen wanted to go home. To lie on her bed and weep. To sit down on her rocking chair in the corner of the sitting room and howl. She wondered if she might start howling now. She desperately needed some sort of release.

She didn't know how to deal with what she was feeling at this moment. Of course, she was relieved that she and Alex had not actually been responsible for anybody's death. She was very glad that Thomas Stenton was still alive – or at least half alive. She hoped the operation had gone well. She wondered if she would summon up the courage to ring his mother and enquire.

But self-disgust was uppermost in her mind. Disgust and a fierce self-loathing for the way in which she and Alex had treated an innocent human being – some poor itinerant, perhaps, who'd taken shelter for the night. A young man who, a mere few hundred yards from warmth and food and basic comfort, had instead died a cold and lonely death. She thought she might never come to terms with that.

Leo Foster said he had to go. He finally found his car keys. He opened the passenger door of the BMW. "I'll speak to you soon," he said, as he shook Robin by the hand. "I must say, I'm very happy with the way it's all turned out."

"Do you think the police will take any further action?" Robin asked him.

"They might, but I rather doubt it. If the papers got hold of this, they could make it all look just a bit embarrassing, for Sanderson and Harris especially."

"How exactly do you mean?" asked Helen.

"A couple of former students found, and gave a decent burial to, the body of a drug-addicted vagrant. Well, so what? No criminal offence has been committed. If identification's made, and if the next of kin come forward, the damage to the body can easily be explained. I mean, it was found on a building site, and mangled by a JCB or two! I imagine they'll want to keep the whole thing quiet."

"I hope you're right," said Robin.

"Trust me," said Leo Foster. "So, Robin, I'll see *you* next month, at the Magistrates' Court – is it the fourteenth?"

"Yes, I think so." Robin winced. "I don't know what got into me," he muttered. "I knew I wouldn't get away with it."

"They'll only tick you off and tell you not to do it again. Colborn probably won't even turn up, much less stand there giving evidence against you." Leo Foster grinned. "I shouldn't lose any sleep, if I were you."

"There's no chance of that," said Robin.

"Goodbye, Helen." Leo Foster offered his hand, and this time Helen shook it. Then he picked up his case and went on his way.

Robin pushed the keys into the ignition. He glanced at Helen, who managed a faint smile. "Right then, my love," he began. "Let's get you home."

Helen met her husband's gaze. "Thank you," she murmured. "Thank you, Robin."

"For what?" asked Robin, frowning.

"For believing me," said Helen.

"Of course I believed you." Robin grinned. "Of course I believed my darling wife," he said.

Epilogue

I suppose I couldn't have expected it to work. Or at least, not in the long term, anyway. But when we found him, after we had stared at the horrible thing for a couple of seconds – and you must believe this – it astonished me that Helen was deceived.

Even in a state of advanced decay, it was obvious that this person could not be the bastard Stenton. For a start, he was too tall, and much too wide. Stenton was a stunted little starveling; I could have picked him up with just one hand. But I could never have carried the bloke we buried. It was as much as I could do to drag him down the bloody path along to the Merchant's House.

But I suppose Helen must have been upset. She had a guilty conscience and this discovery made it look as if her sins had literally found her out. So she was happy to accept that it was Thomas Stenton who lay rotting and stinking under the paving stones. Now she could beat herself up and feel how wicked she had been. She actually wanted to take some blame.

I don't know if I still love her. Perhaps I ought to hate the woman for what she's done to me. But I suppose it's not her fault. She doesn't dress like a common tart, she doesn't flirt, she doesn't encourage men. There's just something about her, which even someone as stupid as Paul Graham can understand. They ought to bottle it, then they could sell it to ugly, stupid women. They'd make a bloody fortune.

I saw her yesterday. She was in her car, stopped at the lights, the sprogs were jumping around in the back, and she was telling them off, like mothers do. She looked okay, her colour's better, her face has lost that gaunt and haunted look. The boy looks just like her, but the girl's a podgy little pudding. I stopped and stared, but I don't think they even noticed me.

It's as if I'm stuck in a groove. I can't go forward, but of course I can't go back. Perhaps I'll get a dog. It'll need to be quite old, because I don't want it chasing Ivy, or upsetting her new kittens. A labrador would be nice; a chocolate-coloured labrador. I'd call her Esmeralda. Or perhaps I'll just get a mongrel from the local Animal Rescue people in Avon Ferry Road.

I need something or somebody to love. I'm sure I'd love a nice, well-meaning dog. Perhaps I could move to a bigger house, with a bigger garden, get a couple of dogs?

A woman is out of the question, anyway.